PRAISE FOR THE *NE...*
LIBRARY L...

"A sparkling setting, lovely characters, books, knitting, and chowder! What more could any reader ask [for]?"
—*New York Times* bestselling author Lorna Barrett

"Terrific . . . intelligent, fun, and lively."
—*New York Times* bestselling author Miranda James

"Sure to charm cozy readers everywhere."
—*New York Times* bestselling author Ellery Adams

"[A] fast-moving, tricky tale that kept me guessing at every turn. . . . A must-read!"
—*New York Times* bestselling author Kate Carlisle

"The characters are fully fleshed out and the coastal setting is appealing. A really enjoyable read."
—*New York Times* bestselling author Rhys Bowen

"Full of sass, charm, and page-turning suspense!"
—*Woman's World*

"[A] superbly crafted mystery novel by a true master of the genre. . . . Very highly recommended."
—*Midwest Book Review*

"What a great read! . . . McKinlay has been a librarian, and her snappy story line, fun characters, and young library director with backbone make for a winning formula."
—*Library Journal*

"Fans of this series will love the scenes leading up to the wedding ceremony and the myriad ways the incidental characters have knit themselves into a supportive community." —*Booklist*

"Plenty of well-defined characters add charm and bite to a thorny mystery." —*Kirkus Reviews*

"A gifted storyteller, Jenn McKinlay writes a mystery that combines the challenges of wedding planning with the search for the killer in a very engaging narrative." —Fresh Fiction

"Rarely does a clean-as-a-whistle cozy qualify as riveting, but this one definitely does." —*Publishers Weekly*

"A mystery set in a library just feels right. . . . McKinlay lets the first third of the story breathe, effectively ramping up the tension. . . . And the conclusion is a wild ride indeed." —*BookPage* (starred review)

"Jenn McKinlay really knows how to keep readers enthralled until the very last page of her books. I loved this one." —*Suspense Magazine*

"Sweet and tart, irresistibly engaging and cleverly entertaining." —*New York Times* bestselling author Hallie Ephron

"Jenn McKinlay is a treasure. . . . Her books are always charming, endearing, and instantly engaging—but McKinlay's secret sauce is her deep understanding of human nature, her superb talent for storytelling, and the most

desirable of skills: her unmatched ability to entertain, enlighten, and delight."

—Hank Phillippi Ryan, five-time Agatha Award
winner and author of Trust Me

"Jenn McKinlay mingles an appealing protagonist, small-
town politics, and the terror of a stalker with the joys of true
love and a library. A master class in the cozy mystery!"

—Lucy Burdette, national bestselling author of
A Deadly Feast

KILLER RESEARCH

Jenn McKinlay

BERKLEY PRIME CRIME
New York

BERKLEY PRIME CRIME
Published by Berkley
An imprint of Penguin Random House LLC
penguinrandomhouse.com

Copyright © 2021 by Jennifer McKinlay Orf
Excerpt from *The Plot and the Pendulum* by Jenn McKinlay copyright © 2022
by Jennifer McKinlay Orf
Penguin Random House supports copyright. Copyright fuels creativity, encourages
diverse voices, promotes free speech, and creates a vibrant culture. Thank you for buying
an authorized edition of this book and for complying with copyright laws by not
reproducing, scanning, or distributing any part of it in any form without permission.
You are supporting writers and allowing Penguin Random House to continue to
publish books for every reader.

BERKLEY and the BERKLEY & B colophon are registered trademarks and
BERKLEY PRIME CRIME is a trademark of Penguin Random House LLC.

ISBN: 9780593101780

Berkley Prime Crime hardcover edition / November 2021
Berkley Prime Crime mass-market edition / September 2022

Printed in the United States of America
3   5   7   9   10   8   6   4   2

This is a work of fiction. Names, characters, places, and incidents either are the product
of the author's imagination or are used fictitiously, and any resemblance to actual persons,
living or dead, business establishments, events, or locales is entirely coincidental.

PUBLISHER'S NOTE: The recipes contained in this book are to be followed exactly
as written. The publisher is not responsible for your specific health or allergy needs
that may require medical supervision. The publisher is not responsible for any adverse
reactions to the recipes contained in this book.

If you purchased this book without a cover, you should be aware that this book is stolen
property. It was reported as "unsold and destroyed" to the publisher, and neither the author
nor the publisher has received any payment for this "stripped book."

For Cindy Burnham Jacques. You've been in my life for more than forty years, and so many of my favorite memories begin and end with you. I'm so glad our eleven-year-old selves found each other. You're one of the best people I know, and I'm honored to call you my friend.

KILLER RESEARCH

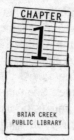

Lindsey Norris pushed a cart full of food toward the back room of the Briar Creek Public Library. It was her turn to provide the eats for the library's weekly crafternoon meeting. She had established the crafternoon club just after becoming Briar Creek's director a few years ago. It was one of many programs she had implemented, hoping to make the library a gathering place for the community.

This particular group was small but enthusiastic, and the women who belonged to it had become some of Lindsey's dearest friends in the small Connecticut shore town. The group met every Thursday at lunch, and they discussed the chosen book of the week while sharing food and making a craft. This week's book was *Pride and Prejudice* by Jane Austen, and Lindsey was thrilled. She'd been trying to get the crafternooners to read Austen for months and they'd finally agreed.

As she navigated the narrow hallway, she was forced to swerve to the right as an enormous hamburger wad-dled toward her. Lindsey squinted. Yes, the head pok-ing out of the top of the sesame seed bun was none other than her children's librarian, Beth Barker. The costume thing was nothing new for Beth, as she was known for dressing up as everything from a teapot to a bat for her story times. She was a firm believer in go-ing the extra mile to engage her young audience, which made her reading programs a packed house. None of this was a surprise to Lindsey as she had been Beth's roommate during their information studies grad-uate school years, and even then, Beth had approached her children's literature courses with the same over-the-top enthusiasm. The burger outfit, though, that was a new one.

"All right, you've got me stumped," Lindsey said. "I know the books that go with a duck costume, a dino-saur and even a rocket, but a hamburger? What are you reading at story time today that goes with this?"

Beth grinned at her and adjusted the lettuce leaf be-neath her top bun. "Well, my favorite is *Burger Boy* but there's also *Bun, Onion, Burger*. Both books get kids thinking about lunch and food, and eating responsibly. Then for the young entrepreneurs in the crowd, there's *Hamburger Heaven*, which is all about making a small business into a success."

"Impressive. Picture books always pack a punch of information," Lindsey said. She glanced at her cart. Today's menu to celebrate spring was loaded with egg salad finger sandwiches, cheddar-broccoli tartlets, pesto-stuffed cherry tomatoes, and lemon cheesecake squares. "Now I'm wishing I'd just ordered a sack of burgers."

Beth slowly backed away with her hands up as if to ward off an attack. "Don't get any big ideas. I'm made of felt, I tell you," she said. She hugged the pillow-like layers that made up her burger costume to her already large pregnant belly. Then she caught her reflection in the office window behind Lindsey. "Uh-oh, it's like the baby knows I'm dressed as a burger, because I'm suddenly starving—like, I'm going to have a mental episode if someone doesn't put a burger in my hand right now."

"Can't help you with that," Lindsey said. She gestured to the cart. "All I have are finger sandwiches and tartlets."

"How very Austen of you," Beth said. She leaned in close to examine the cart, and gingerly took one of the egg salad triangles. "Turns out the baby isn't that particular. This is just for taste-testing purposes, natch."

Lindsey laughed. "Of course."

"Ermagawd, so good," Beth said. She devoured it in two bites, and a look of sublime bliss crossed her face.

Lindsey took a napkin and put another sandwich and a tartlet in it. Then she handed it to Beth and said, "To tide you over during story time."

"You're a goddess, have I told you that lately?" Beth asked.

"Yes, when I approved your summer reading program budget last month," Lindsey said. "But for the record, it never gets old."

Beth grinned. The distinct sound of a toddler giggling emanated from the main library, drawing her attention, and she said, "I hear my crowd arriving. Gotta bounce. See you at crafternoon."

"Break a burger—or would that be a bun?" Lindsey called after her.

Beth stuck an arm out of her costume and bent it as if to make a muscle while cradling her food in her other hand.

Lindsey watched as Beth waddled across the library to the story time room. Her burger bun swung like a pendulum as she tipped from side to side while walking. Beth's baby was due in two months, which was a scheduling challenge for her as she juggled being the children's librarian while also acting as the campaign manager for Ms. Cole, the head of circulation at the library, who was running for mayor of Briar Creek and the Thumb Islands.

It was no small task to make over the image of the woman formerly known to the library staff as "the lemon" (for her puckered disposition and old-school ways) into a viable candidate for mayor, but Beth was giving it her all.

Lindsey wheeled into the crafternoon room to find Paula Turner, a library clerk, already seated at the main table. She was a crafter to her core and was setting up the day's project supplies. Not being crafty by nature— a major understatement—Lindsey glanced with mixed emotions at the table, namely one part curiosity and one part dread.

"Happy crafternoon," Paula greeted her. "Since it's your week to host, and I know you don't love crafting, I picked a super easy Austen-inspired craft. Ribbon bookmarks."

Lindsey glanced at the piles of materials in front of

Paula. Velvet and lace ribbons of every conceivable color, ribbon clamps and loads of charms in silver and brass and some beads and crystals, too. She saw an old-fashioned key, a jade bead, an open book, a teardrop crystal and an antique portrait of Jane Austen in a frame no bigger than a quarter. She immediately felt her spine relax. Lindsey picked up a length of lavender velvet and ran it through her fingers. This seemed like something even she could do.

She grinned at Paula. "You might make a crafter out of me yet."

"That's the goal," Paula said. Her thick braid was currently dyed a fabulous shade of turquoise, and the sleeve of tattoos that ran up her arm was colorful and book inspired. There was no doubt that she gave the library all of its coolness.

"Lindsey!" A breathless Ann Marie Martin appeared in the doorway. "We've got a situation!"

Lindsey glanced at Paula and gestured to the food. "Do you mind?"

"Not at all," she said. "I'll keep watch."

"Thank you," Lindsey said. She hurried to the door and fell in step beside Ann Marie, her library assistant, as she led the way back to the main library. "What's the situation?"

"Mayor Hensen is here," Ann Marie said. "He and Ms. Cole are having an impromptu debate right in the middle of the library."

"Oh, no," Lindsey said.

They were six months out from the local election, and things were heating up. The town of Briar Creek had no term limits, so the incumbent, Mayor Hensen, was planning to run for his third term. So far, he had refused to debate Ms. Cole publicly and could most often be found at the country club, schmoozing with his cronies. He seemed to feel that Ms. Cole was no threat to his campaign, and therefore couldn't be bothered to treat her as a real opponent.

Lindsey suspected he was in for a bit of a surprise given that the turnout for the upcoming election looked to be higher than usual, and much of the town's younger generation was actively engaged and looking for a different sort of leadership. Sadly, since Mayor Hensen was technically her boss, Lindsey had to remain completely neutral whenever she was on duty at the library, even though privately she was one hundred percent Team Cole.

"I'd deal with it myself but one of our computer terminals is missing a cable, and we have an eager line of patrons waiting for a session, plus I think dealing with the mayor is above my pay grade."

"Fair point." Lindsey glanced at Ann Marie. "Wait. We're missing a cable?"

"Yup, it's the weirdest thing. It's like someone just ripped it right out of the back of the computer. I'm trying to scrounge up another one, but they're back in storage and I didn't want to leave the current situation unsupervised."

"Good call."

Lindsey kicked into high gear as she hurried into the main room. In Briar Creek, the library wasn't known so much for its quiet as it was for being the heartbeat of the community. When she'd taken the job, the library was run by an older gentleman, Mr. Tupper, and he considered the library a place for quiet introspection and research, which was lovely but not really meeting the needs of residents.

Given how the world was changing, Lindsey knew that the library's survival depended upon the value the community placed on the library itself. Books were Lindsey's favorite part of the library, for sure, but it was the children's programs, the adult programs, the free Wi-Fi, internet terminals and the sense of community that the place offered that kept the public coming back again and again.

Story time was underway, and the private study rooms and the computer terminals were all in use, minus the one that had a dark screen and an OUT OF ORDER sign taped to its monitor because of its missing cable. Lindsey made a mental note to check back with Ann Marie after crafternoon on its status. Honestly, why would someone take a cable? It boggled.

There were several people in the reference section, doing research, and the new books and DVDs had their usual crowd of people jockeying for the latest releases. Overall, it was a very average day in the library, except in the main room.

Every single person in the main room of the library was standing still with their attention on the circulation department as they stared at the two people facing off over the service desk. Mayor Hensen with his thick head of hair and abnormally white teeth on one side and Ms. Cole on the other in her usual monochromatic outfit, today's being black, with her silver hair swept back from her face in a becoming bob. Beth had been working on Ms. Cole's look with mixed results, but today she was on point as her black slacks paired well with her black top, even though it was admittedly rather severe.

"Ms. Cole, how long have you been with the library now?" Mayor Hensen asked. His voice was conversational enough, but Lindsey could hear a faintly disdainful edge to it.

"I've been with the library through six mayors," she said. Ms. Cole leaned back on her heels and stared at him over her reading glasses as if to say, *Your point?*

"Wow, that's like . . ." His voice trailed off while he did the mental math. Lindsey half expected him to count it out on his fingers.

"Over forty years," she said. "Would you like to borrow my calculator to do the exact math?"

Mayor Henson frowned at her. It was clear he didn't like her tone. A giggle from a patron in the new book area did not help the situation.

"That's not necessary," he said. He smiled, although it looked forced, and gestured wide to encompass the entire building. "A forty-year career is impressive. Clearly, you're very good at your job. And after *all these years*, you're the institutional memory of the place. Why, you're the face of the library. In fact, I don't think folks would recognize the building without you to greet them when they come in."

Lindsey didn't think she was imagining the ageism Hensen was throwing out there for anyone who was listening. One glance at Ms. Cole, and Lindsey knew she'd heard it, too.

As Ms. Cole studied the mayor, one eyebrow ticked up on her forehead, signaling her annoyance. *Uh-oh.*

"Hello, Mayor Hensen," Lindsey said as she joined

Ms. Cole behind the desk, hoping to ward off a full-blown confrontation. "What brings you by today?"

"I'm the mayor," he said. His tone was slightly annoyed, as if he couldn't believe he had to remind her of his position.

"Not for long," Ms. Cole muttered.

The mayor's head snapped in her direction. "What was that?"

"Not—" Ms. Cole began, but Lindsey cut her off.

"Not for nothing." Lindsey smiled—well, she showed her teeth at any rate. "Not for nothing, you're the mayor. Now, is there something in particular that I can help you with?"

Hensen eyed her suspiciously and then puffed up his chest as if inflating with his own self-importance. "I'm not here to use the library. I'm simply representing my constituents by exercising my duty as a public servant to check on all of my departments."

Ms. Cole opened her mouth to speak, and Lindsey stepped on her foot, not too hard, just enough to get her attention.

"Well, it's always a pleasure to see you," Lindsey said. She came around the desk and strode up to Hensen's side, subtly encouraging him to start walking in the direction of the exit. "Have I shown you the latest display by our young entrepreneurs group? It's fabulous."

Hensen sent one last glare at Ms. Cole and fell into step beside Lindsey. They paused in front of a glass display case, where Lindsey pointed out each exhibit, hoping the information overload would push the mayor into a speedy departure. They were halfway through the case when he interrupted her.

"What's she playing at?" he asked.

"I'm sorry?"

"She's too old to be a mayor," he said. "The position requires someone with vim and vigor, stamina, and he should be—"

"'He'?" Lindsey interrupted.

Mayor Hensen waved his hand at her. "Don't get all Helen Reddy on me. You know what I mean."

"I believe you mean the position should be filled by a man," she said.

"No, no," he protested, not very convincingly. "Although, come to think of it, Briar Creek has never had a female mayor."

"Then we're overdue for one," Lindsey said. She glanced at him. He didn't get her pun. Was there anything more tiresome than having to explain clever wordplay when a listener didn't get it? Because it was simply unacceptable to let it go unacknowledged. She sighed. "Overdue. Because we're in a library, get it?"

"Ha ha," Mayor Hensen said. He sounded like a cat choking on a sock. The feigned amusement disappeared from his face in an instant. He stared at Lindsey with a sudden intensity that made her jump. "You want her to win, don't you?"

"Uh . . . I . . ." Lindsey stammered. His question was inappropriate at best and put her in a terrible position at worst.

She wasn't going to lie. Ms. Cole would make a much better mayor than Hensen, and not just because she would be a strong ally for the library, but because she loved Briar Creek, she cared about the residents, she was extremely well organized and she had the rare ability to get people to do what they were supposed to do without having them kick up a fuss.

Hensen lacked all of those skills. It was no contest as to which of them would be a more effective mayor. But Lindsey couldn't say that out loud, nor did she want to lie just to appease Hensen's ego. Thankfully, he didn't give her a chance.

"You want to have a woman on the inside," he said. He reared back, looking as if she'd slapped him. "I see how it is. You want to be close to the seat of power. You think she'll give you your dream budget. What will it include? Unlimited book orders? Training for all of your staff? New equipment? More employees? Longer hours of service?"

He sounded outraged at the mere idea of the library getting any of these things. Lindsey blinked. All of that was on her wish list and were items she'd been lobbying for since she'd arrived.

"May I just say that unless you're actually trying to drum up votes for your challenger, accusing the library director of preferring Ms. Cole as a candidate for mayor because the library will get a bigger and better budget, whilst you're standing in the middle of said library, is not your best play, Hensen," a voice with a distinctive British accent spoke from behind a nearby bookcase.

Lindsey craned her neck and saw Robbie Vine, Briar Creek resident and famous British actor, leaning negligently against the shelf.

"You stay out of this," Mayor Hensen snapped. The library had gone quiet as patrons were, again, watching the drama unfold. "You're not even a citizen and can't vote."

Robbie pushed off the bookcase and rose to his full

height. "Lucky for you, mate, because I wouldn't be voting for you."

Hensen gasped, and Lindsey heard a giggle, which she was certain came from the circulation desk but didn't dare look to confirm. She stared right at the mayor, not glancing away and not meeting Robbie's gaze, for fear of breaking into a laugh herself. As if he suspected that she was barely keeping a lid on it, the mayor glared at her.

"You are not allowed to express any political opinions within the library," Mayor Hensen said. He pointed at her, and Lindsey was surprised to find that a stubby finger and a squinty eye could come across as so aggressive. "It's a part of every town employee's contract."

"I haven't expressed any opinions *within the library*," Lindsey said, emphasizing the important part of the town's policy on employees expressing political opinions while on the job. "You asked me a question, which I haven't even answered."

"Well, that's incidental," he snapped.

Lindsey sighed. If there was one part of her job that she didn't enjoy, it was the politics. Figuring out who in the town had the power to make or break the library. She found it annoying and exhausting as the players constantly shifted with the wind, especially with Mayor Hensen, who seemed to tilt toward whoever flattered him the most.

She firmly believed that decisions should be made and things should be done because they were for the overall good of the residents of the town—not because so-and-so donated a chunk of money to someone's campaign, allowing their personal interests to override everyone else's quality of life.

"Mayor, it's time for your lunch meeting at the VFW." Herb Gunderson, the mayor's right-hand man, strode through the doors of the library.

The mayor yanked on the lapels of his jacket and scowled in the direction of Ms. Cole. When he spoke, his voice carried across the room. "That's right, *I* have a luncheon to attend."

Ms. Cole glanced up and smiled at him with a great big toothy grin. The lemon never smiled like that. It made Lindsey nervous.

"Have the roast beef on sourdough," Ms. Cole called back to the mayor. "That's what I had when I was there last week. Delicious!"

The mayor's nostrils flared and he stomped toward the exit. The automatic doors swooshed shut behind him, taking all of his hot air and his sidekick, Herb, with him.

"Was he always such a pompous ass?" Robbie asked. "Or am I seeing him in a new light?"

"I've only known him during his second term, but he didn't seem to be so overbearing when I was first hired on," Lindsey said. "I'm not sure why he's being so aggressive now."

"It's an identity thing," Violet LaRue said. She was tall and lean, with her silver hair scraped into a bun at the nape of her neck. A former star on Broadway and one of the first African American actresses to win a Tony Award, Violet always entered a room as if she were taking a curtain call.

She and Robbie were old theater friends as they had toured the world together in several shows before she retired to Briar Creek, where she ran the community theater. Now she was one of Lindsey's longtime craft-ernooners and a dear friend.

"Violet's right. He's in crisis. I'm sure he feels that if he's no longer mayor, he won't know who he is anymore," Nancy Peyton, Violet's best friend, said. "It's making him scared and he's lashing out. It happens to the best of us when we lose our sense of self or purpose."

Lindsey nodded. She occasionally forgot that Nancy, with her bright blue eyes and head of thick gray hair, had been widowed at a young age. Having formerly rented an apartment in Nancy's three-story captain's house, Lindsey knew firsthand that even all these years later, Nancy still struggled with the loss of the life she thought she'd have with her boat captain Jake. Having just married her own boat captain, Lindsey paused to think about what could happen to her husband, Sully, out there on the water. It was devastating to consider.

"That makes sense," she said. She'd never thought of the mayor as a particularly mean man, but he'd certainly become rather high maintenance since Ms. Cole had gotten her name on the ballot. If Lindsey remembered right, he'd run unopposed during the last election. Since politics had recently become the world's new spectator sport, Lindsey imagined the days of running unchallenged were long over. "I'm afraid it's going to be a long six months until the election."

"Agreed." Violet nodded. "But Ms. Cole has the fortitude of a bison. She can endure the strain of it."

"And we'll be here to help," Nancy said. She glanced over at the circulation desk where Ms. Cole stood frowning at the doors through which the mayor had departed. She waved to get her attention, and when Ms. Cole glanced over, Nancy gave her a double thumbs-up.

Ms. Cole broke into a grin, and it transformed her. Her eyes twinkled and her lips parted as she let out a laugh that was surprisingly contagious. Lindsey was having a hard time reconciling the new boisterous Ms. Cole with the tart old lemon who had given her such a hard time when she first arrived in Briar Creek.

It occurred to her that the Ms. Cole she'd met when she arrived in Briar Creek wasn't the real Ms. Cole after all. Perhaps that stern woman was just who she'd been at the time and now, with a fuller life, she'd blossomed into who she truly was. Lindsey knew she couldn't take credit for the complete transformation, but she definitely felt as if she'd contributed at least a little.

Remembering her egg salad sandwiches and cheddar-broccoli tartlets, she pointed to the watch on her wrist and said, "Isn't it time for crafternoon?"

Violet and Nancy exchanged a glance. Together, they began to walk toward the crafternoon room. "Just an hour to talk about Mr. Darcy," Nancy said. "Not nearly enough time."

"Agreed, he's definitely worth several hours of discussion," Violet said.

"And if we could watch the movie version with Colin Firth and study—" Nancy paused and they glanced at each other with sly smiles.

"The lake scene," they said together and then burst out laughing.

"See you at the meeting, Lindsey," Violet called over her shoulder.

"Right behind you," Lindsey said. She turned back to Robbie. "Thanks for getting me out of that pickle with the mayor."

"No problem, he's such a gherkin," he said.

Lindsey laughed despite herself. "That was terrible."

"And yet, you laughed," Robbie said. His light green eyes twinkled at her, and he swept the reddish blond hair off his forehead when it fell into his eyes.

"I'm obviously starving and getting light-headed," Lindsey said. "I can't be held accountable for laughing at terrible jokes. Still, thank you for deflecting him. Your timing was excellent."

"He seemed like he was winding himself up for no good reason."

"As I said, I think we're in for a long six months."

She turned to head to the crafternoon room but then remembered they had plans for the evening. "You and Emma are still meeting Sully and me at the Blue Anchor for dinner, right?"

"Wouldn't miss it," he said. "Between the two of us, Emma and I can barely fry an egg without burning it. A nice seafood dinner will be a welcome change from our own cooking."

Lindsey bit her lip to keep from laughing. She and Sully had been to Robbie and Emma's house for dinner, and he wasn't wrong about their cooking. They'd ended up ordering pizza when Robbie's steaks turned into charcoal briquettes and Emma's potato salad was on the crunchy, undercooked side.

"See you at six, then!" she said. She turned to go, crossing the room while scanning to see that everything was as it should be. She was about to turn down the hallway when a patron called her back.

"Lindsey, can I have a word . . . Nah, forget it."

Lindsey stopped and turned. Standing by the computer terminals was Ivy Kavanagh. She was on the upper end of middle-aged, born and raised in Briar Creek.

Lindsey knew her mostly because they ended up at a lot of the same town functions, as Ivy was very civic minded. She ran an international charity that was dedicated to reforestation, and she seemed to know how to dip her fingers into the deepest pockets. She was trim and fit and hanging on to her youth with a tight fist.

"Forget what?" Lindsey asked. She smiled at Ivy. Being on the tall side, Lindsey was always pleased when she met another tall woman. In Ivy's case she was just over medium height, but she wore her short white hair in spikes, giving her a few extra inches.

"Well, I don't want to talk out of turn," Ivy said. She looked uncomfortable and glanced around as if to make certain no one could hear them. "But you don't think the mayor would do anything to harm Ms. Cole, do you?"

Lindsey blinked. "Why do you say that?"

Ivy put her hand on her throat. "I'm sorry, but I couldn't help but overhear, and if Mayor Hensen's identity is really as wrapped up in being the mayor as your friends say, then he may perceive Ms. Cole as a threat that has to be eradicated."

Lindsey stared at Ivy. Did the woman know something about the mayor? She wanted to ask but wasn't sure how.

She would have dismissed Ivy's words immediately, but she'd seen enough murderous behavior over the years to know that there was no telling what a person would do if they felt sufficiently aggrieved. But this was Mayor Hensen and, yes, he was a bit of a blowhard and, sure, he had dismissed her concerns when she was dealing with a stalker last year, but he wasn't necessarily evil, just ineffectual. She shook her head.

"No," she said. "I'm sure Mayor Hensen didn't mean to come across as so overbearing. I mean, he isn't that bad. I can't believe he'd ever actually harm anyone."

"If you say so," Ivy said. She shrugged as if to say she hoped Lindsey knew what she was doing. "But if I were you, I'd guard her back."

Lindsey watched Ivy walk away. She strode with purpose right out the front door, and again Lindsey wondered if she knew something about the mayor that she wasn't sharing.

"Hey, yoo-hoo, anyone in there?" Robbie snapped his fingers in front of her, and Lindsey jumped.

"Sorry," she said. She sucked in a breath and shook her head. "I was lost in thought."

"Clearly—I had to say your name three times," Robbie said. "I just got a text from Emma saying she'll be late but to go ahead without her."

"Oh, okay," Lindsey said. "Robbie, you don't think the mayor would hurt Ms. Cole, do you?"

He shook his head. "No . . . er . . . I don't know. Maybe or maybe not. He certainly looked at Ms. Cole as if he'd *like* to do her some harm. I can tail him if you'd like."

"No," she said. "But you're not the only one to say that."

"Then you'd best be careful. He is still your boss. See you later."

He stepped through the open glass doors, and they swooshed closed behind him. Lindsey watched him go and felt her insides clench. She hated to admit it, but Ivy was right. There had been a moment when the look on the mayor's face was . . . unsettling and Robbie had seen it, too, so it wasn't just her imagination.

She shook her head and hurried to her meeting. Things had been so quiet for the past several months. She was not going to start looking for trouble when there was none. Maybe Ivy had picked up on a vibe. Lindsey had felt it, too, but she'd discourage all talk of the mayor in this regard from now on. It would do them no good to obsess about what he said and did. Robbie had always helped Lindsey with her investigations in the past. It was amazing what a library director had to do sometimes. Obviously, they both needed a new hobby.

CHAPTER

2

BRIAR CREEK
PUBLIC LIBRARY

I don't get it," Paula said. "What is the allure of Darcy? I mean, he's kind of a jerk."

"Ah," Beth gasped. The top bun of her hamburger costume flapped as if to emphasize her outrage. "He is *Darcy*! He is the perfect male."

"Is he? Is he really though?" Paula persisted. "I mean, sure, he's rich and all, but he's not the warmest sort of man, now is he?"

Beth blinked as if she couldn't comprehend such heresy spoken about one of her most beloved book boyfriends. The crafternoon room had gone very quiet. Nothing could bring out stronger emotions in their group than character loyalty.

"I think I'm going to have to rethink our entire relationship," Beth said to Paula.

Paula laughed and shook her head. Her eyes sparkled when she said, "Well, that answers that."

"What?" Nancy asked with a frown.

"Who of the crafternooners is most in love with Fitz-william Darcy," Paula said. She winked at Beth, who blushed a hot shade of pink.

"You set me up," she said. But then she laughed. "Yeah, it's me."

"Can you imagine the library in Pemberley?" Lindsey asked. "Even if Darcy is flawed, I could overlook a lot for a man with a library like that."

Nancy laughed. "Does Sully know your head can be turned by a vast collection of books?"

"Yes, which is why we have one ground rule in our marriage," Lindsey said. "Books are considered an essential expense, assuming I feel the need to own a volume outside of borrowing from the public library, which I frequently do."

"We're getting off track," Beth said. She wrestled her burger costume off, dumping it in the corner of the room. Underneath, she was wearing a maternity blouse and pants. She folded her hands on top of her belly and said, "I'm sorry, but I have to insist that when Darcy says, 'In vain I have struggled. It will not do. My feelings will not be repressed. You must allow me to tell you how ardently I admire and love you,' he becomes the best book boyfriend of all time."

"Admittedly, that is a lovely sentiment," Paula agreed. "But at that point in the book, he still thinks she's not truly worthy of him because of her low-class family."

"Redemption," Violet said. "His character arc needs redemption from his pride and prejudice. I agree with Beth. It is delightful to watch Elizabeth Bennet stand her ground and demand to be treated with the respect she deserves. Truly, it was a glorious take at the time the novel was written."

"Jane was ahead of her time," Lindsey said. "Did you know that when her novels were published, they didn't use her name as the author? Her first novel was published as being by 'A Lady' and her second, our selection this week, was credited as 'the writer of *Sense and Sensibility*.' None of her novels were published under her name until after her death and then only at her brother's insistence."

"She died young, didn't she?" Beth asked. "Only forty-one."

"Yes," Paula said. "Unknown causes, although they suspect it was Addison's disease or possibly lead poisoning since so much lead was used in household items during the Regency period."

"You have to wonder how many more novels she would have written," Nancy said. "Maybe even a sequel to *Pride and Prejudice*."

"I read that the original title of the book was *First Impressions*," Beth said. "But Austen was a great admirer of Frances Burney and her novel *Cecelia, or Memoirs of an Heiress*. There's a quote from that novel which reads, '"The whole of this unfortunate business," said Dr. Lyster, "has been the result of pride and prejudice."' I'd never heard of Frances Burney before, but I'm on the lookout for that novel."

"We don't have it?" Lindsey asked.

"No, but I already put in a request through interlibrary loan," Beth said. "It was republished in 2017 by a London publisher called Forgotten Books, which is an amazing treasure trove of old out-of-print volumes. Seriously, they even have books of household tips for the domestically impaired woman in the eighteen hundreds. Talk about a historical rabbit hole. Needless to say, I'm ridiculously excited to get it."

"You know, forgotten books as a subject would make a wonderful display," Lindsey said. "We could gather little-known or long-neglected novels and nonfiction books and put them on a shelf in the front of the library—"

"Sorry I'm late," Ms. Cole said. She strode into the room with her copy of *Pride and Prejudice* in hand. "There was a reporter from the *Gazette* here asking questions about my campaign." She looked momentarily befuddled. "I really can't believe I'm doing this."

"Why not?" Nancy asked. "You're more than qualified."

"Hensen has been the mayor *forever*, and I don't see the town flourishing under his leadership. Mostly, I think he just likes to ride around in the convertible during the Memorial Day parade," Violet said.

"Exactly," Beth agreed. "We need a mayor who understands the community, and that's you, Ms. Cole. Why, I'll bet you've issued library cards to just about every resident in town. You know the families, the businesses, the impact of summer tourists, and you've been witness to the growth of the area over the years. No one knows Briar Creek better."

"Agreed," Paula said. "I know we're not supposed to talk politics at work, but is there anything we can do to help you with your campaign at the moment?"

Ms. Cole started to shake her head and then she paused. "There is one thing."

"Name it," Nancy said.

"At Beth's suggestion, I ordered a batch of yard signs and picked them up at the printer's today," Ms. Cole said. "If any of you are willing to put them in your yards, that would be helpful, you know, to get the ball rolling."

The normally indomitable Ms. Cole looked unaccountably shy, and Lindsey knew that running for mayor and asking for help with her campaign was making her feel excruciatingly vulnerable.

"Absolutely," Nancy said. "In fact, I'll take several as I have friends who'll want to support you as well."

"Me, too," Violet said. "The community theater is behind you one hundred percent."

Ms. Cole let out a sigh of relief. "Thank you."

"Do you have them with you?" Paula asked.

Ms. Cole nodded. "In the trunk of my car."

"Excellent. Why don't we end the meeting early and collect the signs now?" Nancy suggested.

"I'll pick mine up later when we have our strategy session," Beth said to Ms. Cole. "I'll start the cleanup in here while you're handing out the signs." She flashed a peace sign at the group. "Vote Cole!"

Nancy clapped her hands together. "Let's get to it."

"Hang on, I'm almost done," Lindsey said. She had chosen a length of blue velvet ribbon that was the exact shade of her husband Sully's eyes. She'd found the perfect charm to attach to it. A tiny ship's wheel in antiqued brass. He was a big reader of the Patrick O'Brian Aubrey/Maturin nautical historical novels set against the Napoleonic Wars, and she knew he'd appreciate her efforts with the bookmark.

"I can't quite get it," she said. She was using the needle-nose pliers to open the jump ring that would hold the charm onto the ribbon clamp, which she'd clipped onto the end of the velvet ribbon. She could feel everyone watching her, and it only made her clumsier. The jump ring slipped out of the pliers. "Nuts!"

Paula held out her hands. "Can I assist?"

Lindsey handed over her ribbon with the clamp and the pliers. She watched in envy as Paula made quick work of attaching the ring and then the charm. Lindsey would have been annoyed, but it was well-known that she was not a crafter, and besides, the bookmark looked so cool she couldn't be upset.

Paula held it out to her, and Lindsey smiled. "Thank you. Someday we'll find a craft I can manage."

"Have you considered quilling?" Violet asked as they all headed toward the door.

"Does that have something to do with porcupines?" Lindsey asked. "Because I would have to take a hard pass on that."

Violet laughed and shook her head. She turned to Paula and said, "Can you explain?"

"Yes, in fact, it's a very Austen-approved craft. Strips of colored paper are coiled, folded and shaped and then glued into pictures."

"Oh, that does sound very lady of leisure," Nancy said.

Lindsey frowned at Paula. "Paper crafts. I clearly need to spend more time in the 745.5 area of the library."

"And I know just the books to show you," Paula said.

"Oh, goody," Lindsey said with a marked lack of enthusiasm that made the others laugh.

The group made its way out the staff entrance at the back of the building to the parking lot. Ms. Cole led the way to her car, which was parked in the corner of the lot in the designated staff area. She abruptly stopped, and Lindsey had to veer to the right to keep from plowing into her.

"Are you all right, Ms. Cole?"

"No." Ms. Cole pointed to the dark blue sedan that Lindsey knew was hers. "Someone tampered with my car."

"What? How do you— Oh."

Lindsey followed the line of her gaze and saw that the yard signs Ms. Cole had mentioned were all over the ground around her trunk.

"How did they get into your car?" Violet asked. She sounded indignant as they strode across the lot as one.

"There were too many signs to close my trunk properly," Ms. Cole said. "I had it tied shut with a piece of rope I keep in the car for that sort of thing."

"It looks as if your trunk is still tied," Nancy said. "Could they have taken them out around the rope?"

"I don't think so. It was tied tight," Ms. Cole said. "And it's odd, isn't it? If they went to the trouble of pulling my signs out of the trunk, why would they retie it closed?"

Paula bent over and started picking up the thick corrugated plastic signs, but Lindsey held up her hand and said, "Wait."

They all turned to look at her and she explained, "Possibly, it's just vandalism, but on the off chance it's something else, we shouldn't touch anything, at least, not without taking photos first. If this becomes a pattern of behavior where vandals strike the library parking lot, we're going to want a record."

"But who would vandalize Ms. Cole—?" Nancy began to ask but then stopped.

Ms. Cole narrowed her eyes and glanced back at the library. "Mayor Hensen."

Violet gasped. "Really? Do you think so?"

"Of course, it all makes sense," Paula said. She clapped her hand to her forehead. "He never comes into the library unless he has a meeting, and he deliberately provoked you about your campaign today, making certain everyone in the library stayed in the building to watch, which kept everyone out of the parking lot except for people arriving, but he could have worked around that."

"Except, if he was in the library, how could he have vandalized her car?" Nancy asked.

"His henchman, Herb Gunderson, did it," Paula said. "When he entered the building, he was huffing and puffing as if he'd been exerting himself. I'll bet the mayor told him to do it while he distracted everyone."

"That's an awful lot of speculation there," Lindsey said. While she wouldn't put it past the mayor to ask Herb to do something like that, she had a hard time believing Herb, a straight shooter and a stickler for the rules, would have done something so out of character.

"It fits though," Ms. Cole said. "The timing of it at any rate."

She had Lindsey there. "All right, let's get some pictures of all of this before we pick up the signs."

Paula had her cell phone out in a flash and worked the area, taking photos of the car, the signs on the ground and the surrounding area. She was going full-on crime scene tech, which Lindsey appreciated, but she could only imagine what the Briar Creek police chief was going to say when presented with seventy-five pictures of the back of Ms. Cole's car.

"All right," Paula said. "I think I got every possible angle."

"Really? Are you quite sure?" Violet asked.

"How about an aerial shot?" Nancy joined in the teasing. "You can climb up on the roof of the car for one."

"Ha ha," Paula said. "You joke but if Lindsey's right and we become the target of vandals, we'll be glad of a complete record from when it began."

"Okay, let's get these cleaned up," Lindsey said. She put her hand on Ms. Cole's arm and asked, "Are you all right? I know it's terrible to think of someone violating your things, but it doesn't look as if they damaged them, so that's something."

Ms. Cole nodded in quick jerky movements that indicated she was upset but trying to rally. "I suppose it's just the price of politics these days. It does seem to bring out the worst in people."

"Don't you fret, Ms. Cole." Paula held up her phone. "We'll find out who did it."

"It might have just been some teenagers looking for trouble," Lindsey said. The fire in Paula's eyes was making her uneasy.

"Perhaps," Ms. Cole said. Clearly, she was still thinking the mayor was involved.

"Or possibly, it could have been completely random. Maybe someone was just looking to see if you had anything of value in your trunk," Violet said. She glanced at the other women. "That sounded better in my head, somehow."

Ms. Cole chuckled and the tension in the group was eased. "You're right. I'm just being silly. I can't imagine the mayor would stoop to vandalizing my yard signs. I'm just rattled from our earlier confrontation."

She stepped forward and tugged on the rope that held the trunk shut. It was tied securely, and she worked on the knot while Lindsey and the others gathered the signs that looked as if they'd been thrown onto the ground in haste but were otherwise in fine condition.

Maybe the person had been hoping Ms. Cole had a flat-screen television in her trunk and when they found political signs, they tossed them on the ground in a snit. Still, why would they have tied it shut again? That was just strange, especially if they were in a hurry to get out of there.

Lindsey held a stack of signs in her arms as she waited for Ms. Cole to finish. When she pulled the rope free and the trunk popped up, Paula stepped forward and then stopped. Her head whipped toward Ms. Cole, and her voice was tight with shock when she asked, "Is that . . . a body?"

CHAPTER
3

BRIAR CREEK
PUBLIC LIBRARY

hat?!" Nancy yelped and they all pressed closer to see.

Lindsey only got a glance of what appeared to be a man before Ms. Cole stepped back from the car, holding out her arms and pulling them all with her.

"There is a man in my car," she whispered as if she were afraid she might wake him. "We need to call the police."

"Ms. Cole, we have to see if he's all right," Lindsey said. "He could be in trouble."

"Oh, he's in trouble all right," Nancy said. "He's in a trunk." She was pale and her hands were trembling. She put her signs down on the ground and turned to Paula, and said, "Call an ambulance, please. Hurry."

Lindsey dropped her signs, too, and turned to Ms. Cole. "I need to check on whoever is in there."

"You're right." Ms. Cole shook her head. "I just . . . Be careful, Lindsey."

She dropped her arms, allowing Lindsey access to the back of the car. Lindsey stepped forward. The trunk was deep and dark. Several of Ms. Cole's signs were still in there, and just beyond them was a man.

He was folded up, his limbs at awkward angles and his body half curled. He was facing the opening so Lindsey had a clear view of his face in the sunlight. Alarmingly, his eyes were open, bloodshot and staring past them with an arrested expression as if he'd been caught by surprise.

"Oh, dear," Nancy gasped and turned away. Violet swept a protective arm about her friend, knowing how sensitive she was about death.

Lindsey leaned forward. She could hear Paula talking to the dispatcher for an ambulance. Even though help was on its way, they couldn't just leave the man there unattended. They had to be certain that he couldn't be helped before they abandoned him completely.

She reached forward and pressed her fingers against his wrist. The cuff of his shirtsleeve beneath his suit jacket was bunched up, exposing the skin. Lindsey pressed down, feeling for a pulse. There was nothing. She moved her fingers up under his jawline, clenching her teeth as she did so. She suspected it was a futile effort but she tried anyway. Again, nothing. In a last-ditch effort, she put her hand on his chest, hoping to find a heartbeat. It was still.

There was no rise and fall to his chest. He wasn't breathing. His skin was cold. His body looked stiff. She pulled her hand away. Whoever he was, he was gone. As she shifted away from him, she noticed an abrasion just visible beneath the collar of his shirt. She gently moved his collar aside and felt her breath catch. They were ligature marks going all the way across his throat, red and violent against the pale, peachy skin. It was clear he had been strangled. Lindsey felt her stomach drop, and her insides went icy cold.

She glanced at Paula and asked, "Did you call for an ambulance?"

"Yes," she said. Lines creased her forehead in concern.

"We'd better make a direct call to Chief Plewicki," Lindsey said. She braced herself before adding, "I don't think the EMTs will be able to help him."

Paula's eyes went wide and she glanced down at her phone. With a swift shake of her head, as if she was trying to center herself, she started pressing numbers.

"He's dead, then?" Ms. Cole asked.

"I'm afraid so." Lindsey nodded. They glanced back at the body in the trunk. "Do you recognize him?"

Ms. Cole studied the man in the navy suit with his short gray hair and clean-shaven face for several long moments until the sound of an incoming siren broke the silence and her concentration.

"No, I don't recognize him," she said. She glanced at Lindsey. "You?"

Lindsey shook her head. "No."

Violet had taken Nancy off to the side, but it was clear that neither of them recognized the man either, and when Lindsey turned to ask Paula, she anticipated the question and shook her head.

"He wasn't a library user, that's for sure." Paula was still clutching her phone in her hand like she was planning to use it to ward off evil. She noticed Lindsey's glance and said, "The chief is on her way."

As if Paula had conjured her out of the air, a police car came screeching into the parking lot, and Lindsey saw Chief Emma Plewicki in the driver's seat. She parked several spaces away and came out of her vehicle in a rush. Despite being the chief, she wore the standard-issue navy blue slacks and dress shirt of her officers. Her dark hair was in a loose bun at the nape of her neck and securely fastened beneath her hat with the narrow brim and the shield visible on the front. Her belt was weighted down with all of her gear as she strode forward in her thick-soled shoes.

Lindsey met her halfway and fell into a hurried step beside her.

"What seems to be the trouble?" Emma asked. "Molly, the dispatcher, said you found a body, but I am hoping, really hoping, that the transmission was garbled."

Lindsey slowly shook her head. "Sorry. You heard right. We came out to grab some of Ms. Cole's yard signs from her car and found them on the ground, and when we untied the trunk, we found him."

"Show me," Emma said. Lindsey led Emma toward the trunk and the man inside. To her credit, Emma didn't even flinch. She pulled a pair of blue latex gloves out of her pocket and tugged them on while moving in close to examine the man. Lindsey pulled Ms. Cole and the others back from the car. They stacked the signs they'd gathered off to the side while they waited.

Lindsey watched Emma with a feeling of unreality. They'd just been discussing *Pride and Prejudice*, debating the merits of Mr. Darcy, and now they were outside the library, watching the chief of police examine the body of a stranger found in Ms. Cole's car.

The middle-aged man wasn't someone Lindsey

could recall ever seeing before. Of course, it could be that he looked very different in death than he had in life. She felt a shiver start at the base of her spine and shimmy its way up her back to sit at the base of her skull like a cold finger pressing against her skin. Poor Ms. Cole. Of all the cars for him to have landed in, why hers?

But of course it was because her trunk had been tied shut. It was easy access for someone who wanted to dispose of a body. Judging by the marks around the man's neck, he had been murdered in one of the worst possible ways. Strangled to death.

Lindsey glanced at her friends. She could see by the grim expressions on their faces that they were thinking along the same lines she was. This man, this stranger, had been murdered and dumped, but by whom and why?

The sound of the ambulance arriving broke the silence that engulfed them. Lindsey turned and faced the entrance to the lot. She raised her hand over her head to wave them in as if the police car wasn't obvious enough.

The emergency vehicle pulled up beside them, and the EMTs popped out. Emma stepped back from the trunk and headed them off. Lindsey could hear her having a whispered conversation with the lead EMT while the other two gathered their equipment.

"Lindsey," Emma called out to her. "Can you take everyone back into the library? I'll be there shortly to get your statements."

"Sure," Lindsey agreed. "We'll be in the meeting room." She turned and gestured for the others to come with her. "Let's get out of their way."

Nancy and Violet didn't hesitate and headed for the library as if fleeing the scene of a crime, which judging by the dead body in the trunk, they were. Paula lagged, staying with Ms. Cole, who seemed reluctant to leave.

"I'm sure Emma will give us all the information she can as soon as possible," Lindsey said.

"I know, but it just feels wrong to leave when there's a . . . dead . . . deceased person in my car," Ms. Cole said. She seemed torn between going and staying, and Lindsey didn't want to push her but didn't think it was mentally healthy for any of them to stay.

Just when she was getting ready to insist that Ms. Cole go back to the library to wait, Milton Duffy came striding across the parking lot. "Eugenia, my dear, Violet and Nancy told me what's happening. Are you all right?"

Paula and Lindsey exchanged a look. That was quick work. Milton was an octogenarian who was also the town's resident historian as well as a yogi. He was frequently in the library, coaching the chess club or doing a series of asanas. He was also Ms. Cole's significant other. They were an incongruous couple, given that Milton was a seeker of Zen and maintained a live-and-let-live code, whereas Ms. Cole was more like a keeper of the force, meting out consequences if someone was doing something they shouldn't.

As Ms. Cole looked at Milton, he must have seen the powerful emotions she was struggling with. He put his arm around her shoulders and ushered her toward the library, leaving Lindsey and Paula to fall into step behind them. When they arrived back in the crafternoon room, Beth was listening with rapt attention to Violet and Nancy, who were recounting finding the man in Ms. Cole's trunk.

"Who is he?" she asked them. Both ladies shrugged. Beth looked past them at Lindsey in inquiry.

"No idea," Lindsey said.

Violet and Nancy sat down at the table, which was still littered with the remnants of their bookmark craft. Ms. Cole didn't sit and Milton stood beside her as if afraid she might collapse without his support.

Paula began to clean up the ribbons and charms, as if by keeping busy she could manage the anxiety that was coursing through all of them. Lindsey glanced at the cart of food she'd prepared for today. They'd wiped out most of it during their crafternoon, and Beth had already wrapped up the leftovers, which they usually put in the staff room for anyone who wanted them.

Lindsey wanted to pace the length of the room to work off her own energy but didn't want to make anyone else anxious by being in constant motion. Some people were touchy about stuff like that. She glanced at Beth, who looked troubled.

"What is it, Beth?" she asked.

"Nothing, really, except I'm not sure what to do while we wait. Should we alert the rest of the staff or the patrons? Or, worse thought here, do we need to call the mayor?"

Lindsey suppressed a groan, barely. Given their recent encounter, the last person she wanted to reach out to was the mayor.

"I think I'll let Chief Plewicki take the lead on that," she said. "She will likely have more information than I to give him."

They were all silent, mulling over how the mayor was going to react to the news. Lindsey felt her stomach knot at the thought that he might use this in his campaign against Ms. Cole.

"This doesn't look good for me, does it?" Ms. Cole asked. "I mean, that the person was found in my car."

"I don't see how that's your fault," Nancy said.

"She's right," Violet agreed. "Your car was obviously just easy access."

"It's just rotten luck," Milton said. His gaze swept over each of them. "Mostly for him."

Lindsey nodded. He was right. The person who'd suffered the most was the man who'd been murdered.

"You're right," Ms. Cole said. "I shouldn't be thinking about myself right now. That poor man. How awful."

"The marks around his neck . . ." Violet's voice trailed off and she shuddered.

"It was terrible," Nancy said.

The tension in the room ratcheted up as they each recalled the horror of finding the man stuffed into the trunk as if he were of no more significance than a piece of luggage.

"Let's try and dispel some of this stress and tension," Milton said. His voice took on the quiet authority of a man used to leading others into a calmer state of mind. Wearing his usual tracksuit, today's in navy, with his bald head and silver goatee, he had the look of a tall and slender sensei. "We need to be calm and await word from the chief rather than getting ourselves all in a dither. In fact, let's all do some deep breathing exercises together."

The women all turned to face him. Even if someone wasn't in the mood for the exercises, they'd never say so. Milton was the sort of person you couldn't bear to disappoint. Lindsey, who would still rather be pacing, joined the loose circle they'd formed, and prepared to follow his lead.

"Let's focus on our breath," he instructed. "In through your nose for eight counts." He demonstrated and they all mimicked him. "Hold for four, and now release for eight through your mouth. And again."

The room went quiet. The only sound was that of gentle breathing. Lindsey felt her heart rate slow. Her shoulders dropped. Her mind cleared. When Milton had coached them through several rounds, the intensity of the emotions in the room eased.

"That's better," he said. He was studying Ms. Cole closely and he nodded. "You're getting some color back in your face, my dear."

Ms. Cole gave him a small smile, but it vanished almost as soon as it had appeared when Emma strode into the room. Her face was set in grim lines, and Lindsey knew the chief of police well enough to know that this meant she was deeply disturbed.

"Ms. Cole, if I could speak to you for a moment?" she asked.

"Alone?" Ms. Cole asked.

"Yes, please."

"Is that really necessary?" Milton asked. "I'd like to be there in case it's too upsetting for her."

"I'm afraid so," Emma said. She glanced around the room. "I'll be talking to each of you individually, and I'd prefer it to be one-on-one so that I get each person's unique perspective." She glanced at Beth. "Except for you, Beth. Since you weren't there, you're free to go."

"Okay," Beth said. She didn't leave the room, however, and Lindsey suspected it was because she was feeling a solidarity with her crafternoon sisters and didn't want to abandon them.

"I'll be all right," Ms. Cole said to Milton. She patted his hand where it rested on her shoulder, and then stiffened her spine. "Where would you like to do this? The police station?"

"Oh, no, here in the library is fine. If I could use an office?" Emma asked Lindsey.

"Sure, you can use mine," she said. "It's more private."

"Thanks." Emma turned to Ms. Cole. "After you."

The rest of them watched as the two women left.

Beth pushed up from her seat and sidled over to Lindsey as gracefully as she could given her protruding belly. While Milton closed his eyes and continued his breathing exercises, obviously in an effort to calm himself down, Beth lowered her voice and asked, "Straight talk, do you really not know who he was?"

Lindsey glanced at her in surprise and whispered, "Do you really think I would keep that from everyone, particularly Emma?"

"No, I just thought you might not share with the group. You can tell me if you knew him."

"I didn't." Lindsey shrugged. "He was just a middle-aged guy in a suit, although . . ."

Beth rolled her hand in a gesture to continue. "Don't stop. Although what?"

"He looked fit for his age," Lindsey said. She lowered

her voice even more. "But judging by the marks around his neck, he was clearly strangled. So whoever did it must have either surprised him or been very strong."

"Do you mean 'surprised him' as in he didn't see them coming or 'surprised him' in that he didn't suspect them of trying to kill him and was caught off guard?"

"Could be either," Lindsey said. "But it seems like a horrible way to go, being strangled and stuffed in someone's trunk. I wonder if Emma found any identification on him."

"You can ask her," Beth said. She jerked her chin at the door, and Lindsey turned around to see Emma and Ms. Cole returning.

"That was quick," she said. She studied Ms. Cole's face. She looked calmer, as if talking to the chief had steadied her, but she was also pasty pale and there was a tremble in her fingers. It was clear she was still shaken up.

"Eugenia, I am taking you home," Milton said.

Ms. Cole looked at him in surprise. "I can't leave work in the middle of the day."

"Yes, you can," Lindsey said. She glanced at Emma. "I imagine the car is going to have to be impounded?"

Emma nodded and Lindsey turned back to Ms. Cole. "You're going to have things to do, like rent a car and such. Take the afternoon off. We'll be fine."

Ms. Cole frowned. Spontaneously taking time off was not in her comfort zone. "I'd like to finish up my current project. It'll only take about an hour, and then I'll go. But call me if you need me."

"I will," Lindsey lied.

"Thank you," Milton said. "I'll take good care of her."

"I know." Lindsey expected Emma to call her next, but she didn't. Instead, it was Paula, then Violet, and Nancy. Lindsey was alone in the room, as everyone else had gone back to work or home, when Emma returned for the last time.

"Last but not least," Emma said. "Thanks for your patience."

"No problem," Lindsey said. "Do you want to go to my office or should we just talk here?"

"Here is fine," Emma said. She sat in the armchair across from Lindsey in front of the barren fireplace. Lindsey liked this room best in the winter when they got to have cozy fires. The fire chief hated having a gas fireplace in the library, but Lindsey pointed out that there were no books in the vicinity and the room was kept locked. Patrons had to sign up to use it. It calmed him a little.

"So, tell me what happened with as much detail as you can remember," Emma said. She took a tiny digital recorder out of her pocket and set it on the arm of her chair.

Lindsey talked about the crafternoon and how Ms. Cole arrived late because of her interview with the *Gazette*.

"Did you see the reporter?" Emma asked.

"No," Lindsey said. She frowned. That felt like an odd question. "Should I have?"

Emma's face was blank. "No. Continue, please."

"All right, the talk turned to Ms. Cole's campaign for mayor, and we all encouraged her." Lindsey paused to check Emma's expression. It remained clear. "While we were talking about it, she said she had picked up her yard signs that morning and asked us if we wanted any."

Emma nodded. Clearly this checked out with what the others had said.

"We decided to end crafternoon early and headed out to her car so she could give us some signs," Lindsey said. "We were halfway across the parking lot when Ms. Cole noticed her signs were on the ground." Lindsey paused. She didn't mention that Ms. Cole had suspected the mayor of tampering with her car. It had proven to not be the case, and Lindsey didn't want to bring attention to the squabble between Ms. Cole and the mayor earlier in the day. It seemed irrelevant after the discovery of a body.

"And when you got to the car?" Emma asked.

Lindsey described Ms. Cole untying the rope and then opening the trunk. She told Emma how she had gasped and pulled them all back away from it. Emma nodded. Clearly the others had mentioned this as well.

"Not a completely unreasonable response," Emma said. "She must have been shocked."

"Absolutely, we all were." Lindsey then described stepping up to the trunk herself to see if she could render any assistance to the man. She told Emma how she tried to find the man's pulse with no success while Paula called for help.

"What time was that?" Emma asked. "The medical examiner might want to know in case it helps determine time of death."

"Maybe twelve fiftyish," Lindsey said. "I wasn't really paying attention."

"That checks out. I arrived at five minutes until the

hour and I came straight from the station after Paula's call," Emma said. "Did you know right away he was dead?"

Lindsey nodded. "I suspected, and when I checked for his pulse and found none, I saw the marks around his neck. Then I knew."

"Knew what?"

"That he'd been murdered."

CHAPTER

4

BRIAR CREEK
PUBLIC LIBRARY

As usual, Emma's face was devoid of any hint of what she was thinking. This was not going to work for Lindsey. A body was found on library property in the trunk of one of her staff members' cars. She needed more than the stone face.

"He was murdered," Lindsey repeated.

Emma studied her face and then slowly nodded her head. "It would appear so."

"Again, I saw the marks around his neck, Emma," Lindsey said.

"And the medical examiner will determine whether they are the cause of death or not."

She was good, Lindsey thought. Emma Plewicki was very talented at playing it close to the vest, which made her an excellent chief of police.

"Did he have any ID on him?" Lindsey asked.

"You're cute," Emma said.

Lindsey sighed. "Is there anything you can tell me?"

Emma's expression became thoughtful. "We have a deceased person in the trunk of a local resident's car."

"Sounds like the local news headline," Lindsey said. She considered her words carefully before she spoke. Emma was the head of the police department and Lindsey was the head of the library, so essentially, they had the same boss, Mayor Hensen. "Do you suppose there might be someone with something to gain by having a body found in a person's car?"

It wasn't that she was accusing the mayor of putting the body in Ms. Cole's car, but it certainly wasn't going to help Ms. Cole's campaign when word got out, and there was only one person who would benefit—her opponent.

"Are you asking me if a certain someone might be involved with putting a body in a certain person's car?" Emma asked. Her eyes were wide.

"I'm just saying that a certain someone was in the library about the same time that the body might have been put in a certain person's car," Lindsey said.

"Which would make it highly unlikely that they could be involved with a body being stuffed into a trunk in broad daylight on a Thursday afternoon," Emma said.

"Unless they were here because they wanted to make it look like they could have had nothing to do with a body being stuffed into a trunk when, in reality, they'd already done it."

"That feels like a heck of an overreach," Emma said. She rubbed her temples with the tips of her fingers as if warding off a headache. "Besides, we have no idea who the victim—" She abruptly stopped speaking.

Lindsey's eyebrows shot up. "So, you haven't been able to identify the man. No wallet or cell phone?"

Emma looked like she was about to tell Lindsey to get stuffed, but instead she nodded slowly, answering Lindsey's question without actually saying anything.

"Do you think he was robbed?"

"I don't know," Emma said. "It seems unlikely given the probable cause of his death. Robbers don't usually strangle people. They're in a hurry, they want your wallet or your watch, and they want to get out of there. Murder takes time. Plus, in this instance, the killer went out of their way to hide the body. Why not just leave him on the ground or hidden in the woods? Why stuff him in the trunk of a car?"

"Exactly," Lindsey said. "A very specific car."

"Or a convenient car," Emma countered.

"Any idea when the victim died?" Lindsey asked.

"Not yet," Emma said. "According to Ms. Cole she arrived at the library at nine, straight from the sign shop. The body wasn't discovered until almost four hours later. That's a pretty wide window of time to cover. I've got officers interviewing the patrons now, asking if they saw anything or can identify the man."

Lindsey cringed. She supposed it was weird, but she felt protective of her patrons and didn't want them to have to look at a picture of a deceased person and try to remember whether or not they'd seen him that morning.

"We'll try to pull together a list of every person who came into the library today so we can broaden our search, but given the fact that the staff cars are parked in the back corner of the lot with little to no visibility, I'm not holding out much hope."

Lindsey wanted to pepper Emma with a million more questions, but she held back. She knew that the chief didn't know much more than she did, and asking her was just going to annoy her. Emma could be prickly when she got her back up, and they were supposed to have dinner tonight.

Instead, she decided to steer the conversation in another direction and see what shook out.

"If I'd been approved for those security cameras I asked for last year, we might have gotten some video footage," Lindsey said. She didn't look at Emma but frowned at the floor, waiting to see where the chief went with the conversation.

"I know," Emma said. "The mayor asked my opinion of your request, and I told him I approved. Small wonder you didn't get your cameras."

"What do you mean?" Lindsey asked. Was there tension between the chief and the mayor? She was all ears. Anything that would help remove the mayor from office was A-OK with her. Not to put too fine a point on it, but she was betting that with Ms. Cole in charge, if she asked for security cameras, she'd get them.

"Just that when it comes to security, the mayor and I do not always see eye to eye."

"Why do I feel like that's an understatement?" Lindsey asked.

Emma smiled but it didn't reach her eyes. She rose from her seat and said, "That's all the questions I can think of for now, but I'll be in touch if there's more."

"Or you can ask me at dinner," Lindsey said. She rose, too, and began to walk back to the main library with Emma beside her.

"Right," Emma said. "I was already running late.

Now I have no idea how my day will roll out. I should be able to make it to the Anchor for a quick bite, but I'll text you if there's a change of plan."

"Sounds good," Lindsey said.

They stepped out into the hallway, which was deserted, and made their way to the main part of the building. Here, the vibe abruptly changed. A low hum of nervous excitement charged the air.

Lindsey glanced around the room and saw many of the same people who had been in the building before their crafternoon hour still there. A hiss of frantic whispers created background noise as patrons and staff watched Officer Kirkland work the room, interviewing people.

Lindsey saw him stop by the elderly sisters Mrs. Holman and Mrs. Gage, and show them something on his phone. Both ladies looked at the display and then quickly glanced away. Mrs. Gage shook her head vigorously and Mrs. Holman did the same.

The sisters were native Briar Creek residents, locally called "Creekers," who'd left the area when they married. Sadly, they were both widowed within a couple of years of each other. Together they had bought a little cottage by the water and settled in to live out their days on the seashore where they were born.

Lindsey knew that the sisters were partial to British police procedurals, particularly Deborah Crombie's Gemma Jones and Duncan Kincaid mysteries. They were active in the local food pantry and volunteered at the nearby hospital in New Haven on the information desk. They were both considered pillars of the community, and Lindsey hoped that their good opinion of the library didn't suffer now that they were being questioned by a police officer about a body found in the library parking lot. Mercy, they did not teach a class in this at library school.

"What do you want to bet she did it?" a whisper came from behind Lindsey.

She whipped her head around to see Pamela Kirby, one Lindsey's least favorite patrons, standing by a colorful display of picture books that Beth had put out. Pam was a close personal friend of the mayor's wife, Sarah Hensen, and she tried to use that relationship to jump ahead on the holds list for the more popular library items. It never worked, especially with Ms. Cole, and there was some bad blood between them because of it.

The woman standing beside Pam looked uncomfortable as everyone in the vicinity could hear what was being said, and she slowly sidled away as if trying to make it clear that she wasn't with Pam.

"I mean, look at her," Pam said, oblivious to the woman's departure. She tossed her shoulder-length black hair that she wore teased up to look supersized and said, "I mean, she's so evil-looking with the gray hair, no makeup, stocky build and frumpy attire. She totally looks like a murderer."

Pam jutted her chin in the direction of Ms. Cole, and Lindsey felt a white-hot spurt of anger surge through her. She took a step forward to confront Pam, but Emma caught her by the elbow, halting her.

"Easy," she said. "I know you want to protect your staff, but Ms. Cole is going to have to deal with this stuff as the campaign heats up, so she'd best learn to defend herself now."

"Plus, you want to hear what that awful woman says," Lindsey said.

"That, too."

Lindsey glanced at the circulation desk to watch Ms. Cole. She stood with her head bowed, a faint blush staining her cheeks. It was clear she'd heard what Pam said.

"How lucky for us that the cops are here and can arrest her," Pam continued in an even louder voice. She was clearly projecting so that Emma and Kirkland could hear her.

Neither of them acknowledged her. In fact, Emma had her phone out and appeared to be scrolling through her messages while Kirkland went on to the next cluster of patrons to question them about the body in the trunk.

The murmurs in the library got louder and louder as people watched, wondering what would happen next. Pam glanced around the room, looking for an ally. No one would meet her stare, and Lindsey suspected that Pam was not well-liked in their small community, where she enjoyed wielding her privileged life like a billy club on the less fortunate.

Lindsey remembered seeing Pam in action at a local school board meeting. She'd wanted the school board to fire a teacher because the teacher had given her daughter a failing grade when her child hadn't shown up for class, done any of the work or taken the final. The meeting had ended with Pam screaming that she knew the mayor and she'd have all their jobs. When her gaze veered in Lindsey's direction, Lindsey quickly turned to Emma.

"I think there's about to be a scene," she whispered.

"Good," Emma said. It was then that Lindsey noticed Emma had the video camera on her cell phone on even while she pretended to be flicking through messages.

"Genius."

"That's why I'm the chief."

Lindsey glanced up and saw Pam's eyes flash in anger. She clearly did not like being ignored. She stiffened her spine and strode up to the circulation desk. The lethal points of her high-heeled shoes dug into the industrial carpeting as she went. She wore a tight skirt and a low-cut blouse, and was fully accessorized with thick gold jewelry and a designer handbag that dangled off her elbow.

Disregarding the three patrons standing in line, Pam pushed her way to the front. The man standing there looked surprised but backed up a step when she shot him a furious glance.

"So, it looks like your pathetic bid for mayor is over now that you'll be arrested and carted off to jail," Pam said.

Ms. Cole slowly lifted her head. Her face was serenely composed, a small, tight smile on her lips the only sign that she was upset. Even the color from her cheeks had receded, leaving her looking calm and collected and, with a tilt of her head, confused.

"I'm sorry, if you'd like to talk to me, Mrs. Kirby, you need to wait your turn." She gestured to the end of the line.

"I'm talking to you now." Pam's voice was thick with sarcasm.

Lindsey blinked. She doubted she'd be able to keep her own cool under such nastiness, but Ms. Cole looked completely unperturbed, which was always the best way to handle a bully.

"You might be talking, but it isn't to me," Ms. Cole said. "Because I am busy assisting this gentleman here. You've cut in front of people who have politely waited their turn, so that you can say vicious things to me that have no basis in fact. This is neither the time nor the place for such unacceptable behavior, and I suggest you leave if you don't have any real library business to conduct."

Pam's nostrils flared, and Lindsey had to keep herself from doing a fist pump at Ms. Cole's masterful handling of the situation.

"You can't talk that way to me," Pam snapped.

Ms. Cole lowered her reading glasses and peered at Pam over the top of them. "I just did."

Pam sucked in a huge gulp of air. Then all hell broke loose.

In a tantrum more expected from a toddler than a grown woman, Pam began to shove the stacks of books Ms. Cole had been checking in off the service desk with as much force as she could.

"Stop that!" Ms. Cole ordered.

"Make me!" Pam demanded. "My taxes pay for all of this. I'll do whatever I want."

She turned around and grabbed the book out of the waiting man's hand and threw it across the room.

"Hey!" he cried.

"That does it," Emma said. She kept the video rolling as she started across the room. Lindsey followed.

Officer Kirkland was moving forward as well. Both Mrs. Holman and Mrs. Gage had stepped forward and formed a human shield, blocking Pam from any more items on the desk. When she tried to reach around them to shove more books off the counter, they slid in that direction, keeping her out of range.

"Get out of my way," Pam snarled.

"No," Mrs. Holman said. She spread her arms wide. "How dare you vandalize something that belongs to the entire community!"

"Honestly, the nerve," Mrs. Gage said, mimicking her sister's stance. "Besides, the amount of your taxes that goes into this library annually is about sixty bucks. I'd gladly give you that so that you never ever come in here again."

"How dare you—" Pam began, but Emma cut her off.

"Let's go, Mrs. Kirby," Emma said. "I think you need to come with me."

"What for?" Pam asked.

"Destroying public property for one," Emma said. She pointed to Ms. Cole, who was holding up a book—its cover had fallen off under Pam's assault.

"I'm not paying for that," Pam said. "That's not my fault. She probably did it when no one was looking."

Emma gestured around the room and said, "I have plenty of witnesses to the contrary."

"They're all liars," Pam insisted. "Those books fell."

Lindsey saw the man who'd been standing in line slap his forehead with his hand as if he couldn't believe the blatant lies that were pouring out of Pam's mouth.

"No, they didn't," Mrs. Holman said, and her sister nodded. "And we'll swear to it."

"As if anyone would believe you," Pam hissed. "Two withered-up old crows."

Lindsey frowned. Judging by the vitriol Pam was

spewing, she had a real issue with women of a certain age. She tried to remember that angry people are usually angry because they are feeling hurt or fearful. Neither one of those emotions seemed to underlie Pam's fury, however.

"I believe them," Emma said. "What's more, I have video of your behavior, so let's go. We can call your husband from the police station."

"Unhand me," Pam said when Emma took her elbow.

Emma let go and frowned. This was her *I've had it* face. She leaned close to Pam and said, "Either you can go under your own power or I'll take you in in handcuffs. Your choice."

"You wouldn't dare," Pam taunted her.

This was a mistake. Emma didn't bluff about using handcuffs. She unhooked the Smith and Wesson cuffs from her belt and deftly clipped one onto Pam's wrist.

"Get it off!" Pam demanded.

"Nope," Emma said. She spun Pam around and clipped her other wrist, leaving her handbag to dangle from the chain of the cuffs. She glanced at Lindsey over her shoulder. "Send me a total for the damaged materials, please."

"I'll be happy to," Ms. Cole answered for her.

As Pam was escorted from the building, one of the patrons started a slow clap. It grew in volume until Pam was twisting in Emma's arms and cursing them all.

"Well, that was a much more dramatic library visit than I'm used to," Mrs. Holman said.

"I'll say," Mrs. Gage agreed. She turned and glanced over the circulation desk. "Are you all right, Ms. Cole?"

"Perfectly." Ms. Cole gave them a tight smile. "All in a day's work when you deal with the public—the good, the bad and the ugly."

"Well, you handled yourself beautifully," Mrs. Holman said. "If you didn't already have my vote for mayor, you'd have it now."

"Mine, too," the man who'd been in line said. "That's the sort of leadership this town needs. Someone who is unflappable in the face of . . . well . . ." He stopped as if he had no words for what they'd just witnessed. Lindsey was right there with him.

Ms. Cole bowed her head. "Thank you. If you'll all excuse me, I need to get a book truck to sort these items."

Lindsey watched Ms. Cole leave the desk. She looked perfectly fine, but on closer inspection her hands were shaking and Lindsey knew she was rattled. It was very rare to have a patron attack a staff member like that in a small-town library. It did happen occasionally, although it was usually Lindsey, as director, who took the brunt of their ire.

She knew exactly how Ms. Cole was feeling. She followed her into the workroom, where Paula was sitting with headphones on while she fine sorted a book truck. Lindsey tapped her on the shoulder, and Paula pulled out her earbud. The faint strain of Mozart could be heard. Lindsey explained the situation and Paula shot to her feet.

"Is Ms. Cole all right?"

"She will be. In the meantime, would you mind watching the desk?"

"On it," Paula said. She left her cart and hurried out front.

Lindsey wound her way through the workroom,

where the staff had desks to work on their various projects. A door at the back led to the break room, and Lindsey found Ms. Cole in there, fixing a cup of tea using the hot water feature on the watercooler and a very large mug with a tea bag plopped inside.

"Chamomile, I hope?" Lindsey asked.

A flicker of a smile crossed Ms. Cole's lips.

"I think you should go home for the rest of the day, Ms. Cole," Lindsey said. "I know you wanted to finish your project, but it'll keep. It's been an awful day, and I'm sure you have things to attend to that are impossible to do here."

"That's not necessary." She shook her head. "I won't run because of Pam Kirby. I can finish my project first, really, I can."

Lindsey didn't argue with her because she knew from experience that if she pushed, Ms. Cole would just dig in her heels. When it came to the library, Ms. Cole always put her work first and any concern expressed over her well-being would be pushed aside.

"If you change your mind, you can leave whenever you'd like," Lindsey said.

"I appreciate that," Ms. Cole said. She fussed with her tea, putting in two teaspoons of honey and stirring until the honey dissolved. Lindsey didn't want to leave until she knew Ms. Cole was okay, but it felt just the teeniest bit awkward to stand here watching her make her tea.

"I'm not sure what to do," Ms. Cole said, breaking the silence. "Pam Kirby's outburst reminded me of what a hostile environment politics can be, and while I feel like someone needs to jump in and make changes, I'm not sure I'm the person for the job."

"Why can't it be you?" Lindsey asked. She felt a surge of renewed fury that Pam had abused Ms. Cole to the point of doubting herself.

"I don't know if I want to have my life scrutinized by the entire town," Ms. Cole said.

"Pam isn't the entire town," Lindsey countered. "She's just one very loud, aggressive resident."

"Perhaps, but she said what others who oppose my candidacy will say. That since the man was found in my trunk, I must have murdered him."

"But that's ridiculous and a blatant lie," Lindsey protested. "No one will believe them."

Ms. Cole looked up from her mug and met Lindsey's gaze. "I wish that was true, but we're living in strange times where if a person repeats a lie often enough, people start to believe it."

"No—" Lindsey began, but Ms. Cole cut her off.

"Yes, they will. The opposition will use this incident to fabricate a lie about me, and then they'll bludgeon me with it until even my friends will wonder if I'm a murderer."

Lindsey wanted to argue the point, but she could see that Ms. Cole wouldn't be swayed. And, truthfully, politics was a dirty game, and it seemed the people who got ahead were the ones without scruples. That left Ms. Cole out of the race right there.

"I can't tell you what to do about the mayoral race," Lindsey said. "I can only tell you that you've got my vote and the votes of a whole lot of other people who believe in you."

"Even after they find out a dead man was found in the trunk of my car?"

"Yes, even then," Lindsey insisted.

Ms. Cole sipped her tea. She looked thoughtful.

"Lindsey!" Paula appeared in the doorway. Her eyes were wide and her face pale. She was winded as if she'd run to the break room.

"What is it?"

"We have a problem," Paula said. "The mayor is here and he is refusing to leave the premises until he speaks with Ms. Cole."

Lindsey turned to Ms. Cole. "Change of plan."

"Indeed." She sipped her tea and considered her options. "I'll call Milton back. I sent him home. He can pick me up outside the back door."

"I'll get your things," Paula said.

"And I'll go stall him," Lindsey said.

"Wait," Ms. Cole said. "Is this the best way to handle this? I don't want it to seem as if I'm running away. That might make it look as if I have something to hide, and I don't."

"No," Lindsey said. "I don't think there is a person in town who could find a body in the trunk of their car and be expected to just go on with their day per usual."

"I know I couldn't," Paula said.

"All right, then," Ms. Cole said. "If the mayor needs to speak with me, tell him I'll be available when I return to work tomorrow."

Lindsey nodded. She left Ms. Cole to arrange for her

ride and headed back to the main room. She braced
herself. Usually, she saw the mayor once a week at the
department head meetings in the town hall. They went
around the big table and shared their statistics and a few
anecdotes about their department. The mayor then ap-
prised them of anything they needed to know that was
happening in town, upcoming events, budget concerns
and so on.

To have the mayor visit the library twice in one day,
it was too much. While Lindsey didn't dislike Mayor
Hensen, despite his ageist and sexist opinions, she
couldn't help but feel he'd become ineffectual during
his second term and it was time for someone new.

She crossed through the workroom and glanced out
the windows that looked over the library. The mayor
was standing at the desk, rocking up and down on his
toes as if he were trying to contain his excitement about
something. Namely, that his opponent had had the mis-
fortune to find a body in the trunk of her car.

Lindsey suppressed a sigh. She had a feeling this
was going to be unpleasant. Back in the early days of
her professional career, when she'd worked in an aca-
demic setting, she'd gotten good at managing egos and
agendas. That muscle had atrophied, however, and she
needed to get her game on if she was going to effectively deal with the mayor.

"Mayor Hensen," she said as she stepped out of the
back room. "Two visits in one day. This is unusual."

The patrons who'd been in the building during the
scene with Pam Kirby had cleared out. Probably to go
share the juicy gossip with their friends and neighbors.
Lindsey didn't blame them. Pam Kirby getting hauled
out in cuffs was a spectacle and then some.

She glanced around the room. The patrons in the building at the moment didn't seem to have any idea that there'd been so much drama a few moments ago and were going about their business, paying no attention to Lindsey or the mayor, which suited Lindsey just fine.

"I'm here to talk about the incident," Mayor Hensen said. He assumed a very concerned expression while still rocking up on his toes.

"Which incident would that be?" Lindsey asked. If she let him spell it out, she might have a better idea of how to play it.

"Why the one that involved the police, of course," he said.

"Hmm," Lindsey hummed. It occurred to her that he might not know that his wife's best friend had been carted out of the library by the chief. She decided not to enlighten him. "Very unfortunate."

"'Unfortunate'?" Mayor Hensen sputtered. "I'd say finding a body in one of your staff persons' cars is more than unfortunate."

Lindsey studied his face. He was not checking the volume on his voice, and several people had turned to see what he was talking about. That was what he wanted. He wanted to wear the guise of concern while making sure everyone knew what was happening. Lindsey was certain he had planned to haul Ms. Cole out here to the main room and make a scene. Not on Lindsey's watch.

"Now, I'd like to speak to this staff person and discover for myself—" he began, but Lindsey interrupted.

"I am so glad you're taking this seriously," she said.

"Well, of course, I am," he said. He smiled, and it

was all white teeth and no warmth, rather like a wolf in a fairy tale.

"Excellent," Lindsey said. The mayor looked taken aback at her enthusiasm. "Since you are so committed to the safety and well-being of the library staff and patrons, I'd like to revisit the security cameras that I asked for in my budget last year."

"What? No, I wanted to speak—"

"About where they should be placed?" Lindsey interrupted him again. Her mother would have been appalled by her lack of manners, but Lindsey was not about to let him take over the conversation and turn it into a smear campaign on Ms. Cole, which she suspected was his plan. "Follow me. I'm sure all of our town residents will be pleased that you're taking the security of their library so seriously."

Without giving him a chance to refuse her, Lindsey strode to the front of the building. She knew she could stall him by the front door long enough for Ms. Cole to escape. She stepped outside back into the afternoon sunshine. The daffodils that the Friends of the Library planted along the side of the building were full to bursting after the recent rain. They seemed so incongruously cheerful after the events of the day.

"The security company that I had come and give me a bid said that they would recommend a camera be mounted here." Lindsey pointed to the spot above their heads. "It would have a three-hundred-and-sixty-degree capability so that anyone coming or going could be monitored as well as the walk-up book drop."

"I don't care—"

"About the cost to keep our community safe?" Lindsey asked.

Two mothers with their babies in strollers walked by and Lindsey smiled at them in greeting. Mayor Hensen did the same, although this smile lacked its usual wattage.

As soon as they disappeared into the building, he turned on Lindsey. "Stop doing that."

"What?"

"Finishing my sentences in front of others," he said.

"Oh, my apologies. I'm just so happy to have you on board to upgrade the security of the library."

"I never said that."

"Oh, but I'm sure you did."

"No, I didn't," he argued. "I came here to speak with Ms. Cole about the dead man found in her car. To say that it is suspicious to have such a thing happen . . ."

As the mayor droned on, Lindsey glanced past him to see Milton and Ms. Cole driving away. Ms. Cole sent her a thumbs-up, and Lindsey felt her shoulders drop and her spine relax. Whatever the mayor had thought he was going to do to Ms. Cole had been neatly thwarted.

". . . to that end, I feel that Ms. Cole should be put on leave, and I'll expect you to back my position on this."

"Why would she be put on leave?" Lindsey asked, frowning at him.

"I just explained that we can't have a town employee on duty who might be tied to a murder," he said.

"She's not tied to a murder!" Lindsey snapped. She could feel her grip on her temper slipping.

"The body was found in the trunk of her car!"

"That doesn't tie her to the murder any more than it would tie you to a murder if a body was found in the trunk of your car."

"I appreciate that you're trying to protect your staff person," Mayor Hensen said. The condescension in his voice was thick enough to patch drywall. "But the public must be protected at all costs."

"Excuse me," Lindsey said. "What are you saying?"

"That until further notice, and for as long as I deem it necessary, Ms. Cole is on a leave of absence," he said.

W hy that slimy, hairy wart on a baboon's backside," Robbie Vine cursed as Lindsey recounted over dinner what the mayor had said to her outside the library.

"I think that's an insult to the wart," Sully said. He frowned. "What do you think the mayor is playing at?"

"Politics," Emma said. "Pure politics. He stopped by the station after he got done at the library. Apparently, his wife called him to report my 'abuse' of her friend Mrs. Kirby."

"What happened?" Lindsey asked.

The four of them had succeeded in meeting up at the Blue Anchor, although Emma had been delayed because of the case, and were settled into a big booth beside the window, which overlooked the bay and the archipelago known as the Thumb Islands that was scattered off the shore of Briar Creek. It was here that Lindsey's husband, Sully, ran a water taxi and offered boat tours of the islands. With the increasingly warm weather arriving, his business was in high demand, and Lindsey knew that dinners with friends were going to become rarer as he took on more and more sunset cruises.

"He tried to tell me I had no business hauling in Pam

Kirby, but I had video on my side," Emma said. "Not to mention a truckload of witnesses."

"I don't suppose that went over well," Robbie said.

"No," Emma confirmed. "I'm afraid I might have made an enemy, if not of the mayor, then most definitely Pam Kirby."

"The same Pam Kirby who got bounced from the school board for her funky math skills?" Mary Murphy stopped by their table with a basket of hot rolls. She was Sully's younger sister and the wife half of the husband-and-wife duo who owned the Blue Anchor.

Lindsey had no idea how hungry she was until the Parker House rolls were set down on the table. She exchanged a look with Emma as they both reached for the basket but then pulled back.

Emma halted. "You first."

"No, you," Lindsey insisted.

Robbie swooped in and picked up the basket, at which they both protested, "Hey!"

"If you two are going to insist on dithering over who goes first, I'm not waiting for the rolls to get cold," he said. He extended the basket to Sully. "How about it, mate?"

"Thanks," Sully said. The men exchanged a grin.

Lindsey cast Sully a dark look. Robbie had always been more her friend than Sully's, but after their Christmas wedding, which Robbie had officiated at Sully's request, their friendship had bloomed into a solid bruhmance. Lindsey tried not to feel left out of it, but as they buttered the steaming hot rolls, looking quite pleased with themselves, it took some effort.

"Well, that'll teach us," Emma said, and she snatched

the basket from her boyfriend and held it out to Lindsey.

"Thank you."

"So, what's this I hear about Ms. Cole being terminated after murdering some guy they found in her trunk?" Mary asked.

Robbie choked on his bit of roll. "What? How'd you get there?"

"It's all anyone is talking about," Ian said as he joined them, arriving with a tray of drinks for the table. Ian was Mary's husband and also Sully's business partner in the tour boat company, but mostly he could be found behind the bar at the Blue Anchor, pulling beers, mixing cocktails and getting the gossip.

"Well, and I say this as a librarian, there needs to be some fact-checking," Lindsey said. She took the white wine he handed her, barely resisting the urge to down it in one go.

"Exactly. First of all," Emma said. "You shouldn't listen to gossip."

Ian batted his eyelashes at her. "Now what kind of informant would I be if I didn't listen to what was being said around here?"

"You are not an official informant," Emma corrected him. "That being said, I do appreciate the intel."

"So, you are saying that I'm useful."

Mary rolled her eyes. Lindsey met Sully's gaze and they exchanged knowing looks. Ian was the irrepressible personality behind the Blue Anchor, the only restaurant and watering hole in Briar Creek, and not much happened in town that he didn't know about.

"For the record, in case it comes up amid the chatter

of the regulars, Ms. Cole is not a suspect," Lindsey said. She glanced at Emma, who gave a reluctant nod.

"As of right now, we have no suspects," she said. "Or, more accurately, we have no suspects, no witnesses and no identification of our John Doe."

"A stranger?" Ian's eyebrows bounced. "We have a mystery, then."

Emma sighed and reached for her water. "Unfortunately, yes."

"Has anyone been reported missing?" Mary asked.

"Not to us," Emma said. She frowned and glanced around the table. "I'd appreciate it if you hear anything to let me know, but I also don't want rumors to run rampant about town. It serves no purpose and could muddy up the investigation."

"Understood," Ian said. "I will squash all ridiculous speculation, although . . ."

His voice trailed off, and they all leaned closer to him to hear what he had to say.

"'Although'?" Emma's voice was impatient.

"Stories are coming to light about Ms. Cole," he said. He looked uncomfortable, and Lindsey slowly lowered her wineglass to the table.

"What sorts of stories?" she asked.

Ian put a hand on the back of his neck. "Nah, I probably shouldn't say anything."

"Too late now," Emma said. "If you've heard something pertinent to the case, I need to hear it."

"It's just that, well, did you know Ms. Cole has a record?"

"Why do I feel like you're not telling us she has a love for old-school vinyl?" Robbie asked.

"No, this is more the fingerprinted mug shot sort," he said.

"No way." Lindsey shook her head. "I don't believe it."

"I didn't either," Ian said. He spread his hands wide. "But it was Scott Baldwin who told me, and he heard it from his mom, who went to high school with Ms. Cole."

"What was it for?" Emma asked. Her eyes narrowed. It was the look she gave people she brought in for questioning and made even the most honest man squirm—at least, it had that effect on Ian.

He hesitated and his wife nudged him. "You opened that can of worms, time to set them free."

"Fine," he said. He leaned over the table and in a low voice so as not to be overheard said, "He said she got busted for breaking and entering."

CHAPTER

6

BRIAR CREEK
PUBLIC LIBRARY

No." Lindsey laughed. "That is the most ridiculous thing I've ever heard."

"That's what I thought, but Scott said his mother swears to it, and you know how religious she is. She'd never lie."

Lindsey bit her lip. Mrs. Baldwin kept her priest on speed dial and was the most pious resident of Briar Creek by far.

"Considering the source, I'd say it's probably true," Sully said. Lindsey whipped her head in his direction. "But it could also be a misunderstanding. Sometimes the facts aren't as accurate as they seem."

"That seems most likely," Lindsey agreed. She put her hand on his arm and gave it a squeeze. It was nice having a husband who was the voice of reason.

"Those aren't the only rumors flying about," Robbie said. "I was talking to Joe Gillespie, and he said that a very reliable source told him that Ms. Cole was having an affair with the deceased but was afraid that Milton was going to find out, so she strangled him and stuffed him into her trunk, hoping to dispose of the body after work."

Lindsey pushed her fingers against the middle of her forehead. She'd been afraid that outlandish tales would start being woven about Ms. Cole, but honestly, to think that she'd stuff a body in her trunk was just ridiculous.

"That's not even the worst of it," Robbie said.

"No." Emma held up her hands. "I don't want to hear any more."

"What?" Robbie asked. "Of course you do. It gets positively mental."

"What could be worse than accusing her of murder?" Lindsey asked.

"She's a mobster," Sully said in a bored voice.

Robbie glanced at him in surprise.

"I heard that one when I took Heathcliff for a walk along the beach before coming here and ran into Old Man Drysdale."

"How does he figure she's a mobster?" Emma asked. She reached for another roll and then handed the basket back to Lindsey.

"He said she's so stern over the overdue fines that he always figured she was mobbed up somehow," Sully said. He shrugged.

"Like she laundered money through the library and if you didn't pay your library fines on time, she'd have someone come and break your legs because she needed the cash to hide her crimes?" Lindsey asked.

"Exactly," Sully said.

Lindsey exchanged an annoyed glance with Emma, who rolled her eyes.

"The one I heard is even more outlandish," Robbie said. "Get this. Louis Hobbs, you know the chap who works at the post office, said that he heard from Stacy Steele that Ms. Cole is a Russian asset, trying to infiltrate the government."

"As the mayor of a tiny shore town in Connecticut?" Lindsey asked.

Robbie shook his head and laughed. "Daft, I know."

Lindsey looked at Emma. "This is a real problem. If Ms. Cole gets wind of this—"

"She won't," Emma said. "We'll find out who our victim is and then we'll catch whoever did this and no one will ever remember the crazy things they were saying about Ms. Cole."

"I hope you're right," Lindsey said. "Because she might not take it well if she thinks the entire town has turned against her."

"I don't think it's the entire town," Mary said.

"No, just a few fringe types," Ian agreed.

Lindsey glanced around the table at her friends. She didn't know if they were just trying to make her feel better or if they genuinely believed that everything was going to be all right. She wanted to believe it would be, but there was a lot hanging in the balance, such as Ms. Cole's bid for mayor, Lindsey's relationship with the current administration and the future of the library depending upon who won this contest. If Mayor Hensen was reelected, it was quite possible he'd treat the library in a punitive manner to get even for Ms. Cole challenging him.

She wanted to enjoy her dinner of lobster bisque and crab cakes, but even the amazing food couldn't wash away the lingering anxiety. Sully, as if sensing her inner turmoil, hustled them out of the restaurant by paying their tab as soon as the waitress had cleared their plates.

"Come on," he said. "Let's go home."

They said their good-byes, climbed into his old pickup truck and motored through the small shore town to their cottage on the water. The night air was sweet with just a hint of the incoming tide's brine. The stars sparkled against the inky dark sky, and there was a gentle quietness to their sleepy village that always made Lindsey feel at peace.

She loved Briar Creek. In the years she'd lived here, it had become her home. She enjoyed her work and felt a deep connection to her community. Did everyone who lived here agree about everything? No. But it seemed that there was a commonality found in how much the residents valued their town and their quality of life. All of that could change if Emma wasn't able to find the murderer, and if Ms. Cole was wrongly accused of a crime she didn't commit. Lindsey wasn't a worrier by nature, but she found herself feeling a bit anxious about the fallout of the John Doe being found in Ms. Cole's car.

As soon as they pulled into the driveway, Lindsey heard her boy barking. She hopped out of the truck, meeting Sully on the walkway to the house. He clasped her hand in his as if sensing she needed some reassurance. She gently squeezed his fingers with hers, letting him know he was appreciated.

They climbed the steps to the house and saw their hairy black mongrel leaping from the door to the low window where he could look out and see them. His nose shoved through the curtains, pushing one aside, and Lindsey could just see him in the porch light, looking at her with one eye as the other was covered in sheer fabric, making him appear equal parts adorable and mischievous. Then he darted back to the door as if he just couldn't believe that they were home.

"Three, two, one," Sully counted down before he opened the door. "Impact."

Lindsey braced herself. Heathcliff, her rescue puppy and now full-grown dog, barreled out the door right for her. He stood up on his hind legs, his tail whipping back and forth so fast it made a breeze, while he hugged her around the knees with his front paws.

Lindsey bent over and rubbed his soft fur just where he liked it. "How's my good boy? Did you have a good day? I missed you so much."

Content with her affection, Heathcliff hopped down and then ran down the steps to investigate the front yard. A rabbit must have hopped through, because he followed an invisible trail with his nose to the ground.

Lindsey turned to Sully and said, "You don't believe any of those stories about Ms. Cole, do you?"

"About her being a murderer or a mobster?" he asked. "No."

"I notice you didn't include the breaking and entering charge in there," she said.

He winced. "Yeah, about that."

He paused and Lindsey stared at him. She waved her

hand in a circular motion, indicating he should keep going.

"Don't leave me in suspense," she said.

"The thing is, I don't know any details, but I do remember hearing something about Ms. Cole having a colorful past and that there's an arrest in her background rings a bell."

"And you never told me this?" Lindsey cried. "This is some significant information to withhold about one of my employees."

Sully held out his hands in a gesture of surrender. "I'm sorry. I honestly forgot until today and everyone started blabbing about Ms. Cole and the body in her car. Speaking of which . . ."

"Yes?"

"Are you okay?" he asked. "I haven't had a chance to ask you, and that had to be traumatic, to put it mildly."

"I'm fine . . . no, not really fine, but not scarred for life either. Mostly, I'm just freaked out that someone managed to stuff a body into a car in the parking lot of the library and no one saw a thing. That's what disturbs me most."

"Understandable," he said.

He put his arm around her and pulled her close, keeping her warm. Lindsey leaned in, tucking herself in tight. The April evening had gotten chilly and there was a dampness to the air that indicated rain was coming.

She watched Heathcliff patrol the yard, from end to end, as he did every night, checking to make certain that no danger lurked in the hedges. If only the library had a dog like Heathcliff on duty, maybe today wouldn't have happened.

She leaned back and glanced up at Sully. "You know what really peeves me?"

"No."

"I put a request for security cameras in my budget last year and the mayor said no. He felt they weren't necessary in this 'sleepy little village.'"

"Oh, man, those would have been handy. Think of all the ridiculous stuff that gets shoved into the book drop." He gestured to Heathcliff. "Like him. And the bike rack—there's always a theft on that broken old thing. And, of course, you'd have video of whoever stuffed the body inside Ms. Cole's car."

"Exactly." Lindsey shook her head. "I pointed out all of that, except for the body, of course, but the mayor couldn't be budged. So annoying."

"Of course, the irony is if you'd had those cameras, not only would they show who was guilty, but it would squash the rumors going around about Ms. Cole because she'd obviously not be the person in the video. In a dark and twisted way, Mayor Hensen did himself a heck of a favor by saying no. He can insinuate anything he wants about Ms. Cole and hope it sticks until the election."

"It's maddening," Lindsey said.

Heathcliff broke off from his final patrol of the front yard and raced back to them. He wagged his way through their legs and into the house, where he promptly demanded a treat. Sully ruffled his ears as he handed him his nightly biscuit.

"He's really done a remarkable job with training us, don't you think?"

Lindsey laughed. She feared it was true. Heathcliff did rule the house. She watched as he trotted with the self-esteem of a lion over to his bed to enjoy his biscuit.

She wondered if she could bottle that confidence. She had a feeling she was going to need it.

I'm withdrawing from the campaign," Ms. Cole said.

"What?" Beth cried. "You can't!"

"I think it's for the best," Ms. Cole said.

"It's not," Beth protested. "Tell her it isn't, Lindsey."

Lindsey glanced across the table at Ms. Cole. She was dressed all in red today, but her short-sleeved orange red sweater clashed violently with her cranberry-colored slacks. The combination made Lindsey's eyes water.

The three of them were having a staff meeting to go over the events of the week at the library and determine how best to handle the publicity surrounding the body found in Ms. Cole's car. So far, they hadn't come up with anything other than to deny, deny, deny, which didn't seem like it would be very effective. Lindsey was refusing to honor the mayor's request to put Ms. Cole on leave. She hadn't mentioned it to Ms. Cole and had a call in to the human resources department to see what she could do to delay any paperwork from being sent over.

Lisa Duncan, the HR rep who managed the library staff's paperwork, was a huge fan of Mhairi McFarlane's novels, and Lindsey had promised her first dibs on the latest if she could drag out the process for a day or two. No, she was not above bribes.

"I can't advise you on what to do, Ms. Cole," Lindsey said. "But given that it's only been twenty-four hours since we found the body, and we still don't know who the victim is or how they ended up in your car, it feels premature to abandon your campaign just yet."

There, that felt diplomatic and not an overreach of her position as library director.

Ms. Cole shook her head. "I appreciate the support, I do, but the mayor isn't going to stop using this like a weapon, and you know how people are. Even if the rumors are untrue, there are people who will believe them, and they will use that against me at every turn, making everything I am trying to accomplish pointless."

"It won't be for nothing. It'll be for the greater good of the town. No one could ever believe that you are responsible for the dead man in the car," Beth protested. "It's just preposterous."

Ms. Cole gave her a closed-lipped smile and said, "Oh, yes, they can. Apparently there are rumors swirling about that I'm a murderer, a mobster or an anarchist—or was it an arsonist? I have no idea."

"A what?" Beth looked shocked.

"We live in a small town," Lindsey said. "This is entertainment for a lot of people."

"Making up lies about someone?" Beth crossed her arms over her chest.

Ms. Cole reached over and patted her arm. "You of all people know what it's like to have your behavior scrutinized and then twisted to fit a false narrative."

A few years prior, Beth had been considered a suspect in her boyfriend's murder. Things had been very tense in the small library during that investigation, as it was before Ms. Cole and Beth had become friendly and were at the barely-tolerating-each-other stage in their relationship. It had made Lindsey's first few months as the new director quite the challenge.

"I am," Beth agreed. "Which is why I am telling you it is too soon to quit. You have to give Chief Plewicki and the other officers a chance to figure out what happened."

Ms. Cole looked doubtful. "I don't know. I'm not sure I'm comfortable with being a suspect in a murder investigation and a candidate for mayor."

"If you think about it," Beth said, "it's not really that different."

Lindsey and Ms. Cole shared a confused look.

"How do you figure?" Lindsey asked.

"Well," Beth said. "If she becomes mayor, she'll be murdering someone's budget." She made the *ba-dum-bum* sound of a drum accompanying a punch line. Ms. Cole looked pained.

"All right, seriously speaking, both situations are going to shove you into the limelight, both are going to cause people to scrutinize you from head to toe. Speaking of which—we've talked about your wardrobe and how to put together outfits. This was not on the approved list."

"What's wrong with my outfit?"

"Not all reds are the same, nor do they all match," Beth said. Her look was stern.

Ms. Cole turned to Lindsey. "This from a woman who regularly dresses up like a teapot or a bat."

"Those are costumes, whereas this is your impression on the voting population of Briar Creek. Now, I have your calendar for your next few public events—"

Ms. Cole shook her head. She started to gather her folders from their meeting, making it clear she was about to depart. "I'm sorry, Beth. You've worked so hard on my campaign and I really thought I stood a chance, but I just can't do this."

Without another word, she left the meeting room. Beth sat openmouthed, staring after her. She then whipped her head around and looked at Lindsey.

"We have to change her mind."

"As her supervisor, I don't think I can without it being an overreach of my position," Lindsey said. "Plus, I think we should respect her wishes."

Beth propped her chin on her hand. "How do you think things are going to go for us if Hensen is reelected?"

"I'm sure it—" Lindsey paused. What was she sure of? Nothing. She had no idea how this was going to play out. In fact, Beth was right to question the future. The mayor had already made it clear that the thought of a library employee running against him was akin to a mutiny. Lindsey had no idea if he was going to be punitive about that in the future. And if Ms. Cole dropped her bid for mayor, would anyone run against him, or would he be unopposed like in the last election?

"Exactly," Beth said. "I think Ms. Cole has a real shot against him. She has plans and ideas and listens to the community. Hensen is still coasting on the promises he made to win his first term, most of which remain undelivered."

"We can't discuss it with her on work time," Lindsey said.

"That's fine," Beth said. "We'll drop by her house tonight. I'll warn Milton that we're coming so he can make certain she's there and fit for company."

"Or we could just tell her that we're going to stop by," Lindsey suggested.

"No, then she'll have all day to come up with reasons for why she has to withdraw from the election. This is better. The element of surprise will get her off balance, and then she won't be able to argue against our Power-Point of reasons why she should remain in the race."

"You're always five moves ahead of everyone else." Lindsey glanced down at Beth's belly. "That poor baby is never going to be able to outmaneuver you."

Beth grinned. "I should hope not."

"All right, I'll reach out to Milton, but if we do stop by Ms. Cole's house after work, you have to leave her alone for the rest of the afternoon. She'll be more amenable to us when we plead our case if we don't badger her now."

"Agreed," Beth said. "I have my teen crafternoon club, so I won't have time to pester her."

"Oh, what are you reading?" Lindsey asked. Since working at the public library, she'd developed an appreciation for young adult fiction.

"*Uglies* by Scott Westerfeld," she said. "So much to unpack in that series."

"Agreed," Lindsey said. "I bet it will be a lively discussion."

"And our craft will be to use the 3D printer on loan from the high school makerspace to make chess pieces." Beth wagged her eyebrows. "I have a line of boys wanting to try out that printer. It's going be great."

Lindsey marveled at Beth's ingenuity. Children's librarians were a sly bunch. However she could lure teens, particularly boys, into the library, she would. Lindsey had watched in awe as Beth had revitalized their programs, coming up with such winners as a race between handmade wooden race cars, catapult competitions and a UFO night where anyone with a telescope was invited up onto the roof of the library to seek out extraterrestrial life.

"I don't doubt it," Lindsey said. She tried not to think about the possibility that Beth might not come back after she had the baby. There was simply no replacing the irrepressible children's librarian, plus Lindsey would miss her best friend. She shook her head. She refused to worry about something that wasn't going to happen for months.

Right now she needed to focus on the problem at hand. Of course, if Ms. Cole became mayor, she'd be leaving the library, too. Lindsey hadn't had much turn-over since she arrived. In fact, other than the teenagers who shelved the books and Paula, who was Ms. Cole's assistant, she hadn't had to hire anyone at all.

Of course, even if Ms. Cole didn't become mayor, she might be wrongly accused and convicted of murder with the same result being that she'd leave the library. Lindsey wandered back to her office, trying not to be alarmed at the pace at which everything suddenly seemed to be changing and her inability to stop it.

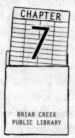

CHAPTER

7

BRIAR CREEK
PUBLIC LIBRARY

Have you ever been to Ms. Cole's house before?"
Lindsey asked Beth when Beth parked in front of
the small cottage. It was still a new experience for
Lindsey to be driven by Beth. In an effort to be environmentally friendly, they'd both ridden bikes around
their small village for years, but with Beth's pregnancy,
her husband, Aidan, had insisted she start using a car
since she was going to need it for the baby anyway.

"No," Beth said. "Which is weird if you think about
it. I mean, I've worked with her for almost ten years. At
some point you'd think I'd have dropped by."

"Not necessarily," Lindsey said. "When I was at the
university, I knew people who had worked together for
decades who had never been to each other's houses."

"So odd," Beth said. She hefted herself out of the car
and Lindsey did the same.

Ms. Cole's white house with black trim was as neat
as a pin. A stone wall enclosed the yard, and daffodils

bloomed in a narrow garden bed all along the inside of the wall. Beth unlatched the white wooden gate, and they walked up the cobbled path to the front door.

Three steps led up to a small portico with a security door and then a thick wooden door, painted black to match the trim. Rosebushes heavy with buds lined the front of the house, with four bushes on each side. Very precise, very controlled and very Ms. Cole.

"I am only surprised the house and the trim aren't painted in noncomplementary shades of green or yellow," Beth said.

Lindsey glanced at the yard and noticed the precisely cut lawn. She also noticed that there were no signs reading "Vote Cole" planted anywhere in the yard. She hoped this didn't indicate that Ms. Cole had already officially pulled the plug on her campaign and that they were now too late.

Beth pressed on the doorbell and they waited. The sound of someone approaching could be heard, and then the door opened. Ms. Cole stood there, blinking at them.

"Is everything all right?" she asked. Her eyes went wide. "Is the library okay?"

"Everything at the library is fine," Lindsey said.

"We're here to talk about your campaign," Beth said. "I have been busy working the phones trying to get the people in town who've been dismissive of your bid for mayor to take you more seriously."

"I don't see how having me suspected of murder is going to do that," Ms. Cole said. She looked resigned, as if the fight had already gone out of her.

"Eugenia," Milton said, appearing behind her. "Don't leave our guests on the doorstep, invite them in."

"Oh, of course, sorry," Ms. Cole said. "You surprised me. I'm afraid I wasn't prepared for company."

"It's quite all right," Milton said. "I made enough tea for everyone."

Ms. Cole's eyes narrowed as she stepped back and gestured for Lindsey and Beth to enter. "Did you know about this, Milton?"

"Please don't be annoyed with him," Beth said. "I told him we were stopping by. Didn't give him a chance to refuse, in fact."

"Which is fine because I wouldn't have," Milton said.

Lindsey and Beth followed Milton and Ms. Cole into the house. They passed through the formal parlor that looked as if it didn't see much use, through a large modern kitchen, where Milton left them to attend the tea, and out to a large sunroom, which was clearly an addition built onto the original house.

It was a beautiful space all enclosed in glass, overlooking a backyard as perfectly groomed and manicured as the front. The room was full of plants and comfy wicker furniture, and Lindsey spotted Milton's influence as a small fountain with a statue of the Buddha parked in the middle of it trickled happily into a large stone basin in the corner.

A piercing squawk made both her and Beth jump.

"Mercy!" Beth put her hand over her heart. "What was that?"

"Fred and Ethel," Ms. Cole said.

"Who?" Beth blinked.

"Over there," Lindsey said. She pointed to the corner. An enormous cage was nestled amid several lush bamboo plants. Peering at them through the delicate metal bars were two tropical birds.

"Ah!" Beth gasped. "Lovebirds."

"Rosy-cheeked lovebirds," Ms. Cole clarified. "The one on the left is Fred, and the one on the right is Ethel."

"How can you tell them apart?"

"Fred has a cowlick," Milton said as he entered the room, bearing a tea tray. He set it down on the coffee table and glanced at Ms. Cole. "Would you prefer that I stay or leave?"

"Stay, of course," she said.

Milton sat on the love seat next to Ms. Cole while Lindsey and Beth took the two armchairs. He nodded and began to pour their tea. Lindsey sighed in relief. She hadn't wanted to get Milton in trouble for helping them ambush Ms. Cole.

"I'm not saying I'll change my mind," Ms. Cole said. "But I'm willing to listen."

"Excellent." Beth took her tea from Milton with a thank-you and launched into her latest campaign plan. "Now, you know that I've had some trouble getting a few of the more entrenched civic societies to take your candidacy seriously."

Ms. Cole nodded. "The Elks Lodge, the Rotarians and the Daughters of the American Revolution to name a few."

"Well, I called them all today, offering to have you come and speak at their monthly meetings, and every single one of them said yes."

"Why?" Ms. Cole looked perplexed. "I mean, if they didn't care about me before, why do they want to have me there now when I'm potentially a suspect in a murder investigation?"

"Notoriety," Milton said. "Having you there will get their lagging members to attend the meeting, and they think they'll get the inside story on what happened to the man in the trunk." He paused. "Which reminds me, are you available for our next historical society meeting?"

Ms. Cole swatted his arm in an affectionate tap and chuckled. "Oh, you."

Milton looked delighted to have made her laugh. Milton, a widower for many years, shocked the town when he found companionship with Ms. Cole, but it was clear there was a great deal of love and friendship there. Lindsey exchanged a small smile with Beth.

"I think the best way to get ahead of the gossip and to keep Mayor Hensen from using it to his advantage is to let the townspeople ask you questions. That way you'll appear to have nothing to hide, and it will prevent your opponent from making it look as if you do."

"Do you really think Mayor Hensen will take the tragic events of yesterday and turn them into leverage for his campaign?" Milton asked.

"I know he will," Beth said. Her voice was grim, and Lindsey studied her over the rim of her delicate teacup. What had Beth heard?

Both Ms. Cole and Milton gave her their full attention, and Beth took a fortifying sip of her tea before she began. "Before the body was discovered in the trunk, rumors had already begun. I didn't want to tell you because I didn't want to alarm you. But the fact is I think Mayor Hensen has begun a disinformation campaign, and this only adds fuel to his fire."

"What could he possibly say about me?" Ms. Cole asked. "That I'm diligent about collecting overdue fines?"

"Yes." Beth nodded. "But, of course, there's a ridiculous spin that you are actually a mobster skimming off the top of the profits or using the fines to hide laundered money."

"What?" Ms. Cole gasped. "That's preposterous and not a little insulting."

"It is," Lindsey said. She kept her voice even when she added, "But I heard that rumor, too."

Ms. Cole gave Milton a horrified look. "A mobster? Me?"

He smiled, his eyes crinkling in the corners. "Well, you do have a very attractive ferocity about you."

Ms. Cole turned a faint shade of pink and looked exasperated with him, but Lindsey could tell she was also pleased.

"That's not the only rumor," Beth said. "It's just one of the most ridiculous."

"What are the others?" Ms. Cole asked.

"Oh, I don't think—" Lindsey tried to halt the conversation right there.

Ms. Cole turned to look at her. "Are they worse?"

Lindsey shook her head. "Just nonsensical speculation, nothing to pay any attention to whatsoever."

"Might as well spill it," Beth said.

"Yes, I believe I want to hear it, too," Milton agreed.

"Agreed. Better to know than not," Ms. Cole said. She looked at Lindsey with an inquisitive expression very similar to the lovebirds in their enormous cage, who were busily flittering from perch to perch.

Lindsey blew out a breath. She had no idea how Ms. Cole was going to take it that people were saying she was a two-timing murderess. This could go very, very badly.

"It was so dumb," she said. "Someone said that they suspected that you were cheating on Milton with the man found in your trunk, and to keep him from telling Milton, you strangled him, stuffed him in your trunk and planned to dump him after work. See? Completely out there with no basis in fact whatsoever."

Both Milton and Ms. Cole stared at her, and Lindsey wondered if her seat was actually getting hot or if it was just the laser-like intensity of their scrutiny making her feel overheated. When she didn't think she could stand it for another second, Milton barked out a laugh and then clapped his hand over his mouth.

Ms. Cole pressed her lips together, fighting to stay serious. She lost and a peal of laughter broke through. They leaned together as they chuckled. Then they met each other's gaze and broke into more fits of laughter. Beth glanced at Lindsey and shrugged.

"I'm sorry," Ms. Cole said. "It's just the idea of me as either a mobster or a murderess is just so out there."

Lindsey felt her shoulders drop from around her ears. Honestly, if people were saying that sort of thing about her, she wasn't so sure she'd be able to laugh it off as easily as Ms. Cole.

"That's the attitude we need to take to your constituents," Beth said. Her eyes sparkled. "Please don't give up now, Ms. Cole. Briar Creek needs you."

Ms. Cole heaved a sigh. "I would argue that it doesn't, but if these are the rumors the mayor is scattering about me, then he'll just do worse to his next challenger. Without a term limit on the books, the man will likely try to be mayor until he turns his toes up." She glanced at Milton. "I don't think I have a choice. I have to stay in the race."

"That's my girl," he said. His grin was full of approval when he reached over and patted her hand, giving her fingers a quick squeeze.

"Yay!" Beth cheered and clapped. At the sudden movement, her belly swung a bit to the side, and she braced herself with her feet. "Let's talk about your schedule, then. On Monday, you've been invited to speak at the Chamber of Commerce. This is an important one as all the town business leaders will be there, so I need you to look like one of them."

"Meaning?" Ms. Cole looked bewildered. "Aren't they mostly middle-aged businessmen?"

"Mostly, but there are several women, who also dress to impress, if you know what I mean."

"Not really, no." Ms. Cole shook her head.

Beth clasped her hands in front of her in a gesture that looked almost imploring. "Ms. Cole, I need you to dress like someone they can relate to. A lot of politics is about building a rapport with the voting public. Because it's the Chamber of Commerce, I need you to wear the sort of clothes that would signal to the members that you're one of them."

"Such as?" Ms. Cole asked.

"It's simple, really, black slacks and whatever color top you'd like, but black slacks." Beth didn't add *because they go with anything*, but Lindsey understood where she was going with it.

Ms. Cole nodded. "I have a matching black top I can wear."

Beth pressed her lips together as if she were holding in her words until she could think of something to say that didn't come out at the volume of a yell.

"I think Beth is suggesting that you wear a different

color top with your slacks," Milton said gently. "Maybe that turquoise blouse you look so pretty in."

Ms. Cole stared at him as if she couldn't get his words to make sense. "But turquoise is blue. That won't work." Ms. Cole shook her head. Lindsey saw Beth flinch but she didn't say a word, which Lindsey suspected was likely killing her. "I have a pair of blue slacks that I could wear with it."

"Dark blue?" Beth asked. "As in navy blue? Because that would work."

"Yes, dark blue."

Beth exchanged a meaningful glance with Milton, and he gave a slight nod. Lindsey took this to mean that he would make certain that Ms. Cole was dressed for success on Monday.

"All right," Beth said. "You have the weekend to prepare for any questions, and people will ask questions. How about I come over on Sunday and we do a practice session? You'll want to prepare about ten to fifteen minutes focusing on you, your history in town and your vision for the future, then we can open it up."

Ms. Cole nodded. She seemed completely at ease with the idea. Lindsey, who would rather deep dive with sharks than speak to a group of more than three people, could feel a fine sweat break out on her skin on Ms. Cole's behalf.

"Is there anything I can do to help?" she asked.

"I'm so glad you asked," Beth said. "I was hoping you and Robbie could be there as well as a show of support but also to hand out flyers to anyone who wants one."

"I'm sure I can put Ann Marie in charge of the library, and I'll take my lunch hour at the meeting so I'm not attending on work time."

Ms. Cole smiled at her with a look of genuine warmth. "Thank you, Lindsey, I appreciate it."

"Happy to help," Lindsey said. And she meant it.

Beth went over a few more events for the week, and by the time they left, Ms. Cole seemed to be back to her indomitable self. Beth drove Lindsey home, departing with a wave. Lindsey turned to face her small house, and before she took more than two steps, the front door opened and a voice called out, "Incoming!"

Lindsey braced herself as Heathcliff threw himself out of the house, down the front steps and across the lawn. His paws got muddy as he dashed across the yard, soggy from a recent rain. He stood on his back legs and wrapped his front paws around Lindsey's knee. His tail wagged nonstop, and his tongue hung out the side of his mouth as he stared up at her in adoration. She was quite certain that no one except for Sully had ever loved her as much as this dog.

Obligingly, Lindsey bent down and hugged him before rubbing him all over. Heathcliff responded by wiggling in and out of her arms until Sully joined them. Lindsey rose, smiling up at her husband.

"Everyone should have someone look at them the way Heathcliff looks at us," she said.

"You, mostly," Sully said. "He tolerates me, but you he adores, and I know exactly how he feels."

He kissed her then and Lindsey breathed him in. It occurred to her that no matter where she was, so long as she could smell that particular scent of briny sea and bay rum that belonged exclusively to Sully, she was home.

"How did it go with Ms. Cole?"

"Really well," she said. "Beth had her talked back into running in a matter of minutes."

"Beth missed her calling as a salesperson." Sully picked up Lindsey's tote bag full of books and work materials and put his arm around her shoulders, leading her gently to the house while Heathcliff wheeled away for a quick patrol.

"Thank goodness, because the library would be lost without her," she said. She glanced at him. "Actually, it occurred to me today that she might not come back to work after the baby. Talk about some impossible shoes to fill."

"Let's worry about that if and when it happens," he said. "Right now, we have a bigger problem."

"We do?"

"Yes." He stopped walking and turned to face her. "They've found what they suspect is the murder weapon."

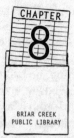

The item used to strangle the John Doe?" Lindsey asked. She felt her eyes go wide. "What was it? Where did they find it?"

"Easy," he said. "This is all secondhand information, so I don't know how reliable it is."

Sully opened the front door and Lindsey stepped through. She kicked off her shoes, setting them on the mat by the door, then slid off her lightweight jacket, hanging it in the coat closet. Sully toed off his running shoes and then opened the front door again for Heathcliff, who came bounding inside.

Lindsey's mind was in a whirl as they left the foyer and headed for the kitchen. She sat at the counter while Sully took a bottle of wine and a beer out of the fridge. He poured her a generous glass of Riesling, twisted the cap off the bottle of beer and took a swig, not bothering to pour it into a mug. Lindsey took this as an indicator of how bad the news was. She took a fortifying sip of the crisp sweet wine.

"Okay, I'm as ready as I'll ever be," she said. "What do you know?"

"Not as much as I'd like, and certainly not as much as Emma, but when I picked up Dennis Monk in the water taxi this morning, he had been talking to Clint Olsen—they were friends in grade school—and Clint told him that he heard from Mary Sturgis that Officer Kirkland's mother told her—"

"Wait." Lindsey reached for her wine. "My brain is starting to turn counterclockwise." She took a healthy sip. "Okay, continue."

"Mary said that Mrs. Kirkland told her that whoever killed the John Doe strangled him using the rope that tied Ms. Cole's trunk shut."

Lindsey frowned. "You mean the same rope that tied the trunk shut when we found the victim?"

"Yes," he said. "That one and . . . Wait, you might want to take another slug of wine."

Lindsey closed one eye as she studied him. He looked like a person about to deliver some seriously lousy news. She took his advice and lifted her glass. After she swallowed, she felt the warmth from the alcohol in the wine bloom in her chest. "Okay, I'm as ready as I'll ever be."

"If the rope proves to be the murder weapon, they think the chief will have no choice but to charge Ms. Cole with the murder."

"But why?" Lindsey asked. "She already said she used the rope to tie her trunk shut. Why would she then use it to murder somebody? We're talking about Ms. Cole being a murderer. It's pre-pos-ter-ous." She drew out each syllable of the word because it required emphasis and it made her feel better.

"I don't know anything else," he said. "My gossip ran out of info at 'they think they know what the murder weapon is.'"

"Are they positive the rope is the murder weapon?" Lindsey asked.

Sully shrugged. "I think it's up to the medical examiner to confirm but the gossip certainly seemed to think it was."

"All right, this is actually good news," Lindsey said.

Sully raised his eyebrows. "How do you figure?"

"Just because the rope might be the murder weapon, that doesn't mean Ms. Cole is the killer. It could be that the murderer did use the rope and then their DNA—a hair, blood, something—might be on it and they can use that to catch the real killer."

"That's true." Sully nodded. "Of course, because the rope belonged to Ms. Cole, it could be her DNA that they find on it."

Lindsey frowned at him.

"Sorry." He grimaced and turned to open the refrigerator, assessing the contents. "Stir-fry for dinner?"

"Sounds good," she agreed but, truthfully, she wasn't that hungry. She was very concerned that Ms. Cole was going to be charged for a crime she didn't commit and there would be nothing they could do to help her.

Sully gathered his vegetables and a cutting board, along with his very large knife. He put a pan with a dollop of oil in it on the stove to heat up and went to work chopping his ingredients. Lindsey watched while he cooked, grateful for the bazillionth time that she'd married a man who was comfortable in the kitchen. She couldn't imagine the drudgery of having to cook dinner every single night.

"There might not be any evidence that ties the rope to the murder," he said.

"Are you trying to make me feel better?" she asked.

He shook his head and then nodded. "Maybe a little," he said. "The bigger question for me is: Did the murderer strangle him in the parking lot? Then I could see the rope being a handy weapon of choice, but if he was murdered elsewhere, then they were just looking to hide his body, and Ms. Cole's car was a convenient spot."

Lindsey felt a chill go down her spine with an icy zip. Families parked in that back parking lot. If the murder had happened on library grounds, parents with their children could have been unloading their cars to go to story time when the murder was taking place. If anyone had witnessed it . . . She shook her head. She didn't want to think about what could have happened. It was already bad enough.

"Given the amount of traffic that area has with people coming and going, even just to use the drive-through book drop, it feels like it couldn't have happened on the premises," she said.

"Especially at midday," he agreed.

"So, the murderer had the body in their car, somehow managed to spot that Ms. Cole's car had an accessible trunk, dumped the body and then presumably fled the scene with no one the wiser." Lindsey pondered this possibility. "I don't understand why they'd want to dump the body in her car. Why not out in the marshes? Or out in the woods? Why in the center of town and at the library, no less?"

"Maybe it wasn't an intentional murder and they panicked," he said. "I think we'd have to know the identity of the victim to know why he was murdered."

"You're right. I don't think we'll understand anything about why he was murdered until we know who he is, er, was," Lindsey said. She watched as Sully tossed minced garlic into the hot oil. The aroma burst into the room, kick-starting her appetite. She pushed her wine away so she didn't overindulge before eating.

Sully set a warmed up bowl of unshelled edamame in front of her, and she gingerly split a casing and nibbled on the lightly salted legumes.

"Do you think it's a random happenstance that the body was shoved into Ms. Cole's car?" she asked.

Sully glanced at her as he dumped diced chicken into the oil. Steam rose, and his wavy reddish brown hair began to curl just as it did on humid days when he was out on the water. His bright blue eyes held hers, and he turned to face her when he asked, "Are you saying that you think someone tried to frame Ms. Cole, specifically?"

"No . . . maybe . . . I don't know," she admitted. "It just feels so coincidental, and then maybe not so much."

"You think her trunk being tied shut wasn't just bad luck, then?"

"It would appear that way on the surface," Lindsey said. "But with the election coming . . ."

"Whoa, whoa, whoa." Sully held up a hand. He took a long swallow of beer and returned to the frying pan to stir the chicken. When he turned back, he said, "This sounds like you're accusing Mayor Hensen of orchestrating this whole thing."

"No, I just feel like it's entirely too convenient that

the first person to run against the mayor in years has a body found in the trunk of her car just as her campaign is beginning to get some traction," Lindsey said. She pushed her long blond curls away from her face, twisting them into a messy bun that she secured with the hair band she always wore on her wrist. "Does that make me paranoid?"

"No. It's worth due consideration," Sully said. "But the ramifications are staggering. If Mayor Hensen had anything to do with that body . . ."

"Yeah, that's where my whole theory falls apart, especially since he was inside the library at the same time that the body was being put into Ms. Cole's trunk," she admitted.

Sully turned back to the stove to finish cooking while Lindsey worked her way through a pile of edamame pods. She knew she was reaching. She'd worked for the mayor for several years now, and she'd never gotten a murder vibe off him. But did stone-cold killers always give off an essence of killer?

Or was she just tying two things, the election and the murder, together because they were both occupying so much of her brain space lately? They could be entirely unrelated, except . . . Would the townspeople be looking at Ms. Cole as a suspect if she weren't running for mayor? Or would she just be that old lemon who worked at the library who had the bad luck to have her car used to dispose of a body? Lindsey had a feeling the answer was the latter, which was why she couldn't separate the two from her mind.

As Sully finished cooking, Lindsey set the table and prepared to feed Heathcliff, who was looking at her from under his thick black fringe as if he might starve to death. She smiled and, when Sully delivered their food to the table, put Heathcliff's on his place mat in the corner of the dining room.

"What do you think the town is thinking?" Lindsey asked. "Beth has Ms. Cole going to the Chamber of Commerce lunch on Monday to speak, and I'm worried that it will just be a bunch of inappropriate questions and stale sandwiches."

"I don't know, but I'll be there," Sully said. "I'm happy to report back."

"No need," she said. "I promised Beth and Ms. Cole that I'd attend, too, as a show of support."

"Excellent. We can enjoy the tasteless ham on rye together," he said. He glanced at her. "Do you think the mayor will be all right with you attending?"

"The official town policy is that employees are not allowed to discuss politics while at work," she said. "So, I will be there on my lunch hour not representing the library but merely as a resident of the town."

"Hensen won't like it," he said.

She shrugged helplessly, and Sully reached across their small dining room table and took her hand in his. "It'll be okay. You'll see."

Lindsey squeezed his fingers with hers. He was right. There was no sense in assuming the worst, not yet at any rate. Plenty of time for that tomorrow.

Ginny, I am so sorry about what happened at the library the other day," Ivy Kavanagh said. "It must have been quite the traumatic experience."

"Thank you," Ms. Cole said. They had just taken their seats at the Chamber of Commerce luncheon, and

Ivy was their table host. "I'd like to say it was just another day at the library, but it wasn't, and I can honestly say I hope I never experience anything like that ever again."

"Indeed. I do commend your fortitude in carrying on with your campaign." Ivy picked up her water glass and held it up in a toast. "You are going to be a formidable opponent for our mayor and, if I may so say, it's about time," she said. "To your success."

Ms. Cole lifted her glass and tapped it against Ivy's. "Thank you very much. I appreciate the support."

When she smiled, it was clear that Ms. Cole was relieved. Lindsey was, too. Every public appearance now seemed fraught with the potential for disaster. This was going to be the longest political campaign ever.

The talk around the table turned to other things, and Lindsey felt herself relax, thinking they just might get through this without an incident.

"I feel like I'm eating a rubber bottle opener between two slabs of cardboard all held together with flour paste," Sully said. He dropped his ham sandwich onto his plate and leaned close to Lindsey. He eyed her salad. "How are the greens?"

"They taste like the plastic bag they came in," she said.

"Shall we drop by the Anchor after this and split a pile of French fries?" he asked.

"Make it a double and yes, please, yes," she said. She pushed her salad away. "And maybe some fried clams on the side and a bowl of chowder."

"That's my girl." Sully laughed.

"Shh," Beth hushed them from across the table. She

turned in her seat to face Ms. Cole. "The president of the Chamber of Commerce is going to introduce you. Let me check your teeth."

"My what?" Ms. Cole blinked at her. "What am I? A horse?"

"You do not want to go up there with spinach in your teeth," Beth said. "Come on, let me see."

Ms. Cole reluctantly showed her teeth, and Beth gave her a swift nod. Ms. Cole looked at Lindsey with one eyebrow higher than the other as if to say, *Really?*

It was a struggle for Lindsey to keep from laughing out loud. She glanced away and felt her heart thump hard in her chest. Walking through the front door were Mayor Hensen and Herb Gunderson. As far as Lindsey knew, they hadn't been on the agenda for the Chamber of Commerce lunch.

"What the heck?" Beth muttered. Lindsey glanced quickly at her friend, who looked as perturbed as she felt. "What is he doing here? He's not supposed to be here."

"Well, he's not here for the sandwiches," Sully said.

Ms. Cole smiled, not looking at all ruffled by the appearance of the mayor. Ivy Kavanagh, however, looked aghast, and she glanced at David Simmons, the president of the organization, who was sitting at the next table. He was busy chatting up Micky Cox, who was also known as the lobster lady since she drove a food truck that served the best lobster rolls in the area, although no one had the heart to tell Mary and Ian that the Blue Anchor had competition. Lindsey could have really used one of those lobster rolls right now.

After Ivy hissed at David to no avail, she flapped her

paper napkin at him and he finally glanced up. She pointed at the doorway, where the mayor stood surveying the scene. David's jaw dropped. It was clear the mayor's arrival was a surprise to them all.

"What do you suppose he wants?" Ivy asked.

"To undermine me," Ms. Cole said. "Let's not let him."

She gave Ivy a pointed look. It was the same look that sent people out to their cars scrounging for change off the floor to pay their fines.

"Of course, you're right," Ivy said. She tossed her napkin onto the table and hopped up from her seat. "I'm going to have David introduce you now."

Ms. Cole gave her a nod of approval, and Ivy's spine stiffened with the boost of confidence. Lindsey observed that the ability to get others on board with her plans was one of Ms. Cole's gifts, primarily because her plans were generally for the greater good of the community, but also because she knew how to get people to feel invested. She was going to make an excellent mayor.

Ivy stopped by David's chair and whispered in his ear. He glanced over at Ms. Cole, who sent him a benevolent smile, and then he nodded and rose from his seat, striding toward the podium.

Lindsey watched the mayor out of the corner of her eye. He didn't move from just inside the door, and she got the feeling he was waiting for something. That couldn't be good.

The small podium had a mic attached, and David's voice boomed, "Hello." He cleared his throat and began again. He introduced himself and the other board members. He talked about some events the chamber would be participating in, and then he gestured toward Ms. Cole.

"I'm very pleased to introduce this month's guest, Ms. Eugenia Cole. Many of you will recognize her from the library, where she's worked for almost forty years. A native of Briar Creek, Ms. Cole is here to talk to us about her vision for Briar Creek's future and how she plans to manage it if she is elected to the position of mayor," David said, his eyes darting to Mayor Hensen still standing by the door, before he continued, "this November. Please give her a warm Chamber of Commerce welcome."

The applause was friendly, and Ms. Cole wound her way through the tables, greeting the people she knew, which was just about everyone, as she made her way to the front of the room. She was wearing navy slacks and the turquoise top Milton had suggested. Her silver hair was brushed back from her face, and she had applied just enough makeup to accent her finer features. She looked calm, poised and professional.

As everyone quieted down, Ms. Cole addressed the room. She went right to the heart of the matter and talked about how she would like to work with the chamber to bolster local businesses. She threw out numbers and statistics, showing she had done her homework, and then offered up several suggestions to boost tourism and lighten the traffic load on their small two-lane main street.

Her most radical suggestion was to build a public parking lot at the entrance to town and to then have a shuttle run people to and from the parking lot every fifteen minutes. It would make the village pedestrian friendly, remove the traffic problem and alleviate the flood of parked cars that littered every single side street, especially in summer when swimming, boating and fishing were at their peak.

She glanced at Micky, the lobster lady, at David's table, and added that with the reduced traffic in the center of town, there'd be more room for food trucks to park in the spots along the public park and the beach. Micky tucked her shoulder length auburn hair behind her ears and grinned. Judging by the twinkle in her light blue eyes, this was clearly a concept of which she was in favor. She adjusted her glasses on her nose and gave a double thumbs-up. Ms. Cole beamed at her.

Beth glanced at Lindsey and said, "She really is a force of nature on things that could make village life nicer and more profitable."

Beth was not known for her whispering skills, and her words carried across the room to the mayor, who scowled in their direction. Oh, boy, Lindsey was not looking forward to the next department head meeting at the town hall.

Ms. Cole ended her speech by asking if anyone had questions. Yes, this had been a part of the plan, but with the mayor arriving and the mean glint in his eye, Lindsey felt that this part of the program should be abandoned with all the speed of a bank robber fleeing a heist. Ms. Cole obviously did not feel the same sense of urgency.

There was a short silence that followed her question, but their table host, Ivy, rose to her feet and asked, "As you know, my charity, Dig Deeper, is globally committed to reforestation in areas that have suffered wildfire damage, but I am interested in the protection of the planet on all levels. It's my hope that a part of your agenda will be dedicated to that as well. Can you share your thoughts about that with us?"

Ms. Cole nodded. "Thank you, Ivy. As a lifelong resident of Briar Creek, I appreciate all that you do to save the trees, and I have some initiatives that I believe will incentivize the stewardship of not just our section of Long Island Sound, but the planet as well."

While Ms. Cole outlined her plan, Lindsey glanced over at Ivy. She listened intently, smiling and nodding when Ms. Cole said something of which she approved. While the library regularly celebrated Earth Day, which was coming up on April twenty-second, Lindsey wondered if there was something more the library could do to raise awareness of environmental issues. There had to be some sort of program they could do. She made a mental note to revisit the idea later.

"What's your experience with managing a budget?" a man in the front of the room asked. He was an older gentleman in a short-sleeved plaid shirt, khaki pants and a buzz cut.

"I've been in charge of the library's circulation budget for years," Ms. Cole said. "I manage the fines and fees, and the collection of them, and I'm pleased to say I have a ninety-nine percent fulfillment rate."

"We keep track of that?" Lindsey asked Beth.

"She does," Beth said.

Lindsey nodded. That really did seem like something for which Ms. Cole would have a pie chart or a Venn diagram.

When Ms. Cole included the amount of money she earned for the library in fines paid, the man seemed impressed and satisfied. Lindsey had a feeling Ms. Cole had just won a vote there.

"Any other questions?" Ms. Cole addressed the crowd. Three hands shot in the air. She was about to choose one, when Mayor Hensen, clearly out of patience, pushed off the wall where he'd been leaning and asked, "Ms. Cole, I have a question. Do tell us, why did you murder that man and stuff him into the trunk of your car?"

Gasps filled the room. To Ms. Cole's credit, she didn't even bat an eyelash. Instead, she lifted one eyebrow and said, "What's the matter, Mayor? Feeling so desperate that you have to make a scene?"

Hensen smirked and Lindsey felt her skin prickle. This was the smile of a man who was up to no good. Lindsey reached over and grabbed Sully's hand. He clasped her fingers and glanced at her.

"I have a bad feeling about this," she said.

"Yeah, he wouldn't show up here unless he had a plan to disrupt Ms. Cole," he said. He shook his head. "Politics is a dirty business."

Abruptly, he stood up and addressed the podium. "Ms. Cole, I have a question."

"Yes, Sully, what is it?" Ms. Cole remained perfectly unflappable.

"There's been some talk about dredging the marshland

and building a newer marina," he said. "Do you have any insight on that proposal?"

"As a matter of fact, I do," she said. She addressed the room. "While a new public marina is a nice money grab for the town with the revenue from docking fees and such, the destruction of the environment makes it a catastrophe. Instead, there are several properties, such as the abandoned wire factory along Shore Road, that could be bought for back taxes and then revitalized into a marina and possibly a brewery or a pub."

A rumble of approval echoed around the room. A smile broke across Beth's face and Lindsey suspected she was trying not to do a fist pump. Mayor Hensen's expression darkened, and a red flush crept up his neck into his face. He'd been pushing for draining the marshland.

"A brewery, huh?" Sam Gardner said. He was well-known for his home brewing.

"Or another venue that would draw visitors who could be dropped off by the newly running shuttle service," Ms. Cole said.

"You'll need drivers," one man said.

She nodded.

"And mechanics," another said.

She nodded again.

"A brewery, a marina and a shuttle service could create a lot of new jobs," Micky said loud enough for the entire room to hear.

"Exactly," Ms. Cole agreed.

A surge of positivity swept the room, making the mayor's face turn apoplectic. He hissed at Herb Gunderson, "Where is the chief? Shouldn't she be here by now?"

Herb shrugged, looking highly stressed. As if he'd

conjured her, however, Emma Plewicki stepped through the main door into the meeting room. Her appearance did not cause the same ripple of excitement as Ms. Cole's plans for revitalization, and she scanned the room until her gaze lit on Ms. Cole at the podium.

She stepped forward and Officer Kirkland took her place. A middle-aged man in a business suit, who appeared to be with them, paused beside him. Emma approached the podium and gestured that she'd like to speak with Ms. Cole. They stepped to the side, with Ms. Cole looking confused. Whatever Emma had to say made Ms. Cole gasp and put her hand over her mouth. Her eyes went wide as she took in the man by the door. Even from across the room, Lindsey could see that Ms. Cole was shaken.

"Bob?" Ivy cried. Lindsey glanced from her to the door. Clearly, Ivy knew who the stranger was, too.

Before Lindsey could ask about him, Beth leaned forward in her seat. Asking no one in particular, she said, "What's happening? Why does Emma want to talk to Ms. Cole?"

No one answered her.

Ms. Cole returned to the podium and said, "If you'll excuse me, something's come up."

A low murmur filled the room, and Mayor Hensen stepped forward and said, "'Something'? Don't be coy, Ms. Cole. The fact is you're being taken to the police station as a suspect in a murder investigation."

Pandemonium ensued.

Ms. Cole was hustled out the door between Emma and Officer Kirkland. The mayor continued to accuse her of murder, quite loudly, while the room broke out in shouts of surprise, cries of disbelief and a flurry of flashes as people tried to get pictures of Ms. Cole on their cell phones.

"We'd better follow," Lindsey said to Beth. She glanced at Sully. "I'll call you when I know something."

"Do you want me to go with you?" he asked. "I can cancel my afternoon tour."

"No, I'm sure this is just a misunderstanding that the mayor is hyping up for his own advantage," Lindsey said. "But I'll let you know if I need you."

"Please do," he said. He glanced back at the mayor, who was looking supremely satisfied with himself. "Something's rotten. I'll do as much damage control here as I can manage."

"Thank you." Lindsey kissed him quick. "I'll be in touch."

She and Beth scooped up their handbags and dashed from the room, hoping to rescue Ms. Cole from whatever horrible error was taking place. Beth hurried to her car, keeping an eye on the police cruiser that had Ms. Cole and the strange man in the back seat.

"Who was that man who came into the room with Emma?" Beth asked.

"I don't know," Lindsey said. "I heard Ivy call him Bob, but I've never seen him before. He's not local, or if he is, he isn't a library user."

"He couldn't be the murderer, could he?"

"No, he would be handcuffed or in jail," Lindsey said. "I could swear Ms. Cole recognized him, however."

"How could that be if he isn't from Briar Creek?" Beth asked. She zipped out of the parking lot and merged onto the street that would take them to the station. "I mean, Ms. Cole never leaves town. Does she even know anyone who doesn't live here?"

Lindsey shrugged. She had no idea. "Should we text Milton?"

"Yes, definitely," Beth said.

Lindsey fumbled with her phone while Beth parked the car. She sent a quick message, hoping it didn't overly alarm Milton. It was Monday, which was his day to volunteer at the town historical society. She knew that unless he had visitors, he could lock up and be there in a matter of minutes.

She shoved her phone into her handbag, and she and Beth hurried into the station as fast as Beth's extended belly would allow. Lindsey had a hard time keeping up with her, which spoke well for Beth's fitness as she entered the last months of her pregnancy.

They pushed through the front doors to find Molly Hatcher seated at the information desk. She was the face of the police department, their girl Friday, who made the coffee, handled the calls, consoled families and basically made the place run. Absolutely nothing happened without Molly knowing about it. The robust brunette shook her head at Lindsey and Beth as if she knew what was coming.

"I have no idea what's happening, so don't ask," she said. "They all hustled into the building and went right into the chief's office."

"But who—" Lindsey halted her question as Molly shook her head at her.

"Can we go in Emma's office?" Beth asked. "Because I am Ms. Cole's campaign manager, and Emma just scooped my candidate out of what was promising to be a very productive luncheon for her."

"I . . . uh . . ." Molly hesitated, looking conflicted.

"It's unfortunate that you were in the break room

and didn't see us when we came in," Lindsey said. She took Beth by the elbow and led her toward the back of the station to Emma's office.

"Well, at least let me pretend to be getting coffee," Molly said. She hurried around them and down the hall.

Lindsey waited until she was out of sight before knocking on the office door. "Emma, it's Lindsey and Beth. We're here to see Ms. Cole."

There was no answer but Lindsey heard the sound of someone moving. The door opened just a crack and Emma peered out at them. "Not now, you two. Ms. Cole is busy."

"No, it's all right," Ms. Cole said. "There's nothing you can say to me that they can't hear."

Emma glanced over her shoulder. She considered Ms. Cole for a moment and then pulled open the door. Lindsey and Beth tumbled into the room. Ms. Cole was sitting on the couch next to the man who'd been at the luncheon. Officer Kirkland was standing in the corner as if he was watching to make sure no one made a break for it. This was not reassuring.

"Lindsey, Beth, this is my friend Bob Spielman," Ms. Cole said.

Lindsey nodded at him, as did Beth. Then they both turned to Ms. Cole.

"What's happening?"

"How can we help?"

"You can help by sitting down and being quiet," Emma said. She shooed them in the direction of a love seat and sat down in the armchair across from the couch where Ms. Cole and Mr. Spielman sat.

"I just don't understand it, Ginny," Bob said. "How did Henry come to be in the trunk of your car?"

Ms. Cole clutched a tissue in her hands. Her voice was wobbly when she said, "I don't know."

Beth and Lindsey exchanged a surprised glance. Beth opened her mouth to ask questions, but Lindsey shook her head. She had a feeling Emma would toss them out if they disrupted the conversation. Beth nodded.

"Did he contact you?" Bob asked.

Ms. Cole shook her head. "No, I haven't heard from Henry Lewis in years. Not since that fateful day when I didn't go to Washington with you. Even when his grandmother passed away and he was in Briar Creek for the funeral, he never looked me up, and I never tried to reach him either. We remained estranged all these years."

Lindsey felt the mental key slide into the lock and click. The mystery was unlocked. Their John Doe was Henry Lewis. She felt the surprise ripple through her. Henry Lewis was one of Briar Creek's more famous former residents.

"I'm sorry," Bob said. "He never got over the—"

"I know," Ms. Cole interrupted him. It was obvious that whatever they were talking about was intensely personal.

"Never got over what?" Emma asked. Clearly, boundaries were not something she cared about when dealing with a homicide.

Ms. Cole looked pained. "Henry Lewis and I were engaged for a time."

Bob reached over and patted her hand.

"Whoa, whoa, whoa," Beth said. "The guy that was found in the trunk of your car was a man you were engaged to?" Her voice was higher than normal, as if she was trying very hard not to sound screechy and failing miserably.

"It was a short engagement," Ms. Cole said.

That was it. That was all she said. Lindsey blinked. This was bad. So bad, on so many levels.

"You didn't recognize him when you saw him?" Emma asked.

Ms. Cole shook her head. "The Henry I knew was very different from the middle-aged man in the suit. Back in the day, he had long blond hair, a thick beard, and he wore flowing flowery shirts and bell-bottom jeans and sandals. He was always in sandals." She looked at Bob, who was nodding. "He was so different back then. We all were."

He smiled kindly. "We were kids, well, it seems like that now. At the time we thought we were a force to be reckoned with."

"We were going to change the world," Ms. Cole said. They exchanged a look of deep understanding from a shared personal history. Lindsey felt as if the rest of them were intruding on a moment, and she glanced away, noticing that Emma and Beth did the same.

Ms. Cole delicately blew her nose into a tissue and cleared her throat. It was the signal that she was pulling it together. She glanced at Emma and said, "I expect you have some questions."

"I do," she said. "But first, I want to tell you both that I'm sorry for your loss and I won't rest until I find out what happened to Henry Lewis."

Bob inclined his head. His eyes were suspiciously watery and he said, "I appreciate that."

"I suppose we should start at the beginning," Emma said. "What was Henry doing in Briar Creek?"

The door opened, and Molly appeared holding a tray with a steaming pot of coffee and mugs.

"I thought you all could use some coffee," Molly said. She glanced around the room and her eyes went comically wide at the sight of Lindsey and Beth. "Oh, when did you two get here?"

"A few minutes ago," Beth said. "You must have been making coffee and missed us."

"I expect," Molly said. She turned to leave but Emma stopped her.

"It's truly remarkable, Molly, that you knew to bring six mugs," she said. Her knowing gaze met Molly's.

Molly shrugged and said, "It's a gift."

She slipped through the door before Emma could say another word.

Ms. Cole reached forward and poured Bob a cup, pushing the creamer and sugar in his direction. He declined the extras, taking his coffee black.

Emma gestured for Lindsey and Beth to help themselves, but Lindsey was already too amped up by the events of the day, and Beth had given up caffeine during her pregnancy. Another reason not to have children, as far as Lindsey was concerned.

"Henry was in New York City on business," Bob said. "He said he was going to stop by Briar Creek and see Ginny." He paused and gestured to Ms. Cole.

"That's what they called me in high school," she explained. "Did he say why?"

"No." Bob shook his head. "But I encouraged him as I felt it was a long-overdue visit. When he didn't return to work in Maine, I called our offices in New York. They confirmed that he had been there and left and planned to stop in Briar Creek. I called his nephew, who still lives here, but he didn't answer, so I came down to file a missing person's report with your chief, and she's the one who showed me the picture of the man found in your car."

"Henry," Ms. Cole said with a sigh.

"Yes," Bob said, his voice low as if weighted down by grief.

"What sort of business did Mr. Lewis have in New York?" Emma asked. She'd taken out a recorder and held it up to show Bob. He nodded and she switched it on.

"Our business is headquartered in Maine," Bob said. "But our distribution center is just outside New York City. We take turns going down there to oversee the operation."

"What business are you in?" Beth asked. Then she glanced at Emma and said, "Sorry."

Emma shrugged. "Solid question."

"Henry and I are the founders of Nana's Cookies," Bob said.

"What?" Beth cried. "No way. Your oatmeal raisin cookie is my go-to for instant mood elevation."

They all turned to look at her. Beth cringed. "Sorry—again."

Bob shook his head. "No, it's all right. I hear that a lot, actually."

Lindsey knew Henry Lewis was one of the founders of Nana's Cookies. He was one of Briar Creek's claims to fame. She had not known that Ms. Cole had such a personal tie to the company, or more specifically, to the man behind the company.

"He never called you?" Emma asked Ms. Cole.

"No," Ms. Cole said. "I haven't spoken to him since we broke up almost forty years ago. As Bob and I were saying, it didn't end well."

"He wasn't the same after you left," Bob said.

A shadow crossed over Ms. Cole's face. Lindsey suspected it was regret.

Emma glanced between them. "Bad breakup?"

"It was sad more than anything else," Ms. Cole said. "Henry and I grew up here in Briar Creek. We were just good friends as children, but when we both went to college in New Haven, we started to date. We were politically active and had a lot in common."

"We were all active in those days," Bob said wistfully. "People were invested in equal rights, the environment and world peace. It was amazing to be a part of something bigger than ourselves."

Ms. Cole nodded. Lindsey had never viewed her as a rebel. She'd always been very old guard about the library rules and regulations. It was absolutely fascinating to see another side of a woman who, up until today, she'd thought she knew quite well.

"Bob and I met through Henry." Ms. Cole gestured between her and Bob. "He was Henry's roommate. When we started becoming student activists, your girlfriend at the time, Tilda, joined us and rounded out our foursome. We spent most weekends attending rallies, protesting and getting people to sign petitions."

"We made a difference," Bob said.

"Did we?" Ms. Cole asked. "Sometimes I wonder."

They shared a rueful look that spoke of plans and dreams that had gone unfulfilled before Ms. Cole glanced away.

"One weekend, we were all supposed to attend a big march in Washington," she said. "We prepared for weeks. Right when we were about to leave, my mother called. My father had just had a stroke and was in the hospital. I couldn't leave him, and I couldn't leave my mom to care for him alone."

She stared at the wall opposite as if remembering every emotion that had coursed through her on that day. Her eyes were troubled and her shoulders slumped. Lindsey suspected it had been one of those moments when a single decision changed the course of her life. Ms. Cole shook herself out of the past and focused on Emma.

"Henry was furious," she said. "He said that I couldn't help my father and that I belonged at the rally. He told me if I didn't go, he was breaking up with me right then and there."

Bob sighed. "Tilda was furious with him for being so heartless."

Ms. Cole gave him a small smile. "So was I."

"As I recall, I was useless," he said. He glanced at her and said, "I'm sorry. I remember being so obsessed with not being late that I was quite oblivious to what was happening to you. I was not a very good friend to you, Ginny."

"It's all right," she said. She patted his hand where it rested on the couch between them. "Those were extraordinary times."

They shared another look of times past, strife endured, of dreams achieved and laid to waste, and of friendship that excluded everyone else in the room.

The office door abruptly opened and Milton appeared. His silver goatee was trimmed with precision, and today's tracksuit was a crimson red, the reflection of which made the dome of his bald head pink.

"Excuse me, I'm looking for Eugenia." He glanced at the couch and saw Ms. Cole holding hands with a strange man. His back straightened and one eyebrow rose. He did not look pleased. "Is everything all right?"

CHAPTER

10

BRIAR CREEK
PUBLIC LIBRARY

Ms. Cole patted Bob's hand once, then let him go. "It is now. I'm so glad you're here, Milton."

"Come on in," Emma said. Her voice sounded weary. "Everyone else has."

Milton entered the room and sat on the other side of Ms. Cole. She gestured to Bob and said, "This is an old friend of mine, Bob Spielman. Bob, this is my . . ." She paused. She and Milton stared at each other, and she added, "He's my good friend, Milton Duffy."

"I'm a bit more than a good friend," Milton said.

Ms. Cole blushed and Bob looked uncomfortable. Lindsey glanced at Beth, who was trying not to smile. Milton had been single since he'd been widowed several years ago. Ms. Cole was the first woman in town he'd actively dated, and now he looked as if he wasn't happy with the lack of definition to their relationship.

"Milton, the man found in my car—" Ms. Cole paused. She blinked several times and then cleared her throat. "He was Henry Lewis, the fiancé I told you about from my college years."

"What?" Milton looked shocked. He took Ms. Cole's hands in his. "Oh, my dear, are you all right? That must have been a horrible shock. When did you realize?"

"I didn't," she said. "I never recognized him. Bob is his business partner and he came to town because Henry was supposed to be back in Maine on Friday but he never arrived."

"I'm very sorry for your loss," Milton said to Bob.

Bob nodded. He looked emotional, as if he couldn't speak at the moment. He had a good face, with a strong chin and straight nose. His eyes were pale blue but warm and friendly. He seemed fit for his age with no paunch at his middle, and he carried himself well, as if he was comfortable with himself and the successful life he led. Lindsey thought he had probably been very handsome in his youth.

She tried to remember what Henry had looked like, but the trauma of finding his body had blocked out everything but a few fragmented details. She could picture the cuff of his shirtsleeve, the lines embedded in the skin of his neck and his bloodshot eyes staring vacantly at her. She shivered.

"Now that we're all caught up," Emma said. "Let's get back to the discussion at hand, yes?"

Emma turned to Bob. "Was there a reason Henry wanted to see Ms. Cole in particular?"

"Not that I know of," Bob said. "I suspect he was finally willing to let bygones be bygones, and I assumed this trip was just a jog down memory lane because Briar Creek is where he grew up and where his nana lived until she passed. Without her and her magical cookie recipes, there'd be no Nana's Cookies. Besides, he usually stopped in Briar Creek on his way back from New York. It's just that this time he was going to look up an old friend as well. His family's home is still here, and his nephew lives there."

"Lenny Lewis, and, yes, he does," Ms. Cole explained to the rest of them.

Lindsey frowned. She knew Lenny Lewis. Not well, but she'd helped him at the library. He was a big man, very quiet, kept to himself but was always polite. There was something not quite all there about Lenny. He bounced on the balls of his feet with his gaze always somewhere off in the distance as if he could see things no one else could. But he loved books about nature, particularly about the wildlife in the marshes and out in the bay, and Lindsey was always fascinated with the details he shared about whatever creature he was researching.

His latest obsession had been horseshoe crabs. He'd been consumed with how the blood of horseshoe crabs was used in medicine, and Lindsey had printed a stack of articles for him. She had no idea what he was going to do with the information, but like all good reference searches, it left her with more knowledge about endotoxins and how the blood of the horseshoe crab was used to detect them.

"Is he a library user?" Beth asked. She was frowning as if trying to place the name with a face.

"Only occasionally," Ms. Cole said. "He tends to keep to himself. He's what we call a character. Harmless but definitely marches to his own drummer."

Emma glanced at Officer Kirkland. He stepped forward and asked, "Shall I bring him in, Chief?"

"Yes," she said. "We need to know if he heard from his uncle before he arrived in Briar Creek. We also need to know where he was the morning that Henry Lewis was found."

Ms. Cole frowned. "You don't think Lenny had anything to do with it, do you?"

"Everyone is a suspect," Emma said.

"But Lenny's . . ." Ms. Cole's words ran out and she looked to Bob for help. He gave her a concerned look as if he didn't know what to say either.

"Lenny is on the spectrum," Milton said. Everyone turned to him in surprise. He said, "I don't know if it's common knowledge, but he was diagnosed as high-functioning autistic as a teen. I only know this because his parents informed me when I had him in my chess club. He was a loner then, too. Not great at the social niceties. He was rather off-putting to the other teens, but he was absolutely brilliant at chess. He could see ten moves ahead. It was electrifying to watch him play."

Emma nodded. She turned back to Kirkland. "Bring him in but don't say anything. If he doesn't know about his uncle's death, and I doubt he does, then it would be best to have someone break it to him gently." She turned back to Bob. "Were Henry and Lenny close?"

"I don't think Lenny has ever been close to anyone except for Nana," he said. "Even when his parents passed, he showed a remarkable lack of emotion. Henry tried to have a relationship with Lenny but he was unreachable."

"Does he have any family who might look after him when we tell him the news?" Emma asked.

"I don't think so," Bob said. "Nana passed away almost twenty years ago, Henry's parents passed before her, and his brother and his wife—Lenny's parents—were killed in a car accident shortly after Nana died. Henry is divorced and never had children, so Lenny is the last of the Lewis family."

"Henry is . . . er . . . he was . . . divorced that is?" Ms. Cole asked.

"Yes," Bob said. He gave her a kind smile and said, "His marriage was brief. He just never met anyone he cared for as much as you. You were always the one who got away."

"Oh, that's . . ." Ms. Cole put a hand over her heart, obviously too overcome to speak. Milton stiffened beside her and she dropped her hand and said, "That's unfortunate."

An awkward silence filled the room. Lindsey wasn't sure where to look, but Emma had no such qualms.

"Mr. Spielman—" she said.

"Please call me Bob."

"Bob, do you know who stood to inherit Henry's share of your business?"

"Yes, although I don't feel I can give specifics without his attorney present. I can tell you what he told me, and that was that he was taking the billionaire's Giving Pledge—you know, where they pledge most of their wealth to charity. It was Henry's wish to have his entire fortune divided up among his favorite organizations."

"So, there's no heir?"

Bob shook his head.

"Not even Lenny?"

"No," Bob said. "Henry signed over the family home to him and he gifted him some shares of the company, but that's it. As I mentioned, they weren't close."

"Do you know the names of these charities?"

"Let's see." Bob frowned in concentration. "There were a couple of big ones like the American Heart Association and the Juvenile Diabetes Research Foundation. Then there were a couple of smaller more personal ones like New Haven Reads, where they donate books to schoolchildren, and Dig Deeper, which is actually based here in Briar Creek. Ivy Kavanagh, the woman who runs that one, is a childhood friend of Henry's. Her organization raises money to reforest areas decimated by wildfires."

"Oh, we just had lunch with Ivy," Ms. Cole said. "She was the host of our table. You know, I read in the local paper years ago that Henry was a contributor to her charity. Reforestation was one of Henry's passions." Ms. Cole paused. Her voice was strained when she added, "I'll be sure to make a contribution to Ivy's charity in his name."

"He'd like that," Bob said. They shared a small smile. "I will, too."

"Bob, I'm going to need you to create a timeline of the events of Henry's travels as best you can," Emma said. "The medical examiner will give us a time of death, but any information you can give us will help. Also, a list of the names of anyone he spoke with or visited would be good to have."

"I can do that."

"Ms. Cole, we already have your schedule from that morning," Emma continued. "If you never connected with Henry Lewis, then I don't think I have any more questions for you at this time."

Ms. Cole nodded. Milton put a comforting hand on her shoulder.

"I'll be staying in town for a few days," Bob said.

"I'm at the Beachfront Bed and Breakfast if you need to reach me."

"Jeanette Palmer's place," Ms. Cole said. "Ask her to make you some lemon scones. They are the absolute best."

"I will," Bob said. He glanced at Emma, and it wasn't the look of a kindly older gentleman but more the cookie tycoon who was used to getting his way. "I'm not leaving until I know what happened to my partner."

"Excellent," Emma said. Her tone was severe. "That saves me the trouble of telling you not to leave town." Bob blinked in surprise and she nodded. "Yes, that means exactly what you think it means. As his business partner, you're a suspect. I'll be interviewing you shortly for a better understanding of your working relationship, and I'm going to want to talk to your accountants and board of directors."

Bob's chin tipped up. Former hippie or not, he looked every inch the multimillionaire businessman who was not used to being told what to do. Emma stared him down.

"I'm sure you'll do whatever it takes to find your partner's killer," she said.

Bob immediately deflated. Lindsey wondered if it was possibly just an act. She glanced at him and noted that while he was on the later end of middle-aged, he looked well muscled. Could he have strangled his partner and lifted him into the back of Ms. Cole's car? How convenient it was for him—the only person who knew about Ms. Cole's relationship with Henry—that the trunk of her car had been open that day.

Was it possible that their business was in trouble?

Maybe Henry wanted out and Bob didn't want him to go? Or maybe it was the other way around. Lindsey wondered whom she could call in the corporate world who might know what was happening with the gourmet cookie company.

Maybe it wasn't even about business. Maybe Bob and Henry were sick of each other on a personal level. Their partnership had lasted longer than many marriages. Had they just gotten tired of each other but were too financially entangled to go their separate ways?

Lindsey knew it was none of her business, but Ms. Cole was her employee, and more than that, she had become a friend. At first, having a body discovered in *Ms. Cole's* car felt like the desperate act of someone trying to torment her, but now that the victim had a connection to Ms. Cole, it felt even more sinister, and Lindsey's protective instincts were on high alert.

"Of course, I'll do anything I can to help catch whoever did this," Bob said. "Henry was . . . he was more than my business partner. He was my friend. My brother." He broke down. His voice wobbled as he put a hand over his eyes to shield his tears from view.

Lindsey felt Beth stir beside her. She knew the nurturer in Beth likely wanted to go over and give the man a hug. She resisted but Lindsey saw her wipe her own face, and she suspected Beth had a case of sympathy weeping.

"I'm so sorry, Bob," Ms. Cole said. "Why don't you join Milton and me for dinner?"

The only sign of Milton's resistance to this plan was the tightening in the corners of his lips. But he didn't object, quite the opposite. He leaned around Ms. Cole and met Bob's gaze.

"I make a mean vegan meatloaf," he said.

Bob lowered his hand from his face. He nodded. Pulling a handkerchief from his pocket, he blew his nose. "If it's no trouble, that'd be nice. Thank you."

"Mr. Spielman, I'd like you to stay here and work on that timeline. The rest of you can go. But if you think of anything else about Henry Lewis, please reach out."

"We'll collect you from the Beachfront at six," Ms. Cole said.

Bob gave her a warm smile. "Thank you, Ginny. We have a lot of catching up to do."

"Eugenia," Milton said. Lindsey didn't think she was imagining his emphasis on her full name. "We should go. I'm sure Bob wants to finish up here as quickly as possible so he can go and call his wife."

He was staring pointedly at the wedding ring on Bob's finger. Ms. Cole glanced between the two men and nodded.

"Of course," she said. She turned to Lindsey and Beth. "Shall we walk back to the library together?"

"I have my car," Beth said. "I can drive us."

"I can take you," Milton offered.

Ms. Cole smiled at him. "Thank you, but I don't want to trouble you any more than I have today."

"You are never any trouble, my dear," he said. They exchanged a tender look that made Lindsey want to say, *Aw.* She resisted.

"All the same," Ms. Cole said. "I'd best get back to work, and it only makes sense to go with Lindsey and Beth. I'll call you later."

Ms. Cole led the way out of the room, and Beth and Lindsey fell in behind her. They were silent as they walked to Beth's car. Once inside, when the doors were shut, Ms. Cole said, "I have no idea what to make of any of this."

Lindsey leaned forward. She had taken the back seat to give Ms. Cole the front, which was more comfortable.

"Are you all right, Ms. Cole?" she asked. "It must have been quite a surprise to discover the victim found in your car was actually your ex."

"I'll say." Ms. Cole fanned her face. "I think I might be in shock."

Beth turned out of the parking lot and merged onto the street. The library was the next right turn, so she flipped on her signal and pulled into the parking lot.

"I think someone is trying to set you up," she said.

"What?" Ms. Cole asked. "Why?"

"The race for mayor," Beth said. Her voice was grim. "Someone wants you out."

"So they murdered her ex-boyfriend from forty years ago and stuffed him in her trunk? That feels a bit extreme," Lindsey said.

"Exactly," Ms. Cole agreed. "I can't imagine running for mayor of a tiny shore town would warrant that sort of campaign sabotage."

"Mayor Hensen doesn't want to give up his power," Beth said.

"Yes, but how would he know about Henry Lewis and Ms. Cole? How would he know to put him in her trunk? How would he know her trunk was going to be tied shut on this particular day?" Lindsey asked.

"I am not deterred by your logic," Beth said. She stuck her chin out, looking like a stubborn child.

Ms. Cole glanced around at Lindsey with a small smile. They had come so far since Lindsey had first arrived in Briar Creek. It was nice to be allies, although unfortunate that it was because Ms. Cole was a suspect in a murder investigation.

Beth parked the car and they climbed out. As they crossed the parking lot to the staff door at the rear of the building, Lindsey paused to study the spot where Ms. Cole's car had been.

"You didn't recognize him at all?" she asked.

"No," Ms. Cole said. "It had been so many years."

Beth glanced at Ms. Cole as she, too, stared at the spot where her car had been. "You said it was a bad breakup?"

Ms. Cole turned to look at her. Her expression was rueful. "It was a bit more than bad, but of course I didn't think it would do me any good to admit as much to Chief Plewicki. It was all so long ago."

Lindsey and Beth said nothing, waiting.

Ms. Cole sighed and said, "When he left for the rally without me, I promised him I'd go back to him as soon as I could. He didn't believe me and demanded his ring back. I gave it to him. And then it turned out he was right. I never made it back."

"You went home to help your mom," Beth said. "There's nothing wrong with that, and he should have understood."

Ms. Cole grunted.

"Did you ever consider going to find him afterward?" Lindsey asked.

"No, my mother was so fragile after my father died that I couldn't leave her alone," Ms. Cole said. "Besides, I was young and stubborn and felt he was in the wrong and therefore it was up to him to come and apologize to me. As time went by and he didn't, I realized he never would."

"That's . . . that's just so sad," Beth wailed.

Lindsey glanced at her friend. Her face was streaming with tears. She and Ms. Cole exchanged a distressed glance.

"No, it's okay. It worked out exactly as it was supposed to," Ms. Cole said. "I have a wonderful life. I love my town, my library job, and I have a terrific man to keep me company. And, look, I'm running for mayor. My life is amazing."

"Yes, but you could have been married to the love of your life," Beth said.

"If he had truly been the love of my life, I would have gone back to him," Ms. Cole said. She smiled at them both, then turned and walked to the library.

"The guy owned Nana's Cookies," Beth said.

"I know," Lindsey agreed.

"Ms. Cole could have had an entirely different life."

"Sounds like she's okay with the life she's had."

Ms. Cole reached the door ahead of them and turned around. "Are you coming?"

"Be right there," Beth said. She waved at Ms. Cole to go on without them. "I have a stitch in my side. Just need to let it pass."

"Can I get you anything?" Ms. Cole frowned in concern.

"No, I'm fine."

Ms. Cole nodded. They watched as she typed in the security code and slipped through the door.

"Are you sure you're all right?" Lindsey asked.

"Yeah, I'm fine," Beth said. "I need you to hear me out, but I don't want to talk in front of Ms. Cole."

"Okay."

"Now, you know I'm her campaign manager, so it

really pains me to go here, but I feel that all possibilities must be considered so that we can prepare for any outcome."

"All right." Lindsey wondered if her friend was having another hormone surge. "Let's start with what you're talking about—what possibility?"

"That Ms. Cole is the murderer."

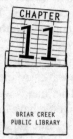

"What?" Lindsey stared at Beth. She had no idea what to say. Could Beth actually be considering Ms. Cole for the murder of her ex-fiancé? It made no sense. Her face must have shown her shocked disbelief because Beth rolled her eyes.

"I'm not saying she murdered Henry Lewis," she said.

"Really, because that's what it sounded like."

"No, what I meant was we need to prepare for the possibility that Ms. Cole is propagandized as the murderer at large. We have to be ready to combat that misinformation."

"It's Ms. Cole," Lindsey said. "No one in Briar Creek is going to—"

"Mayor Hensen will continue to weaponize this incident as sure as I'm standing here with swollen ankles and heartburn."

Lindsey stopped talking. The mayor's behavior

toward her and the library and Ms. Cole had made it
abundantly clear that he did not respect them as people,
and certainly not as colleagues. If the news that Ms.
Cole had once been engaged to the murder victim became public knowledge . . .

Lindsey glanced at the library. "Let's go!"

She hustled up the walkway and into the library. Her
heart was racing and her hands were sweaty, making it
take longer than she would have liked to enter the code
to unlock the back door. She yanked it open, and strode
into the building with Beth right behind her.

The sound of raised voices alerted her to the problem immediately. She followed the sound down the
hallway and through the workroom to the front of the
library. Ms. Cole was standing behind the circulation
desk with Paula while a crowd of reporters stood on the
other side. Their shouts were deafening.

"Ms. Cole!"

"Did you murder your ex?"

"How long were you involved with Henry Lewis?"

"Did you have anything to do with his success in the
cookie business?"

"When was the last time you saw him?"

"Did you lure him here to kill him?"

"Was it years of pent-up rage from rejection?"

"What impact will a dead body being found in your
car have on your election campaign?"

The questions came in hard and fast like a hail of
bullets. Ms. Cole stood blinking at the crowd as if she
couldn't quite believe they were asking such absurd
things.

"Oh, no," Beth said. She surged around Lindsey,
striding forward like she was heading into battle. She

went nose to nose with the reporter from the *Register* who was halfway over the desk in his quest for the scoop. "Back up."

He met her gaze and then slowly slid back to the floor. Beth then turned to Ms. Cole and put her arm around her waist, gently guiding her away from the frenzy.

"Wait," Ms. Cole said. She turned back to the reporters. "I'm prepared to answer any and all questions. What do you want to know?"

"Ms. Cole, as your campaign manager, I am urging you not to take questions at this time," Beth said.

Ms. Cole patted her hand. "It's all right. I believe in transparency, and we may as well get it all out on the table now."

The eyes of the reporters lit up like kids on Christmas morning. The questions were shouted again, and Ms. Cole drew herself up with all the authority of the librarian that she was and said, "Shhhh."

Lindsey almost laughed, she was so happy to see the old Ms. Cole make a well-timed appearance.

"This is a library. There are people here who are working and studying. Now, while I am happy to speak with you, you must comport yourselves with the respect this institution deserves or you may leave. Am I clear?"

Every single reporter went silent and hands shot in the air.

"Perhaps this would be better held in another room," Lindsey said. "If you'll all follow me; we have a study room available."

She led the group to a glassed-in room, with Beth and Ms. Cole following. Beth was whispering frantically in Ms. Cole's ear, and Lindsey suspected she was still trying to talk her out of talking to the reporters.

They filed into the room. The air practically crack-led with tension, and Lindsey noted that the patrons in the library were watching through the glass, hoping to get a look at what was happening.

As the reporters took seats at the table, Lindsey closed the shade, allowing them some privacy. Ms. Cole moved to stand at the head of the table. She inclined her head to the reporter on her left and said, "Let's go one at a time. Please introduce yourselves and tell me what news outlet you represent."

She smiled, and it was a genuine smile as if she'd invited them all here for tea. Lindsey felt a burst of pride bloom in her chest. Ms. Cole was a force to be reckoned with. It was a sight to behold.

"Hi, I'm Mark Jacobs, with the *Courant*." The first man spoke. He looked like he was just warming up. "Can you tell us about your connection to the victim?"

"Of course," Ms. Cole said. "Henry Lewis was an old friend of mine. We both grew up here in Briar Creek."

"'Friend'?" he clarified with one eyebrow raised.

"Childhood friends," Ms. Cole said. "His death . . ." She paused, and a look of pain crossed over her face. "I'm sorry, his murder, is a tragedy that can't be understated."

A ripple passed through the room. Beth looked like she wanted to jump in but Ms. Cole forged on.

"I'm sure you know he was a founder of the company Nana's Cookies," she continued. "His partner, Bob Spielman, is here in town. Together, we are determined to find the person or persons responsible for this heinous act, and we will be sure they are caught and convicted."

She glanced at the next reporter and gave her a small nod.

"Anna Trask, from the *Independent*," the young woman said. "Is it true that you were involved with Mr. Lewis?"

"In another lifetime, I was engaged to Mr. Lewis, yes," Ms. Cole said.

Now the energy in the room was buzzing.

"When was the last time you spoke to Mr. Lewis?" the next reporter asked. Ms. Cole stared at him. He was the same man who had practically crawled over the desk to get to her.

"Sorry, Mike Strickland, from the *Register*," he said.

She smiled again. "Well, Mike, to be fully transparent, I have to admit that the last time I spoke to Henry was the day I broke off our engagement almost forty years ago."

The unexpected answer sent all of the news people into a palpable frenzy.

"Then why was he found in the trunk of your car?" another man shouted.

The look Ms. Cole sent him was quelling. "Sorry, Kyle Rogers from Channel Seven."

"I wish I knew," Ms. Cole said. "Sadly, I have no idea who would want to murder Mr. Lewis or why they'd want to dispose of the body in my vehicle." She waited a beat. "I can't think of anyone, can you?"

"Aren't you campaigning against the incumbent, Mayor Hensen?" Anna asked. Her eyes narrowed in concentration as if she was trying to connect the dots on a particularly difficult puzzle.

"Why, yes, I am," Ms. Cole said. She looked thoughtful. "You don't think that has anything to do with it, do you?"

It was a genius move. Had they not been in a room

of reporters, Lindsey would have applauded. The reporters, realizing that a bigger scoop was out there, rose from their seats as one. In a flurry of thank-yous, they rushed to the door. Lindsey had no doubt that their next stop would be the mayor's office.

When they left, Lindsey, Beth and Ms. Cole stood in the quiet, staring at one another. Beth started to laugh. It was a wheezy laugh of relief and disbelief.

"I can't believe you just did that," she said.

"Did what?" Ms. Cole shrugged. "They asked questions and I answered. I can't be held accountable for any conclusions they might have drawn."

"Brilliant," Beth said.

"Agreed," Lindsey added.

"Maybe," Ms. Cole said. Her expression was grim. "I think turnabout is fair play."

"What do you mean?" Beth asked.

"Don't you think it's odd that the mayor showed up at the luncheon right before Emma arrived with Bob to ask me about Henry?" she asked.

Lindsey nodded. "It was as if he was waiting for something to happen."

"You mean he knew Emma was coming to talk to you," Beth said. "But how?"

Lindsey met Ms. Cole's gaze. "You don't think it was a coincidence that the mayor showed up and asked you if you murdered Henry, do you?"

"No."

"Me either," she said.

"So, you're saying someone in the police department tipped him off?" Beth asked. "Because you know there's no way Emma would have told him that she was coming to the luncheon with Mr. Spielman."

"Possibly." Ms. Cole looked at her. "However he found out, the mayor is definitely using Henry Lewis's death to try to force me to withdraw from the campaign by making me look guilty."

"Crazy thought," Beth said. She put a hand on her belly as if she could shield her baby from what she was about to say. "You don't think the mayor is mixed up in Henry Lewis's murder in some way, do you? Because it's awfully convenient for him that Mr. Lewis was found in the trunk of your car, isn't it?"

Lindsey felt an apprehensive shiver ripple through her. Mayor Hensen, complicit in a murder. She'd worked for him for years, and while they hadn't always seen eye to eye, she'd never gotten a murderous vibe off him. Could she really have been so wrong about him all these years?

"Afternoon, ladies," a voice broke into the silence. Lindsey glanced at the door to see Robbie Vine standing there. "You aren't going to believe this, but a pack of reporters just passed me and they didn't ask me any questions. Do they not know who I am?"

He looked so affronted that the three of them broke into laughter, dispelling the unease. Looking pleased to have made them happy, Robbie grinned.

"Also, I brought biscuits," he said.

Lindsey glanced at the bag of oatmeal raisin Nana's Cookies he held up. Oh, the irony.

A re you telling me that you think Mayor Hensen strangled Ms. Cole's former fiancé and then stuffed him into the trunk of her car just to frame her for murder to take her out of the running for mayor?" Robbie asked.

Robbie and Lindsey were sitting in her office, sharing a pot of tea and the cookies, or, as Robbie called them, biscuits.

"Well when you put it like that, it sounds crazy," she said. She had spent the past fifteen minutes catching him up on the news of the day. "But as Ms. Cole pointed out, who else has anything to gain by framing her for murder?"

"I disagree," Robbie said. "I'm not convinced she was being framed for murder. Just because the mayor has reacted very poorly to Ms. Cole's bid for mayor does not mean he's the killer. I mean, how would he have known that the trunk of her car would be tied shut and therefore accessible? Do we even know if the rope was the weapon yet?"

"No, we don't. I thought the same thing, but I don't believe in coincidences," Lindsey said. "And it is a very big coincidence that the man in her trunk turns out to be a man she used to be involved with almost forty years ago."

"I think the angle to take is to figure out who had a problem with Mr. Lewis," Robbie said. "His business partner, for example. They had to have issues at some point in their business dealings, even the best partnerships do. And he knew about Ms. Cole and the bad breakup. Why, he already admitted that he knew Mr. Lewis was coming here to see Ms. Cole."

Lindsey bit into her cookie. Crunchy on the outside, chewy in the middle, with a generous helping of plump raisins. Divine.

"But was Mr. Lewis really coming here?" she asked. "We only have Spielman's word for it."

"See?" Robbie said. He sipped his tea. "That's how you have to look at this. From every possible angle. No one is to be trusted."

"Including Ms. Cole?"

"Oh, no, she's above reproach."

"You're afraid of her."

"As any good library user would be," he said. "Frankly, she terrifies me."

"She adores you," Lindsey said. Ms. Cole and Robbie were both players in the local community theater under Violet LaRue's direction, and after the town's initial starstruck reaction to Robbie, they had embraced him as one of their own.

"Doesn't everyone?"

Lindsey laughed.

"How can we help Ms. Cole?" he asked. "I don't want to see her campaign for mayor ended prematurely because of this situation."

"We need to get ahead of the rumors that are about to start swirling through town about her. You know how people are. They love juicy gossip and it doesn't matter if it's true or not," Lindsey said. "She handled herself well with the reporters, but the mayor has a lot of friends in town, and it wouldn't surprise me if they try to ruin her reputation ahead of the election."

"I'll keep my ear to ground and squash any nefarious twaddle," he said.

"Thank you."

They sat in companionable silence for a moment, and then Robbie lowered his cup. He studied Lindsey and asked, "What else? I get the feeling you have something more in mind but you're not saying."

"I hesitate to ask," Lindsey said.

Robbie leaned forward in his seat. "We're going to investigate, aren't we?"

"No . . . well, maybe?" Lindsey said. "There are just a few things, and I'm sure Emma is on top of it, but . . ."

"Do not leave me hanging in midair here," Robbie said. "What?"

"It's just so convenient that Ms. Cole's trunk was open when someone happened to need to dispose of a body and that body happened to belong to her ex-fiancé. I mean, as I said before, that sort of coincidence is just too much."

"Agreed. It is awfully random. So, we can assume that whoever the killer is, they had to know of her relationship with him, right?"

"Right," Lindsey said. "But I've worked with Ms. Cole for years and I never knew, so there can't be that many people who did."

"And if this person did, how did they time the murder just so?" Robbie asked. "Were they following her? How long was Mr. Lewis deceased? Was there an alternative plan to dispose of his body and her car was just convenient? And, most importantly, who wanted him dead?"

"So many questions," Lindsey said. "And I'm sure Emma has already thought of them all and is chasing down leads as we speak."

"But we should help her," he said. He put his hand over his heart. "It's our civic duty."

"I thought so, too."

Robbie swallowed the last of his tea and put the cup and saucer on the tray. "Where should I start?"

"Ms. Cole picked up her signs from the sign maker

that morning," Lindsey said. "Maybe they noticed someone skulking about."

"I can follow that lead," he said. "What will you be doing in the meantime?"

"I have a few minutes of my break left, so I thought I'd do a deep dive and see what I could find on Nana's Cookies, the corporation. Bob Spielman seems sincerely distraught at the loss of his partner, but as you said, business can try even the closest of friendships. Maybe there was some bad blood there."

"Excellent. We'll reconvene later, then." Robbie rose from his seat and gathered the tea tray. At the door he paused and said, "Lindsey, do be careful. Whoever killed Mr. Lewis is likely desperate and will not hesitate to come after anyone they think can expose them."

"Likewise," Lindsey said. "Try to be circumspect with your snooping."

"Always," he said. He winked at her and left the office, taking the tea tray with him.

Lindsey glanced at the clock. She had a quarter of an hour to see what she could discover about Nana's Cookies. She opened up the library catalog to access the business databases they subscribed to. She chose to begin with the Dun and Bradstreet Hoovers database. She typed in the company name and waited for the listing.

The history of the nonpublic company was impressively extensive. It hadn't been updated to reflect the passing of Henry Lewis, but that wasn't surprising. She read the company's profile and then decided to do a comparison with the company's website. She opened another window on her computer and did a quick search for Nana's Cookies. When she found it, she followed the links to their "About Us" page. The narrative matched up.

Henry Lewis and Bob Spielman met in college and afterward decided to use Henry's grandmother's cookie recipes to start a small business up in Maine, baking and selling cookies in Portland. Their popularity took off, and in no time they became a national name in the cookie aisle. There were photographs that Lindsey realized were taken shortly after college when they opened their first bakery. Henry had the long hair and beard that Ms. Cole had described, as well as sandals on his feet. She studied the pictures that accompanied the story, watching the two men mature into adulthood. Suits replaced jeans, the long feathered hair was cut into mullets and then standard nine-to-five businessmen's cuts, and the beards were trimmed into mustaches and then shaved off. It was like watching forty years flip by in a blink.

The last few pictures were from Hawaii, where Bob and Henry had opened up their latest bakery a few years ago. Wearing Hawaiian shirts and leis, they had an arm around each other's shoulders and looked to be laughing. If there was any discord between them, the picture didn't show it.

Lindsey glanced at the clock. She was running out of time. She opened up the business magazine database. She wanted to see if *Forbes* or *Fortune* had written any articles about them. There were many from their early days as a startup, using a large portion of their profits for the greater good, like protecting the environment, equal rights and fighting cancer. Several stories mentioned how Henry's grandmother, Nana, died of lung cancer at the age of eighty-seven and that the company was dedicated to raising money to find a cure.

Lindsey scrolled through the articles. There was a lot to unbox here but she wanted to see if there was anything in recent days that might have indicated a problem within the company, such as any claims of harassment or financial malfeasance. There was nothing of the kind. Rather, it seemed Nana's Cookies had tapped into the conscientious consumer movement and their popularity was peaking—particularly with the younger generation who wanted to spend their money where they knew the company was giving back to society. From what Bob had said, all of Henry's wealth would go to his four favorite charities. The man had lived what he preached.

Lindsey glanced at the last oatmeal cookie on the plate on her desk. Yes, there was definitely something to be said for knowing that your purchase of a cookie was going to help plant trees in the rain forest or save a manatee. The cookie just tasted better.

She was about to close the search when her eye was caught by a recent article in *Food Business News*. It appeared that a giant food corporation was considering purchasing Nana's Cookies for the price of three hundred and sixty million dollars.

Lindsey leaned back in her chair. She reread the number. That was a lot of cookies. She thought about the bios she'd read on Henry and Bob. Their mission was all about locally sourcing their organic ingredients, using healthy alternatives to chemicals with no additives and no preservatives, while supporting sustainable farming. How was being owned by one of the world's three largest food corporations going to allow them to maintain their "just like Nana's" corporate philosophy? She downloaded the article, making a note to email it to Emma.

It wasn't surprising that a business as successful as Nana's Cookies was being considered for purchase. According to the article, food giants like Nestlé, Pepsi or Kraft Heinz often scooped up smaller niche companies to expand their product line and keep on trend. The former owners of the smaller companies sometimes stayed on, using the bigger company's sales capabilities and distribution, or else they would cash out with their new fortune and retire off into the sunset.

There was no mention of what Nana's Cookies was going to do. Was that what had happened? Had Bob and Henry disagreed? Had there been a rift in how to handle the future of the company? It would certainly give one of them three hundred and sixty million reasons to kill their partner. Lindsey tried to wrap her head around the possibility that Bob was a murderer. He just seemed so likable.

She glanced at the clock. It was time to relieve Ann Marie on the reference desk. Lindsey closed the door to her office and headed out to the main area of the library. Ms. Cole was in her office just off the workroom and Lindsey waved to her as she walked by. Ms. Cole waved back. Her expression revealed nothing of what she was thinking, but she looked calm as she typed on her keyboard, probably working on the circulation statistics, so Lindsey decided to let her be and not share the information about Nana's Cookies being sold.

There was something to be said for the stoicism of a native New Englander. Not much riled them besides a World Series loss or another region claiming to have the best pizza—everyone knew the best was from New Haven's brick ovens in Wooster Square.

Lindsey met Ann Marie at the reference desk just as she was finishing with a patron looking for tax forms, one of the joys of library life in April. The phone started to ring. Lindsey gestured that she'd take the call, leaving Ann Marie to go take her break.

She picked up the receiver and said, "Briar Creek Public Library, may I help you?"

"Who am I speaking with?" a woman demanded.

"I'm Lindsey Norris, the director."

"Good. You're just the person I was hoping to reach. I want to know what you're going to do about having a murderer on your staff."

"Excuse me?"

"That's right, my taxes pay your salary and her salary, and I expect this Ms. Cole person to be removed from her position immediately."

CHAPTER

12

BRIAR CREEK
PUBLIC LIBRARY

Lindsey sat down in her seat hard. She could feel her temper heat and knew that was the exact wrong way to deal with this situation.

"I'm sorry, what was your name again?" she asked.

"That's not relevant," the caller said. "I want to know what you're going to do about having a murderer on staff."

"As far as I know, I don't have a murderer on staff," Lindsey said.

"Liar! Ms. Cole is a murderer and everyone knows it. How do you know she won't go off and kill someone else?"

Lindsey glanced at the display and noted the number. It was a local area code. She then jotted down the remaining seven digits. Something felt "off" about this call.

"I'm sorry, unless you can give me your name, I have nothing to say to you," Lindsey said.

"My name doesn't matter!"

"I'm going to hang up," Lindsey said. "Have a nice—"

"My name . . . is . . . um . . . Noelle," she snapped.

"Noelle what?" Lindsey asked. She didn't believe for a hot minute that it was the caller's real name. She'd been hoping for a last name so she could determine whether this was actually a library patron or just some ghoul who had watched the news and now wanted to harass the library staff.

"You don't need any more than that," the woman said. Her voice was impatient, and Lindsey braced herself for the rest of the conversation. It wasn't very often that she had to deal with difficult patrons, the hissy fit by Pam Kirby the other day being the exception. Most of the residents in Briar Creek were friendly and operated on a small-town love-thy-neighbor attitude. This woman clearly did not. Her volume was getting louder and screechier when she said, "Now I demand that you fire that woman—that *murderer.*"

"Yeah," Lindsey said. "That isn't going to happen."

"Ah!" the woman gasped. Lindsey rolled her eyes. "I am going to be calling the mayor's office to complain about you!"

"That's up to you," Lindsey said. She opened up the browser on her computer and typed in the number the woman had called from.

"Yes, it is up to me!" the woman said, clearly furious. "I'll have your job, too!"

"You may want to hold up on that," Lindsey said.

"Oh, are you worried now?" the woman asked, satisfaction in her voice.

"No, and you forgot that you're dealing with

librarians, and I just did a reverse lookup of the number you're calling from, and it appears you are using a phone in an office in the town hall," Lindsey said. "Care to explain to me why you're calling me on a landline provided by our taxpayers with unfounded allegations against one of my staff people before I forward all of this information to the chief of police?"

"You think you're so smart, don't you?" the woman hissed.

"Well, kind of, yeah," Lindsey said. She knew it was terrible to enjoy the woman's fury, but she couldn't seem to help it.

"You're not, you're nothing special, why, you're just the frozen pizza of librarians," the woman shouted, and then she hung up.

"Frozen pizza of librarians"? What did that even mean?

Lindsey raised her eyebrows as she lowered the receiver and gently put it back in its cradle. She noted the date and time and the phone number, planning to send it to Chief Plewicki, along with the article she'd found. It seemed highly suspicious that the aggrieved "patron" had been calling from the town hall. She suspected it was one of Mayor Hensen's lackeys, trying to cause trouble for Ms. Cole. Would he really stoop that low? After the luncheon where he'd shown up right before the chief of police, she suspected he would.

Lindsey turned to her computer and opened her email. She found the link to the article and sent it and the phone call information to Emma, hoping she could track the caller down and that the article might give her some useful information on Nana's Cookies.

She was just opening her file to work on the library's

budget when Nancy Peyton, one of the crafternooners and Lindsey's former landlord, approached the desk.

"Just here to pick up my books on hold," Nancy said. "I've been waiting forever for the new Sonali Dev, I just love what she's doing with the reimagined Austen themes, but I wanted to say hi and see how you're doing."

"I'm all right," Lindsey said. "Worried about Ms. Cole but otherwise okay. How are you?"

"Worried about Ms. Cole," Nancy said. "Which is why I made her some butterscotch blondies."

She held up a Tupperware tub and Lindsey smiled. Nancy was known for her cookie-baking skills throughout town. She had a gift that she generously shared with the community.

"Those are sure to cheer her up," Lindsey said. She studied Nancy, who was a native of Briar Creek. "Did you ever think of starting your own business like Nana's Cookies?"

"Oh, heavens, no," Nancy said. "Then it would have become work and I wouldn't have enjoyed it anymore. Besides, I'd have felt like I was stealing someone else's work. Nana Lewis was actually my mentor. She taught me everything I know about baking cookies."

"No way," Lindsey said.

"Way." Nancy's blue eyes twinkled. She sat in the chair beside Lindsey's desk. "Did you know I used to babysit Henry Lewis?"

"You did?" Lindsey knew she shouldn't have been surprised. It was a small town after all, but knowing that Nancy had known the Lewis family so well made it all feel even more personal.

"Oh, yes," she said. "Every Friday night so that Mr.

and Mrs. Lewis could go dancing. Nana Lewis lived with them, but she was too old to chase after two young boys, so they hired me. She and I would bake cookies after the boys went to bed. Those were some of my happiest memories as a teen."

"What was she like?" Lindsey asked. She was suddenly very curious about the woman whose recipes had launched a billion-dollar cookie enterprise.

"Well, she used to sneak outside to have an evening smoke and cocktail," Nancy said. "Every day at five o'clock, she enjoyed a glass of Canadian Club with a splash of water, and I do mean a splash. She ran it under the faucet, barely getting the glass wet."

"Cocktail hour."

"It was a thing back in the day," Nancy agreed. "She only ever had the one glass, but it was a generous pour."

"Do you think she ever expected her recipes to become Nana's Cookies?" Lindsey asked.

"No." Nancy shook her head. "She passed away before Henry took her recipes and began the company. Even his brother and parents had no idea how successful he would become."

"That's too bad," Lindsey said. "I bet they would have been proud."

"I think so," Nancy said. She looked thoughtful. "They seemed like a close family. Not wealthy and not poor, definitely middle-middle class and content to be so. It's a shame about their old house."

"The one Henry's nephew lives in?" Lindsey asked. "Lenny?"

"Yes, it's been earmarked for demolition."

"What? When?" Lindsey asked.

"A few months ago," Nancy said. "It and the cottages

surrounding it are to be leveled so that the Schmitt company can build some fancy town houses."

Lindsey stared across the library. This seemed like a significant piece of information. "Does Emma know?"

Nancy shrugged. "I don't know. Probably. I mean, Milton and the rest of the historical society have been fighting to save the homes, citing them as historic given that the cottage is the origin of Nana's Cookies and all."

"But the neighborhood isn't designated as historic?" Lindsey clarified.

"No." Nancy shook her head. "It's a pity, too, because it's a very picturesque street."

"Do you think Henry came to town about this?" Lindsey asked. "I mean, this was his grandmother's home, maybe he felt that it needed to be preserved."

"Maybe," Nancy said. "Only Lenny would know about that, but he's . . ."

"Aloof?" Lindsey asked.

Nancy smiled at her. "Good word."

"Do you suppose he understands what might happen to his home?" Lindsey asked.

"I know Milton has tried to talk to him about it, but Lenny is hard to reach," Nancy said. "And he doesn't really have anyone to look out for him now that Henry is gone because while they weren't close, I know that Henry always made certain that Lenny had everything he needed."

Her voice broke and she glanced down at the tub in her lap. Lindsey felt her heart pinch. How hard it must be to know that the young boy you'd once looked after had grown up into a successful businessman that someone had felt compelled to murder.

"I'm so sorry, Nancy," Lindsey said. "I know this must be hard."

"Oh." Nancy waved her hand dismissively. "I hadn't seen him in decades. It's not as if I lost a close friend, but still, he was such a nice boy. I remember he had a family of stray kittens that he fed. Every night at exactly the same time, he'd go outside with a bowl of food and then he would sit there, crouched on the ground talking to the cats. Nana and I would watch him from the kitchen window. It took him months to get the cats to trust him but finally one day, the largest of the cats rubbed her head against his knee, and that boy grinned the biggest grin I have ever seen."

A small smile played on Nancy's lips while she was caught up in the memory. "He had a big heart, Henry did. When he loved something or someone, it was totally and completely. He was passionate about the environment, protecting the oceans, and he really did try to use his company for good. I can't help thinking he would have been very unhappy about the proposed demolition of Nana's house and the new development."

"I think I'll mention this to Emma just to make sure she knows."

"Do you really think it has anything to do with his murder?"

Lindsey shrugged. "I think everything is up for consideration at this point."

Nancy nodded. She glanced at Lindsey and asked, "Is it true that he was here to speak with Ms. Cole?"

"So Bob, his partner, says," she answered. "But why now? Why after decades of avoiding her when he came to town would he suddenly want to talk to her?"

"People get nostalgic in their old age," Nancy said.

"Unfinished business, things left unsaid. No one lives without some regret. I heard he was recently divorced. Maybe he was hoping to rekindle the old spark with Ms. Cole."

Lindsey glanced across the room toward Ms. Cole's office. What would have happened if Henry had gotten in touch with her? They'd never know.

What did Emma say about the phone call?" Sully asked.

"I haven't heard back from her yet," Lindsey said. "That's assuming I do hear back from her. You know how Emma is."

"Yes, she doesn't like citizens to get mixed up in police business," he said.

They were walking Heathcliff along the stretch of beach that ran behind their house. It was almost noiseless with just the steady rush of the waves on the sand and the occasional cry of a seagull to break the evening quiet.

Heathcliff was investigating every smell his nose could find. Lindsey watched his tail wag as he pawed the sand. She watched closely to make certain her boy didn't dig up something dead and roll in it. The last time he did that it took three baths and an entire bottle of her most expensive shampoo before they got the stink off him.

"How is Ms. Cole holding up?" Sully asked. He had his arm around her shoulders and matched his stride to hers. She glanced up at him and noticed he was watching Heathcliff as closely as she was.

"Better than I would be if I found my ex in the trunk

of my car," Lindsey said. "Of course, it helps that she didn't recognize him. Still, I have a feeling the mayor is going to use her relationship with Henry Lewis to try and smear her, assuming that whoever called me today called from the mayor's office, which seems likely."

"What about Herb Gunderson?" Sully said.

"What about him?" she asked.

"Do you think he would know who called from the town hall? I mean, I know he's the mayor's right-hand man, but he's also the most principled man I know."

Lindsey nodded. "He is that, and he and I have always gotten along well."

"Maybe you could ask him about the phone number without giving him any information," Sully suggested.

Lindsey leaned back to study his face. "That's a brilliant idea. I could say I thought I was getting an important call from the mayor's office and that it was cut off but I have the number. I'll bet he'd track it down for me. Herb doesn't like loose ends."

"And then you'd have more to share with Emma," he said.

"At which point she will likely tell me to mind my own business," Lindsey said with a laugh.

"Yeah." Sully grinned. Something caught his eye and he looked past her shoulder. His eyes went wide. "No, Heathcliff, no!"

He dropped his arm from around her shoulders and broke into a run. Lindsey saw Heathcliff dragging something from the hole he'd dug. He looked delighted with himself but they were downwind and the sudden gust of foul-smelling air made her eyes water.

"Nooooo!" Lindsey cried, breaking into a run as well.

CHAPTER
13

BRIAR CREEK
PUBLIC LIBRARY

I don't want to insult you, but you look tired," Beth said when she met Lindsey in the break room the next morning. Lindsey was making the coffee extra strong today. "And believe me, I've had enough people tell me that over the last few months that I know how insulting it can sound."

"No offense taken." Lindsey turned to her friend and held up three fingers. "Three dog baths last night. Three."

"Oh, no." Beth cringed. "Poor Heathcliff. Skunk?"

"Dead fish."

"Ulp." Beth made a gagging sound.

"Yeah, there was some of that, too," Lindsey said. "I asked Sully to take him to work today and let the sea breeze blow the rest of the smell off him."

"Good plan," Beth said. "Have you seen Ms. Cole? I called her last night but she didn't answer her cell phone, and when I called her house, Milton answered but he said she was having coffee with Bob."

"Bob Spielman?" Lindsey asked—as if there was another Bob that Ms. Cole would be out with. She shook her head. She needed coffee. She was clearly not operating at full capacity. "Sorry, dumb question."

"No," Beth said. "I said the same thing. She never called me back, so I have no idea how long she was out or what they talked about or anything. Not that it's my business, but I am her campaign manager and feel I should be kept in the loop."

"Not unreasonable," Lindsey said.

"That's what I told Aidan," Beth said. "In any case, if you see her, will you let me know? I have to go set up for story time, but I wanted to talk to her about her speech at the Rotarian happy hour tonight."

"Will do," Lindsey said.

"You're going, aren't you?" Beth asked.

"Wouldn't miss it," Lindsey said. She hadn't planned on going, but given the current state of things, she'd best be there to give Ms. Cole and Beth backup.

"Great. See you later."

Beth left and Lindsey stood staring at the coffee machine wondering how many cups of coffee she was going to need to get her all the way through the day to the other side of the happy hour. She decided it was most definitely a full-pot kind of day.

Lindsey called Herb Gunderson at midmorning, hoping he'd be in his office. His phone rolled over to voice mail. Drat. She left a message for him, letting him know that she had something to discuss with him.

There was a staff meeting planned for that afternoon, and she knew she could corner him then but she would have preferred to do it without the mayor being present. She was going to have to finesse this conversation very carefully.

Herb never called her back, which was odd, and when she left for the staff meeting, she made sure she took the mystery phone number with her. Briar Creek was a small enough town that Lindsey knew everyone who worked in the town hall. While only the department heads attended the weekly meetings, everyone attended the holiday party in December and the barbecue in July.

In all the years Lindsey had been going to these events, she had never met a staff person named Noelle. So either the woman who had called the library demanding that Ms. Cole be fired was lying about her name—which seemed probable—or it was someone just using the phone who didn't actually work at the town hall. But if "Noelle" wasn't a town employee, how had she gotten access to the phone, and what was her endgame? She couldn't possibly think that Lindsey was going to fire Ms. Cole. Either way, Lindsey planned to find out what phone in the town hall was tied to that number and who had used it.

She arrived at the room for the weekly staff meeting and found it empty. She frowned. For as long as she'd been the library director, the weekly meetings had been held at the same time and in the same meeting room. Had today's been canceled? She took her phone out of her shoulder bag and opened her email. There was nothing. Weird.

She left the first-floor meeting room and climbed the

stairs up to the mayor's office. The administrative assistant, Pearl Newsom, was sitting at her desk, staring at her computer screen. Her ash blond hair was cut short and curled around her face. She was middle-aged and had come to work for the town after her four kids had grown up and left. She was always quick with a smile and had a maternal air about her that made the recipient of her attention feel as if everything was going to be okay, even if it wasn't. She was truly a port in a storm, and Lindsey frequently wished she'd come work at the library.

"Hi, Pearl," Lindsey called as she crossed the reception area. "How are you?"

"I'm wonderful," Pearl said. She beamed, looking over her reading glasses at Lindsey. "We're getting closer to Friday, and my oldest is coming into town with his babies. I can't wait. We're going to play on the beach and have a big family cookout." She shimmied with excitement.

"That sounds fun," Lindsey said. She grinned, as Pearl's enthusiasm was contagious. "I hope you enjoy every second."

"Thank you."

"I do have one question though," Lindsey said. "Was the staff meeting today canceled? No one's in the meeting room, but I didn't get an email about it."

"You didn't?" Pearl frowned. "That's weird. The mayor said he would send out a notice to everyone."

"He did?"

"Yes, which was odd because usually he has me do it." She shook her head as if the mayor were a mystery to her. "He must have missed you on the email chain. They're downstairs in the sky room."

"The sky room?" Lindsey asked. This was on the complete opposite side of their usual meeting room. "Was there a reason for the change?"

Pearl thought about it for a moment. "Not that he told me."

Lindsey nodded. She had a bad feeling that it wasn't coincidence that she'd been left off the email or that the meeting location had abruptly been changed. The mayor was trying to flex his power over her, most likely because Ms. Cole worked for her and he knew that she supported Ms. Cole's bid for mayor.

"Thanks, Pearl," she said. "I'd better hurry on down there."

"Have a nice week," Pearl said. She turned back to her computer.

"You, too." Lindsey turned to leave but stopped. She'd planned to ask Herb about the number, but Pearl would be a much better source. She knew everyone in the building and likely had the numbers to the different departments memorized.

"Pearl, I do have one more thing," she said. She reached into her bag and took out the paper with the number on it. "Does this number look familiar to you? I was on the phone with someone named Noelle yesterday, and we got disconnected before I could figure out what department she was in."

Pearl pushed her readers up her nose and studied the number. "That's the tax assessor's office."

"Is it?" Lindsey asked.

"Yes, but there's no one down there named Noelle. I'd know," Pearl said. "But talk to Janice Snyder. She'll be able to tell you for sure. I mean, maybe they had a temp helping them or something."

"Thanks, I'll do that." Lindsey left the office and headed down the stairs. She crossed the building with its stately marble floors and went down another hall-way. She glanced at her phone, saw that she was ten minutes late and picked up the pace. When she reached the doors, the meeting had already begun and the mayor was addressing the room.

As she pushed open the door, the entire room turned to look at her. She smiled and strode in. If the mayor was trying to make her uncomfortable, he was succeed-ing, but she'd be darned before she'd let it show.

"Mrs. Sullivan, nice of you to join us," the mayor said. His mouthful of very white teeth was curved into a smile but it didn't meet his eyes.

"It's Ms. Norris," she said. "Apparently I was left off of the email announcing the room change. Perhaps you sent it to a Mrs. Sullivan?"

She hadn't taken Sully's name when they married, which the mayor knew, as the name change would have been reflected in her personnel file. This was just an-other way to needle her. Ugh, this election could not come soon enough.

The mayor's smile never wavered. "Perhaps, or maybe you just neglected to check your email."

For a nanosecond, Lindsey debated opening her email on her phone and showing the lack of a message, but she decided it wasn't worth it.

Lindsey moved around the table until she got to the first open seat between Sam Rubenstein, the head of fa-cilities, and Officer Kirkland, who didn't normally attend department head meetings. She wondered what had taken the chief away that she'd sent her second in her place.

"Now, as I was saying." Mayor Hensen paused to give her a meaningful look. "There is a fringe group that is trying to stop the latest Schmitt development."

Lindsey felt her ears perk up. Was this the same development that Nancy had told her about? The one that would demolish the Lewis family home?

"By 'fringe' do you mean the local historical society?" Melissa Partridge asked. She was frowning and had her arms crossed over her chest. She was the head of the water department but was also a native Creeker and very active in the preservation of the small town.

"Them and other more radical entities," he said. "To date, Curtis Schmitt has bought most of the properties on the street and plans to pick up the remaining ones in the next few weeks. He will be building a luxury town house community that will bring higher-income residents, which means a tax dollar windfall for the town."

"That neighborhood should have a historic designation," Melissa said. Her chin jutted out stubbornly.

"I appreciate your opinion," the mayor said, sounding anything but appreciative. "But the reality is that it's a crumbling-down eyesore of a street that has what? Ten houses with big yards? Curtis Schmitt is going to put in forty town houses. That's four times the property tax revenue for the town. We need this money for our schools. You aren't against the children and the future of their town, are you?"

Lindsey watched him leverage Melissa with the one thing more important to her than historic properties, and that was her kids. She had three all in elementary school. Lindsey was certain that if Melissa thought tax money was going to education, she wouldn't hesitate for a second to bulldoze the old houses to make way for the new ones. It was a smart play by the mayor even though she disliked how self-serving and manipulative it was. Melissa sat back in her chair, vanquished.

The mayor droned on about some other topics. Lindsey made a note of upcoming closures for town offices and some of the town-sponsored events that were slated for spring and summer. And finally, after a short talk from the human resources department about encouraging all town employees to get their summer vacation requests in as soon as possible, they were dismissed.

Lindsey dragged her feet as she was leaving the meeting room so as not to have to talk to the mayor. He seemed to be on the same page as he jetted out of the room as if someone had lit his backside on fire.

Lindsey tried to time her departure so that she was next to Janice Snyder as she slipped from the room. Janice was a book reader and stopped by the library frequently for a stack of traditional mysteries. She was partial to the food-based mysteries and devoured anything by Bailey Cates, Joanne Fluke and Vivien Chien.

"Hi, Janice," Lindsey said as they exited the room together.

"Hi, Lindsey," Janice said. "How are things at the library?" She glanced at the mayor where he strode ahead of them. "Tense?"

"A little bit," Lindsey said. "But I'm sure it will be fine. Listen, I wanted to ask you about this phone number. Pearl up in administration thought it came from your department."

Janice glanced at the number on the paper. She frowned. "Yes, that's one of our three extensions. Why?"

Lindsey glanced at the other department heads in the hallway and said, "Is there a quiet place we can talk?"

"Sure, come to my office," she said. Lindsey fell into step beside her as they wound their way down the hall and into the tax assessor's office. The receptionist's desk was manned by an older woman named Dawn, who waved at them as they passed. Janice led Lindsey past an empty desk to her tiny office at the back.

Janice closed the door behind them and gestured for Lindsey to sit down. "What can I do for you?"

"Someone called me from that number yesterday," Lindsey said. She sat across from Janice's desk, which was devoid of any clutter apart from her computer and a framed photograph of her family at the beach. It was a level of organization that the librarian in Lindsey admired and also envied.

Janice frowned and glanced out of the office at the empty desk. "The number belongs to that phone on my assistant's desk."

"Is your assistant named Noelle?" Lindsey asked. Maybe this was it.

"No, my assistant was Vince, but he retired and the mayor hasn't approved a rehire yet," Janice said. She looked grumpy. "It's been six months."

"So that desk is always empty?" Lindsey asked.

Janice nodded. "Yes, it's just me and Dawn here, and she stays at her own desk."

"Do you remember if anyone was in here yesterday?" Lindsey asked. "I took down the number when they called and noted it was seven minutes past three."

Janice shook her head. "That's about the time we

ducked next door to the clerk's office. They were having a baby shower for Alexis, so you know . . . sheet cake."

Lindsey smiled. "I understand completely. Sheet cake in the middle of the afternoon can pull you through."

"It should be mandatory," Janice agreed. "We can ask Dawn if she saw anyone in here. She was with me at the shower but she may have been keeping one eye on the office."

"All right," Lindsey said.

They rose from their seats and Janice opened the door. Halfway across the room, she turned back to Lindsey and asked, "Why is this so important? I mean, the person who called you didn't say they were from my office, did they?"

Lindsey shook her head. "No, in fact, they pretended to be a taxpayer who was unhappy with the library and then proceeded to chew me out, which is whatever, but it bothered me that the call came from the town hall."

"Understandable," Janice said. "That whole song of 'my taxes pay your salary' gets so old, doesn't it?"

"Like 'Ninety-Nine Bottles of Beer on the Wall' old," Lindsey said.

Janice snorted and led the way to Dawn's desk. She was inputting numbers into a form on her computer, and Janice waited until she was finished before she spoke.

"Dawn, quick question, do you know if anyone was in our office while we were at Alexis's baby shower yesterday?"

Dawn's eyes got wide behind her glasses. She looked worried. "Yes, actually. I let someone use the phone because she couldn't hear over the noise in the other room. Was that wrong?"

"No, not at all," Janice said. She gave Lindsey a sideways glance, which Lindsey interpreted as *say nothing*. "Do you remember the name of the person?"

"I'll say," she said. "It was the mayor's wife and one of her friends."

CHAPTER

14

BRIAR CREEK
PUBLIC LIBRARY

It took everything Lindsey had not to gasp. Janice reared back as if Dawn had taken a swing at her but then quickly yanked on the lapels of her jacket as if she'd just been about to do that anyway. "Oh, well, of course, it's all right, then. Thank you."

"No problem." Dawn smiled and went back to her work.

"Lindsey, I need to stretch my legs," Janice said. "I'll walk you out."

Lindsey nodded. Janice's tone of voice made it clear that this wasn't optional. Probably, it was a voice honed in steel from dealing with people who argued against her assessments of their property.

They crossed the marble floor of the main entrance and walked out the doors. It was a beautiful spring day with a stiff breeze blowing in from the bay, bringing the briny smell of the sea with it. The sun was warm but the air was cool, making it perfect. The daffodils that lined the stone walkway were bursting, and several robins hopped in the thick green grass as if celebrating the arrival of spring.

"Explain." Janice folded her arms across her chest. The breeze tousled her gray curls, but she didn't bother to keep them out of her eyes. She just turned her head so the breeze pushed her hair in a different direction.

"I'm not sure I can," Lindsey said.

Two employees from Parks and Recreation walked by and Lindsey and Janice nodded but didn't speak until they were out of earshot.

"You told me you had a disgruntled patron on the phone who called from the empty desk in my office," Janice said. "And now we find out that the mayor's wife may have been the person who called. You have to tell me what she said."

"No, I have to tell Chief Plewicki what she said," Lindsey countered. She didn't want to deny Janice the info, but she felt that it needed to be kept quiet. As much as she liked Janice, she didn't know where she stood on the gossip meter of the town hall.

"She used my office," Janice said. "I could go upstairs to the mayor and demand an explanation."

"But you won't because that would give his wife a heads-up and time to concoct a lie to cover herself," Lindsey said.

Janice let out a frustrated huff, and Lindsey knew she had her.

"Tell me this," Janice said. "Was there a threat of danger?"

"No," Lindsey said. "It was an odd call, but if it really was the mayor's wife—and it may not have been, as Dawn did say she had a friend with her—it actually makes more sense, because I believe it was politically motivated."

Janice's eyebrows rose. She studied Lindsey for a moment. "If it helps your situation at all, no one here believes that Ms. Cole murdered her college fiancé even though there are some who are trying to spin the story that way." She inclined her head toward the town hall, letting Lindsey know that it was the mayor supporting the unfounded rumors.

"I'd appreciate it if you could keep this conversation between us," Lindsey said. "And I expect Emma will be coming by to talk with you. Also, it would help if you could keep anyone from touching that phone. Emma might want to take a look at it."

"I'm on it." Janice winked and said, "Tell Ms. Cole I've got her back."

Lindsey smiled. "I will."

She turned and walked down the sidewalk. Her original plan had been to go right back to the library, but now she was going to pop into the police station to see Emma. Maybe this phone call was nothing, but it didn't feel like nothing—not under the present circumstances.

The police station was a squat building nestled near the town hall. Lindsey stepped through the automatic glass doors and looked to the left where Molly Hatcher was usually found at her desk. It was empty.

Lindsey walked down the short hall to Emma's office. She rapped on the closed door and heard a muffled sound from inside. Not wanting to interrupt, she called, "Emma, it's Lindsey. Do you have a second?"

The door was yanked open and Emma stood there,

looking frustrated and in disarray, which was not her usual style. She looked at Lindsey and said, "Get in here."

Okay, then. Lindsey stepped into the room.

"What's wrong?" Lindsey asked.

Emma gestured to the enormous whiteboard on the far side of the room. "That."

Lindsey had never seen a whiteboard in Emma's office before, so she raised her eyebrows in surprise and asked, "Is that new?"

"Yes." Emma spat the answer as if it had offended her. "It was a Christmas gift from Robbie. I think he has delusions that I'm Stana Katic and he's Nathan Fillion."

"From the TV show *Castle*?" Lindsey asked.

Emma gave her a long-suffering look. "Yup."

Lindsey burst out laughing. She couldn't help it. It was so quintessentially Robbie to get the lines crossed between an actor's role and real life. Emma flashed her a smile and then shook her head.

"I can't work a case with this," she said. She gestured to the enormous whiteboard.

"How do you usually work?" Lindsey asked.

Emma gestured to the top of her desk. It was littered with sticky notes. Yellow, green and pink, and they all had notes scribbled on them in Emma's distinctively illegible handwriting.

"If that's your process," Lindsey said, "that's your process. You don't have to use the whiteboard."

"I'd agree but I am having a horrible time trying to keep track of the suspects for this case," Emma said. "And my notes system isn't working so I thought I'd try the whiteboard, but my brain hates it."

"Hmm." Lindsey considered the desk and white-board from her librarian's perspective. "Maybe we can merge the two and you'll see something from a new angle."

Emma shrugged as if to say, *Why not.*

"Okay," Lindsey said. "Let's start with the white-board and write what we know."

She picked up a blue marker from the tray at the bottom of the board.

"Put the facts in the middle so we can use the sur-rounding board for details to be added," Emma said.

"All right." Lindsey wrote the name Henry Lewis, the location of his body and the time he was found.

Emma picked up a red marker and drew an arrow that arced to the right. Below that she wrote the names Bob Spielman, Lenny Lewis, Eugenia Cole and Curtis Schmitt.

"Curtis Schmitt?" Lindsey asked.

"He's the builder who is going to bulldoze the neigh-borhood that includes the Lewis house," Emma said. "I heard that didn't sit well with Henry Lewis."

"So, those are your suspects?"

"Yes, and before you freak out, Ms. Cole is only there because she's his ex and his body was found in her car. I don't believe that she murdered him and stuffed him into her trunk, at least not without help."

"Weird how that's not as reassuring as you might think."

Emma rolled her hand in a gesture for Lindsey to continue with the board.

"All right, let's take your notes and transfer them to the board," Lindsey said.

Emma blanched but Lindsey ignored her. Lindsey

walked to the desk and started picking up the notes. "Decipher, please."

"These are from my canvass of the area where his body was found," Emma said. She studied Lindsey. "Including all of my interviews with the library patrons. In short, no one saw anything, but I have names and they fill out the timeline of the morning."

"All right, let's make a bubble on the board for all of these," Lindsey said. Emma nodded.

They grouped them together, and Emma put them in some sort of timeline that only she could understand, because she was the only one who could read her notes. Then they moved on to random notes about each of the suspects.

Lindsey was relieved to see that Ms. Cole's only connections to the crime were her previous relationship to the victim and the fact that he was found in her car. Even so, without knowing all the facts, it still looked pretty bad.

She glanced at the other names. Bob was Henry's business partner. It made sense. She noticed that the sticky note that Emma put beside him mentioned the deal from the food giant, the one mentioned in the article Lindsey had emailed to her. She looked at the chief.

"Did Bob and Henry disagree about selling out to a corporation?" she asked. Emma didn't look as if she wanted to answer but she nodded. "Who didn't want to sell?"

Emma gave her a quelling look.

"Aw, come on, I'm helping you," Lindsey said. "And Ms. Cole is one of my employees."

"All right, I suppose I can tell you since he was very

forthcoming with it himself," Emma said. "Bob wanted to sell out. Henry did not."

"How come?"

"Bob wants to retire and take the time he has left to enjoy his children and grandchildren," she said. "Henry didn't have any of that. No kids, no grandkids, he worked to live and lived to work."

"Couldn't the food giant have kept Henry on?" Lindsey asked.

"I asked him the same thing, but Bob said that the new corporation wanted a younger person at the helm."

"Ouch."

"Indeed."

"So, there was a rift between the partners," she said. "A three-hundred-and-sixty-million-dollar riff."

"Bob seemed to feel that they were going to come to a resolution," Emma said. She shrugged. "I've asked to speak with his wife to verify his story."

"Is she here?" Lindsey asked.

"She's arriving tomorrow," Emma said.

"You're assuming he's not going to coach her on what to say," Lindsey said.

"I'm assuming nothing," Emma said. "I also have interviews set up with many of the high-level employees and the executive board of Nana's Cookies."

"So, you think Bob did it," Lindsey said.

"As you mentioned, I think three hundred and sixty million is a heck of an incentive," Emma said.

"It'd be half of that if they sold the company and split it."

"Or potentially all of it if one of them died."

"Good point. I can see how that would make him a prime suspect," Lindsey said. She tapped the whiteboard.

"You've got Lenny on here, too. How did he take the news of his uncle's death?"

Emma shrugged. "It's hard to get a read on him. I explained to him about Henry, but he wouldn't meet my gaze, and then he talked about the osprey nests he was planning to set up in the marshes because their habitat is being infringed upon."

"Do you think he understands that he's going to lose his home to Curtis Schmitt and the development?" Lindsey asked.

Again, Emma shrugged. She looked frustrated and weary, and Lindsey could only imagine that chasing down leads was an exhausting way to spend her days.

"All right, so why is Curtis on the board?" Lindsey asked.

"Because according to my informants, he and Henry had a huge fight when Henry told him he was going to see that Nana's house was designated as a historic site and it was going to effectively halt the development."

"Was that true? Melissa Partridge called out the mayor at the department head meeting just now, and he seemed to think that the street wasn't worthy of a historic designation and that there was a fringe group trying to stop the development. He sounded very confident that it was going to go through with Curtis only having to pick up the few remaining properties. Could Henry have stopped the development?" Lindsey asked.

"As you know, Henry had resources to burn," Emma said. "I've discovered he had a team of lawyers at the ready, and it looked as if he was going to achieve his goal to stop the development."

"What about the other homeowners on the street?" Lindsey asked. "If they'd already sold out, but Curtis couldn't go forward with the development, then wouldn't they lose, too? Or the people who'd already bought the town houses under construction—how would the stoppage impact them?"

"Oh, yes," Emma said. "It's a hot mess, which is why I am rather hoping that Bob the business partner is Henry's killer because that would make my life easier. Not that I'd investigate it with that slant—everyone is a suspect until proven otherwise, but still."

"Sully told me that the rope used to tie the trunk shut was being examined. Was it the murder weapon?" Lindsey asked.

Emma stared at Lindsey as if trying to determine whether she should say anything or not. Lindsey tried to make her face inquisitive as opposed to insatiably curious, although it was a struggle, as she desperately wanted to know if the rope tied Ms. Cole to the murder, so to speak.

"No." Emma shook her head. "And this is just between you and me."

Lindsey nodded her head. She'd have agreed to anything to hear what Emma knew.

"The medical examiner found no traces of blood or hairs on the rope. If we could just find the actual murder weapon, we'd have our evidence, and then it would only be a matter of tying it to the killer, but we have no idea how he was strangled. There was nothing else at the scene."

She stepped up to the whiteboard and wrote *murder weapon* with a question mark. The board was getting full now. They stood back and stared at it as if something might leap out at them. Lindsey had nothing and Emma didn't seem to either.

"Well, it was worth a shot," Emma said. "And Robbie will be happy that I've finally broken out the board. He was quite disappointed when I shoved it in the corner and let it collect dust."

"Well, it does seem easier to read than the sea of sticky notes on your desk," Lindsey said.

"Maybe a little," Emma agreed grudgingly.

Lindsey glanced at the clock. The meeting at the town hall and the visit here had rolled into her lunch hour, which was now over. "I have to go back to work. If I hear of anything else, I'll let you know."

"Thanks," Emma said. "I know it's pointless to warn you away from asking too many questions when it's one of your staff who is in the middle of it, but, Lindsey, be careful. Whoever the killer is, they're smart and ruthless. Do not get in their way."

"Roger that," Lindsey said.

She left the chief's office and waved to Molly, who was on the phone, on her way out the door. It was a short walk back to the library, and she chose to go through the front doors as they were closer. As the doors whooshed open and she stepped inside, she ran right into Ivy Kavanagh.

"Sorry!" Lindsey cried out as she reached out to steady the other woman. She gently moved Ivy aside so that other patrons could pass.

"No, it's my fault," Ivy said. She ran a hand through her short spiked hair. "I wasn't looking where I was going."

She looked a bit frazzled, and Lindsey realized that given Ivy was an old friend of Henry's and because he was such a big contributor to her charity, she must be feeling his loss on a very personal level.

"Neither was I," Lindsey said. "So, we can share the blame."

Ivy gave her a faint smile and glanced away and then back. "I'm just not myself since Henry—"

"I understand," Lindsey said. "This must be very difficult for you."

Ivy nodded and then shook her head as if trying to shake off the grief that threatened to swamp her. She straightened her shoulders and said, "It is, but I will carry on because that's what Henry would have expected and wanted. I have a lot of trees to plant in his name."

"Which is a very fitting tribute from what I've come to know about him," Lindsey said. "Please let me know if I can help in any way."

Ivy patted Lindsey's arm and said, "Thank you. I will."

With that, she turned and headed down the steps to the sidewalk. Lindsey watched her for a moment, thinking how fragile life was and how hard it was, especially for the ones left behind with just their grief.

When she entered the library, she glanced around the main room as a feeling of unease crept up her spine. Patrons were browsing books and movies, lounging by the magazines and scattered among the internet computers. The occasional laugh came from the children's area, and most of the quiet study rooms were occupied. Still, the feeling that something wasn't right wouldn't leave her.

She glanced at the circulation desk. Paula was there, helping a customer. She glanced out into the reference area and saw Ann Marie. She was sitting at the desk, working on her computer with no patrons in sight.

Lindsey headed for her office, thinking it must be Emma's whiteboard and the murder of Henry Lewis putting her on edge. She entered the workroom and found Ms. Cole standing there, holding a photograph in her hands. She glanced up and then looked away but not before Lindsey noticed the horror on her face or the tears in her eyes.

"Ms. Cole, what is it?" Lindsey asked.

"Nothing," she said.

She turned away, and Lindsey saw her trying to stuff the photo back into an envelope. Her fingers were shaking too hard, and Lindsey moved to stand beside her and then gently took the picture and envelope out of her hands.

"Talk to me, Ms. Cole."

"Someone sent me this," she said. She gestured to the envelope and photograph in Lindsey's hands. Her voice cracked when she added, "Why would someone do this?"

Lindsey looked at the photo. It was old. Faded from the relentless march of time. But Ms. Cole was easily recognizable, as was Henry Lewis. The photograph was taken on the Briar Creek town beach. The same stretch of sand just across the street from the library that was still there today.

Lindsey glanced at the envelope. It was addressed to Ms. Cole, in care of the library. The label had been printed on a computer, and many stamps had been stuck in the corner, but the postmark was an illegible inky smudge and there was no return address.

"Why would someone send you an old picture?" Lindsey asked. "Do you think they wanted to send you a memento?"

"No," Ms. Cole said. Her voice was low and she shook her head. "It's a threat."

"What?" Lindsey looked back down at the picture.

"Flip it over," Ms. Cole said.

In black marker, in all capital letters, someone had scrawled, I KNOW YOU KILLED HIM. SOON EVERY-ONE ELSE WILL, TOO.

CHAPTER

15

BRIAR CREEK
PUBLIC LIBRARY

Lindsey felt the hair on the back of her neck stand up. She could practically feel the malevolence emanating from the threatening note. She glanced up and out of the windows of the workroom that overlooked the library. Everything was business as usual. Still, she felt exposed. She took Ms. Cole's arm and led her into her office, where she closed the door.

"Tell me about this. When did it get here? What do you think it means? And what do you want to do about it?"

"It came with the daily mail," Ms. Cole said. She sat carefully in one of the chairs in front of Lindsey's desk. "I saw it was addressed to me, so I opened it."

"Who would have access to this picture of you?" Lindsey asked.

"I don't know," Ms. Cole said. "I don't even remember it. Maybe Bob took it or Nana or possibly Henry's brother. They all would have been alive back then."

She twisted her hands in her lap. She glanced out at the library with a haunted expression that broke Lindsey's heart.

"I think we need to call Emma," Lindsey said. She dropped the photograph onto the desk. "We've both touched it so I don't know that there will be any fingerprints, but it's worth checking."

Ms. Cole nodded. "You're right. I just need a minute."

"Of course," Lindsey said.

Ms. Cole drew in a deep breath and closed her eyes. When she started to speak, her voice was so soft Lindsey had to strain to hear her.

"It was such a different time," Ms. Cole said. "It felt as if we could change the world for the better if we just put our minds to it. Henry believed in that. He believed in making the world a better, fairer place for everyone."

Lindsey didn't say anything. She suspected Ms. Cole needed to get this out. She remembered what Nancy had said about Henry Lewis as a little boy and the stray cats. It sounded as if he was always the champion of the underdog.

"The last time I saw him on that fateful day, he looked at me as if I'd broken his heart," Ms. Cole said. "But what was I supposed to do? My mother needed me. I couldn't pick Henry over my mother and father, but that's what he wanted me to do. That's what he expected me to do. I failed him that day."

Lindsey could hear the regret in her voice, and she didn't know what to say, except, "Did you fail him or did he fail you?"

Ms. Cole turned to face her. "At the time, I thought he failed me, but now I wonder."

"Wonder what?"

"I gave up my entire life to move home and take care of my father, and instead of getting my life back at the end of it, I was then expected to take care of my mother," she said. "I didn't have any siblings or cousins or aunts and uncles. There was no one but me. I never married and I never had children because after my father passed away, my mother made it very clear that she needed me, she couldn't function without me, that if I left her, she would die. At the time, I felt that she was my responsibility. It never occurred to me to tell her she had to try and go it alone. How could I? She'd never lived on her own. She didn't know how to write a check or call a repairman or deal with my father's will. None of it. I was twenty and I was supposed to take over all of it. So I did."

Lindsey stared at the formidable woman in front of her, who had sacrificed her own life for the care of others.

"The day we broke up, Henry told me that would happen," she said. "He told me, and I didn't listen. I thought I could go home for a few weeks and then my father would get better and my parents would have it all figured out. Instead, I took care of my mother for the next twenty-two years. By the time she passed, my youth had passed me by, and I was the poster girl for spinster librarian."

Lindsey said nothing. Ms. Cole stared out the window at the library. She turned back with a mirthless smile. "I might have become a tad bitter."

Lindsey burst out laughing, and Ms. Cole's smile warmed into a grin.

"Henry's death hits so very hard, I suppose, because he was the love of my life for a very long time," she said. "I spent most of my twenties pining for him, but also, he was the path not taken. I always wondered what my life might have been had I gotten on the bus with him that day."

They were silent for a few moments. Lindsey didn't know what to say. She didn't want to say the wrong thing, but she wasn't sure of what the right thing was either. Living with regret was a painful journey because there was just no way to go back and fix it. There were no do-overs once a person passed on.

"I just wish I could have talked to him one more time."

Lindsey nodded. The lack of closure, and the reality that there never would be any, had to be hard to bear.

"Obviously, I didn't know Henry," Lindsey said. "But from everything I've heard about him, I bet he'd be very proud of you right now." Ms. Cole glanced at her in confusion and Lindsey added, "Running for mayor, giving 'the man' a challenge. It just sounds like something of which Henry would have wholeheartedly approved."

A single tear ran down Ms. Cole's cheek, and she wiped it away. "Thank you for saying that. I think you're right. He would have gotten a real charge out of me trying to be Briar Creek's first female mayor."

"Then don't let this"—Lindsey gestured to the photo on the desk—"stop you. Someone is trying to get you to quit. Don't let them win."

Ms. Cole nodded. She smoothed the front of her pale

mint green blouse and then yanked the cuffs out from under the chartreuse jacket she wore. It was quite the color combination, but it was so inherently Ms. Cole that Lindsey couldn't help but smile.

"You're right," Ms. Cole said. "Let's call Emma and then get back to work."

Lindsey reached for the phone.

W hat do you know about Curtis Schmitt?" Lindsey asked Sully, sitting across from his desk in his office on the pier. She'd already told him about the photo that was sent to Ms. Cole, and he agreed with her that it was alarming and best left to Emma to discover its provenance.

He was finishing up signing the pile of paperwork his assistant, Ronnie, had left for him before they went to dinner at the Blue Anchor. Heathcliff was sacked out on his dog bed in the corner after a hard day of water taxi duties.

"The developer?" he asked.

"Yes," she said.

"He grew up here," Sully said. "He was a few years ahead of me in school. He was very bright, very ambitious, his dad was a dentist, and his expectations for Curtis were high."

"So, Curtis ripping up historic homes and planting shoddily built town houses must make him so proud," Lindsey said.

Sully raised his eyebrows in surprise.

"Sorry, that came out a bit harsh."

"No worries, I happen to agree." He smiled. "And we're not alone in those feelings. His office is at the end of the pier next to his wife's real estate office, and he's had petitioners out front, gathering signatures to stop the development."

"That must be unpleasant—for him," Lindsey said. "But what a convenient arrangement. He builds and she sells."

Sully finished signing the last paper, clicked his pen and tossed it down on the desk. He rose from his seat and patted his leg. Heathcliff rolled up to his feet and trotted over to him. "You ready for some dinner, buddy?"

Heathcliff wagged and Lindsey stood up. She glanced at Sully. "Any chance we could stop by Curtis's office on the way and say hi?"

Sully heaved a sigh. He glanced down at Heathcliff. "Sorry, my boy, dinner is going to have to wait."

The fuzzy black dog let out a whimper, and Lindsey could have sworn he understood them.

"It'll be quick," she said. "I just want to see if he has any information about Henry Lewis that might be useful."

"Meaning did he have any motive to murder Lewis for causing him problems with the new development."

"That, too."

Together they left the office with Heathcliff trotting between them. The sun was setting, taking the day's warmth with it. Lindsey leaned up against Sully, absorbing some of his heat as they walked down the pier, past the Blue Anchor, to the line of shops and offices that sat along the street across from the restaurant.

The lights were on in both the real estate office and in the builder's. Sully strode right up and pulled the glass door open, holding it for Lindsey and Heathcliff.

There were enormous aerial photographs of the Connecticut shoreline, architectural renderings of housing developments and one lone plant, which appeared to be thriving in front of the windows.

An office administrator's desk stood off to the side, empty. Lindsey guessed that whoever usually sat there was gone for the day. She motioned for Heathcliff to stop beside the door and wait for them.

"Sit," she said. Heathcliff did but with great reluctance, and when he rested his head on his front paws, he made quite a put-upon expression. "It's just for a few minutes." He did not look encouraged.

There were two glassed-in offices at the back. One was dark but the other had lights on. A man with thick, curly white hair, very tan skin and a solid middle-aged paunch was standing while talking on the phone. He saw them through the glass and waved, holding up a finger to indicate he'd be just a minute. Sully raised his hand in return.

Lindsey wandered over to the rendering done all in white of the new development, the one that would flatten Nana's old house. It looked very square and faux midcentury modern. There wasn't much charm and certainly not any of the quirkiness of the old houses with their colorful paint and mismatched front porches, tiny driveways and variety of wooden trims.

Lindsey estimated which one would sit on top of Nana's house and noted it looked like a copy of all the others with nothing even remotely interesting about it.

"Hey, Sully, and Mrs. Sully, what can I do for you?" Curtis came out of his office with his hand extended. He and Sully shook, and then Curtis turned to Lindsey and did the same. "Checking out the new development?

If you're interested in buying one, you'll want to move fast. They're selling like nobody's business, but of course, you'll have to take it up with the wife. She's making all the sales."

"How can you be selling already when you haven't even broken ground?" Lindsey asked.

"We take deposits," Curtis said. "We'll be starting construction soon. Don't you worry."

"Oh, I'm not worried," she said. Sully gave her a watchful look when she added, "But aren't you concerned that Lenny Lewis isn't going to sell to you since his uncle Henry was so opposed to it?"

It was a toss of the fishing line to see if he bit. Curtis did, hook, line and sinker.

"Given that Henry Lewis is now deceased, I don't think he's going to be a problem," Curtis said. He looked irritated.

"That was cold, Curtis," Sully said. "Even for the guy who led the polar bear club every New Year's Day for fifteen years."

Lindsey watched Sully subtly build a rapport with Curtis by mentioning one of the things Curtis was clearly very proud of, his polar bear club days. She would have high-fived him but that would have been weird.

"You're right. Sorry," Curtis said. He looked somewhat abashed. "I didn't mean anything by it, but the development was going great until Henry Lewis showed up, trying to make trouble, and now I have all these petitioners gathering signatures and some of my backers are beginning to balk. The guy hadn't even lived here for forty years, what did he care if we bulldozed his grandmother's house?"

"He probably wanted to preserve her legacy," Lindsey said. "I heard the house has been in his family for generations."

"Well, if it was so important to him, why did he sign it over to his nephew?" Curtis asked. "Lenny doesn't care about keeping it."

Lindsey felt her temper heat. She glared at Curtis.

"Wait." Curtis snapped his fingers. "Now it's all coming into focus." He looked at Sully and said, "I just remembered, you married the librarian."

"Yes, I did." Sully grinned with pride at Lindsey and she smiled back.

"So, you're the one the mayor complains about," Curtis said to her.

"Excuse me?" The smile slid from Lindsey's face.

"You're the one running against him for mayor, aren't you?" he asked.

"No," she said. "And by that, I mean no, not ever."

"You sure?" Curtis asked. "The mayor said you were a know-it-all."

"Easy, Curtis. Did you miss the part where I said she's my wife?" Sully warned him.

Curtis lifted his hands in the air. "Fine, but you'd best leave. The mayor said the librarians were working against him, and I don't want to be a party to that."

"We're not working against him," Lindsey said. "One of my staff people is running against him for mayor, which is an entirely different thing."

"Not to him, and I need him on my side with this development, so I need to stay on his," Curtis said. "I can't help you."

"Unfortunately, you don't have much choice," Sully said.

"I beg your pardon." Curtis drew himself up to his full height of five foot eight, meaning both Lindsey and Sully were still looking down on him.

"You heard me," Sully said. "You can talk either to us or to the chief of police, who I'm sure will be interested in hearing your take on Henry Lewis's death. Now, we have some questions and we'd appreciate your cooperation."

"What? Are you going to go tell the chief what I said about Henry no longer being a problem?" Curtis said. "It's not like that's news. Besides, I already did this dance with Chief Plewicki. I'm not doing it with you."

Sully stepped close and loomed over the smaller man. "Curtis, unless you want to spend all of your free time motoring out to Horseshoe Island to pick up your mother, you'll answer our questions."

"What are you saying, Sully?" Curtis asked. "You can't deny taxi service to my mother."

"Private company," Sully said. He held his hands out in a *what can you do* gesture. "If my taxi is suddenly fully booked and I can't pick her up for her daily shopping runs, well, you know what that means."

"You wouldn't." Curtis looked horrified.

"Wouldn't I?"

"But you know she's a shopaholic," Curtis protested. "I mean, the woman comes ashore and shops every single day. I can't be dealing with that."

Sully just stared at him unrelenting. Lindsey wanted to hug him but she didn't want to interrupt the showdown.

"All right, fine," Curtis said. "What do you want to know?"

"What exactly went down between you and Henry

Lewis?" Sully asked. Curtis looked stubborn but Sully said, "If you've already told the police, what's the big deal with telling me?"

"All right, fine," Curtis said. He paced around the architectural model, glaring at the spot where Nana's house would be. "I approached Lenny because the house is his and he was very interested in selling."

"But isn't that the only home he's ever known?" Lindsey said. "Where did he think he was going to go live?"

"He said something about a houseboat," Curtis said. "The point is, I had him. I had him ready to sell his house to me, when Henry swoops in and stops everything."

"So, you were mad," Sully said.

"'Mad'? Ha! I was furious," Curtis admitted. "But I didn't kill him."

"Really?" Lindsey asked.

"Yes, really, sheesh. What do you take me for?" Curtis said. "I knew he'd have to go back to his cookie empire sooner or later, and I was just biding my time until I could get Lenny back on track."

"Do you really think that's the right thing to do?" Sully asked. "Taking the house of a man with limited capabilities?"

"What? He's fine. A little odd, sure, but perfectly capable of taking care of himself," Curtis said. "Lenny wanted to sell, and I was looking to buy. It's a win-win."

"What did the chief say when you told her all of this?" Lindsey asked.

"She told me not to leave town," he said. "As if I'm going to leave. I didn't do anything wrong. Plus, I can't

leave with this development hanging in the balance—
I'll lose a fortune if it doesn't go through."

"You might want to keep that to yourself," Sully
said. "It doesn't sound good."

"Eh." Curtis shrugged. "All of my investors know
that if I don't get the Lewis property, then this whole
thing is a bust."

"Wait. What?" Lindsey asked.

"Did I stutter?"

"Curtis," Sully warned him.

"What I meant to say is, who are your investors?"
Lindsey asked.

Curtis stared at her. "No. That's too far. That is private information and I am not divulging it."

"Did you tell the chief of police?" Sully asked.

Curtis sighed. "What does that have to do with anything? You are not the police. You are two busybodies,
trying to find someone else to blame the murder of
Henry Lewis on when everyone knows it was his
ex-girlfriend the librarian."

"What?" Lindsey cried. "No, it wasn't."

"Yes, it was," Curtis said. "The mayor even said so.
Oh, snap! Now I remember. She's the woman who
works at the library who wears all the weird color com-
binations, isn't she? She's the killer. And she works for
you, so that's why you're here trying to blame it on me."

Lindsey sent him an annoyed face. "We're not trying
to blame it on you. We're just gathering facts."

"Well, gather this," Curtis said. "Your library lady
killed her old boyfriend and stuffed him in her trunk.
She got caught and that is that. In fact, I should probably thank her since now I can go forward with the
development."

Annoyed by his self-assured cocky attitude, Lindsey turned away. She was done here. She got halfway to the door before a thought occurred to her. She whipped back around and pinned him with a stare.

"Tell me this, is the mayor one of your investors?" she asked.

CHAPTER

16

BRIAR CREEK
PUBLIC LIBRARY

Curtis's face went white, then red, then white again. Sully clapped him on the shoulder as he walked around him.

"Thanks for the confirmation," he said.

"But I didn't—" Curtis protested, but Sully and Lindsey didn't stay to hear the rest of it. They collected Heathcliff where he waited by the door, and exited.

They hurried across the street and over to the Blue Anchor. Because Heathcliff was with them, they ate outside on the large patio under a gas heater.

"What do you make of that?" Sully asked. He opened the menu and looked it over even though Lindsey knew that he knew it by heart. She suspected that what they'd discovered was making him restless and he was fidgeting because of it.

"I think the mayor is invested in Curtis's development," she said. "Which means Henry blocking the purchase of Nana's house was a problem for him, too."

"Enough of one that he'd murder somebody?" Sully asked.

"When the victim has a connection to his campaign rival, and it means he can get rid of her as well as his problem? Maybe." Lindsey glanced around the restaurant to make certain they couldn't be overheard.

"I had the same thought," Sully said. He closed the menu and leaned over the table. "Curtis will tell Mayor Hensen we were there and that we were asking questions. You're going to need to be very, very careful until Lewis's killer is caught."

"I will," Lindsey said. "And you were with me, so you need to be careful, too."

"I promise," he said. He studied her face by the light of the lone candle on their table. "All right, let me have it. What's our next move?"

Lindsey smiled. "I thought you'd never ask. We need to go visit Lenny Lewis."

Why are we here again?" Sully asked as he turned his truck down the narrow lane. "You explained last night, but in the harsh light of morning, I'm questioning our decision-making skills."

"We're here to ask Lenny what he knows about Henry's fight to save Nana's house. I mean, Curtis was forthcoming about his issues with Henry, and even though he was apparently honest, I still think he's a suspect. But clearly he must have an alibi since Emma hasn't arrested him."

"Either he had an alibi or someone lied for him."

"Like his wife?"

Sully shrugged as he parked his truck in front of the small cottage.

"I still think the mayor had the most to gain by Henry's death, so we need to ask if Lenny has had any contact with him as well."

"Agreed," Sully said. "But I'm having a hard time picturing the mayor and Lenny having a conversation."

Lindsey had to admit it was an odd pairing.

Sully stared out the windshield at the well-kept little house, and Lindsey followed his gaze, noting that it looked exactly like the line drawing of the house on the Nana's Cookies label. It hadn't changed at all after so many years. No wonder Henry had been sentimentally attached.

"All right, let's go," Sully said.

Lindsey hopped out of the truck, and Sully met her beside her door. Together they walked through the white picket fence and up to the porch. The cottage was one of the oldest in Briar Creek. Built in the eighteen hundreds, it sported gingerbread scrollwork and scalloped wooden siding up on the eaves. It was painted white with a deep green trim and was meticulously maintained. Lenny certainly took excellent care of his house.

A large shiny new boat rested on a trailer beside the house. Sully gave a low whistle when he saw it. "Fancy. That's a Lagoon 380. It's small for a catamaran but for one person a totally livable space. Pretty pricey though."

Lindsey, who knew nothing about boats except that she preferred to be on them rather than in the water, nodded. Even a layperson like her could see it was a spectacular boat.

She climbed the steps and knocked on the front door. "Hello, Lenny?" There was no answer. "Lenny, it's Lindsey from the library."

There was a sound from the side of the house, and a head popped up behind the side of the boat. "Hi." The head disappeared.

Lindsey and Sully exchanged a glance of confusion. Was he coming back out or was that the total of their interaction with him?

Lindsey decided to go for it and approached the boat. Sully fell into step beside her. She noticed he kept his body between her and the boat as if he would shield her from harm. Always the Navy man, she thought, and she was grateful for him. Truthfully, given the events of the past few days, she'd have been nervous to approach Lenny, Curtis or the mayor on her own. But Bob Spielman, even though he had solid motive, still seemed like such a nice guy.

"Lenny, can you come out?" she asked as they drew close to the boat. "I wanted to talk to you about . . ." She paused. She didn't think mentioning Henry was the way to go here. Instead, she said, "About some books that have come in about . . . horseshoe crabs."

Lenny's head popped back up, making her jump. "I'll be right down."

She felt Sully release a breath beside her, and she knew he'd been feeling just as tense as she was.

Lenny appeared above them. He paused to study them from beneath the cloud of unkempt straw-colored hair that swirled around his face, obscuring his eyes. Lindsey wondered what he was thinking, but forced her lips into a small curve so as not to appear overly cheerful and yet not stern either. Finding the middle ground was exhausting.

"What books?" he asked. "Did you bring them?"

"No," she said. "We were just in the neighborhood, and I thought I'd stop by and mention them as I know you're very interested in horseshoe crabs."

"They're arthropods not crabs."

"Of course, sorry," Lindsey said. She glanced at Sully. He gave her an encouraging nod. "Nice boat. Is it new?"

"Yeah, it came yesterday." Lenny hunched his shoulders. It was clearly the posture of someone who did not want to have a conversation. "I thought you had the books with you."

"Sorry," Lindsey said again. She sensed her lure was going to blow up in her face if she didn't come up with another draw to keep him talking to them. "Your boat looks big enough to live on."

"Yeah."

"The library has an excellent selection of books about boats and seafaring," she continued. She hoped the subject might spark some interest for him. "I can put some aside for you if you want."

He stared at her. He didn't look impressed.

"I know why you're really here," he said. He glanced at them quick before his gaze went back down to his shoes.

"And why is that?" Sully asked. His tone was genial but firm.

"You want to know if I killed my uncle," Lenny said. "I didn't."

"No, Lenny," Lindsey said. Her voice was gentle. "We don't think that."

He glanced at her from beneath his hair, like a bird giving her side-eye, trying to determine whether she'd strike or not.

"Everyone else does," he said. "That's why I bought the boat. I'm going to sail away, away from everyone."

Lindsey felt her heart pinch. With Henry gone, even though they weren't close, Lenny had no one. Absolutely no one.

"What about the house?" Sully asked.

Lenny shifted his feet, kicking a rock back and forth between his beat-up boat shoes. "Curtis Schmitt wants it. He can have it." He stared off at the bay visible beyond the line of trees at the end of the street. "*On a day when the wind is perfect, the sail just needs to open and the world is full of beauty.*"

"Rumi." Lindsey identified the poet with a surprised nod. She appreciated his literary reference even though she knew using the boat to run away was not a solution to his problem.

"Can you help us, Lenny?" she asked. "We're trying to figure out what happened to your uncle. Is there anything you can tell us that might help?"

Lenny shook his head. "I didn't know him very well. He came by to check on the house a couple of times a year but we weren't close." He stared at his boat. "It felt like he wanted me here just to watch over the house because it was Nana's. I miss Nana. She was the only one who understood."

"Understood what, Lenny?" Lindsey asked.

"That I wanted to be free," he said. He glanced past them, down the street, to the sea. "I just want to be free. I tried to tell Uncle Henry that, but he said I had no idea how lucky I was that I hadn't been betrayed by someone

I trusted." He scrunched up his face in confusion as if he had no idea what Henry had meant. "You don't think he meant me, do you? That if I left the house I was betraying him?"

Lindsey and Sully exchanged a look, and then Sully glanced back at Lenny.

"Nah, he just didn't understand that we sailors are born to roam the seas," Sully said. He was clearly trying to take Lenny's mind off Henry's words. He spoke as if he and Lenny were cut from the same cloth. It was clear Lenny knew who he was, that Sully was a sailor, too, and Lindsey saw his shoulders relax just slightly. "Did you feel that Henry was stopping you from being free?" Sully asked. His voice was sympathetic as if he understood what it meant to be pulled by the sea and have people get in the way.

"No, he didn't stop me, but he told me that if he was going to continue to provide for me, you know, with a roof over my head, that I had to watch over Nana's house. He didn't want it, but he didn't want anyone else to have it either."

"So, you were stuck," Sully said.

"Yeah," Lenny spoke to his shoes.

Lindsey pursed her lips. It was an interesting observation. She wondered how much Lenny understood about his uncle's business. "Henry sure made quite a business out of your grandmother's recipes."

"He did," Lenny said. A purple martin cried, and his head turned in that direction as he tracked the bird's flight. His voice was distracted when he said, "It's nice that people like her cookies."

"Did he share the business with you?" Lindsey asked.

Lenny studied her. "Not the business, just the house. But he always made certain that I had what I needed."

"So, the house belongs to you?" Lindsey asked.

"It did." Again he turned his head away, facing the bay.

"But now you have a boat," Sully said.

Lenny nodded. "Henry and Curtis fought about the boat."

"Curtis?" Lindsey asked. "Curtis Schmitt?"

"He helped me get the boat," Lenny said. "So I would have a place to live when he took the house."

Lindsey turned to look at Sully. Curtis had not shared this with them, and it seemed significant.

"Why did Henry fight with him about it?" Lindsey asked.

"Uncle Henry said that Curtis only wanted to help me get the boat because he wanted the house," Lenny said. "Curtis said that was true but that he wasn't the only one."

"Did someone else want the house?" Sully asked.

Lenny shrugged, shoved the hair back from his face and scrunched up his eyes as if he was trying to remember. "I don't know. I can't remember. I didn't understand."

"That's all right," Lindsey said. "It's a nice house. I'm sure there are a lot of people who would want it."

Sully asked Lenny about his boat, which distracted him and made the lines in his face ease. When he seemed calmer, they took their leave with Lindsey promising to put aside some books for him about living aboard a boat.

"What do you make of that?" she asked as they drove back to the center of town.

"I don't know what to think," Sully said. "Of the two men we've spoken to, I'd say Curtis is the more likely to have murdered Henry Lewis than Lenny. I mean, Henry was actively tying up his development, and with a fortune on the line, I can see where Curtis might've gotten desperate."

"But with Henry gone, he's no longer desperate, and it sounds as if he got possession of the house yesterday, which he conveniently neglected to mention," she said.

"Yeah, it appears Curtis bought the house from Lenny for the price of that boat, which is about two hundred thousand," he said. "Nowhere near the actual property value of the house."

"A steal, if you will."

"Curtis said he didn't have to murder Henry, because all he had to do was bide his time, but the sale of the house certainly came about pretty quickly."

"Conveniently quickly."

"Here's what I want to know," Sully said. "If Lenny is Henry's sole living relative and all he gave him from the cookie company was the house that he signed over to him years ago, then who is inheriting the rest of Henry's wealth? Don't the police usually look at who-ever has the most to gain?"

"They do, but Bob Spielman, Henry's partner, said that Henry had been inspired by the Giving Pledge—you know, that pledge a bunch of billionaires made to give away most of their wealth—and had committed almost all of his money to charity."

"So, there's nothing to fight over," Sully said. "And no heir who would kill him to gain the cookie empire."

"In theory, but apparently, the house was still

important to Henry," Lindsey said. She glanced out the window. "I don't want to say this, but . . ."

"You're wondering if Lenny might have killed his uncle so that he could sell the house without Henry interfering."

"Yes, and I feel awful about it," she said.

"It's a legitimate possibility," Sully said. "Emma hasn't arrested him, so maybe he has an alibi, too."

"Maybe, or perhaps he and Curtis are each other's alibis," Lindsey said. "I truly don't know what to think anymore."

"Same," Sully said. "For a guy who sold cookies for a living, Henry had more enemies than you'd think and judging by what he said to Lenny about being betrayed, he clearly felt that someone had wronged him, but who could it be?"

H ey, Chief," Lindsey said as Emma Plewicki approached her at the local Friday evening merchants' association meeting. Lindsey was there for two reasons. One, Sully was a member, as his business worked cooperatively with so many local businesses; and two, Ms. Cole was speaking. Beth was working the room, passing out flyers detailing Ms. Cole's campaign promises. The pamphlet was well done with a great shot of Ms. Cole in front of the library and bullet points listing the features of her campaign.

"Hey," Emma said. She sat in the seat next to Lindsey with a bit more force than necessary.

"You okay?" Lindsey asked. "How's that whiteboard working out?"

"If by that, do you mean is it helping? No. I can't

seem to get a break in this case," Emma said. "I'm going to have to tell Bob Spielman he's free to go back to Maine, and I don't have a clue as to who murdered his business partner."

"It is a weird case," Lindsey said. "With his charitable contributions, no one would profit from Henry's death in the usual way."

"Exactly," Emma said. "Which makes me think it was anger that got him killed. Someone was furious with him. But who and why?"

The two women sitting in front of them turned around and gave them a quelling look.

Duly chastened, Lindsey lowered her voice. "It could very well be Curtis—Henry wouldn't let Lenny sell Nana's house to Curtis, preventing Curtis from going ahead with the development."

Emma gave her side-eye. "Someone's been busy."

"Just keeping an ear to the ground," Lindsey said.

"Well, the problem with that theory is that Curtis has an alibi," Emma said. "He was helping his wife show a house on Bell Island."

"Do we trust his wife?" Lindsey asked.

"When the people they were showing the house to verify their story, yes, we do," Emma said.

"That is hard to argue with," Lindsey agreed.

"Shh." A man shushed them, and Lindsey hunkered lower in her seat while Emma shot the man a glare.

Lindsey lowered her voice and asked the most pressing question on her mind. "Have you had any luck tracing the photograph that was sent to Ms. Cole?"

"No." Emma shook her head. "Whoever did it left nothing on the envelope or the photo. No prints, no hairs, no fibers. Nothing."

"And how about the mayor's wife calling the library from the tax assessor's office?" Lindsey asked. "Anything?"

"She denies it and unfortunately, again, there is no evidence of her being in the assessor's office. She says she was in attendance at the baby shower the entire time and no one who was there is saying differently."

"Well, that disappoints."

"Indeed."

"Good evening," Ms. Cole addressed the room.

Lindsey and Emma straightened up and stopped talking. They watched Ms. Cole address the room full of local businesspeople. Having lived in Briar Creek most of her life, Ms. Cole knew everyone, and she knew the histories of their businesses. The marina owner's father had been friends with her father. The local bakery was run by a woman Ms. Cole had gone to school with. She acknowledged how these small local businesses made Briar Creek a wonderful place to live.

Lindsey could feel the crowd warming up to her. The stigma of finding the body of Henry Lewis in her car was now more a point of sympathy than suspicion. Ms. Cole was one of them. She understood how taxes affected them and how having a thriving economy mattered to their livelihoods. Lindsey glanced at Beth, who was standing just off to the side. She was absolutely beaming with pride, like a mom watching her child in a school performance.

Ms. Cole was just wrapping up her talk when there was a commotion by the entrance. Lindsey glanced over her shoulder and groaned. It was Mayor Hensen. Oh, no, she had a feeling they were in for public ambush part two. She leaned close to Emma and said, "There isn't another big reveal about to happen, is there? You don't have another business partner of Henry's off in the wings, do you?"

"Not that I know of," Emma said. She frowned. "What is he playing at?"

A murmur rippled through the room as everyone noticed the mayor. Ms. Cole finished her talk and then saw Hensen. Maintaining her poise, she leaned closer to the mic and asked, "Can I help you, Mayor Hensen?"

As if he was just waiting for this opportunity, he took a few steps forward. Everyone in the room turned to look at him, and he visibly swelled with the attention.

"Yes, you can help me," he said. "Please explain to me and the rest of the room why a convicted criminal should be mayor of our peace-loving town?"

"Excuse me?" Ms. Cole blinked.

"No, I will not," Mayor Hensen said. He turned so he was addressing the crowd of merchants. "Ms. Cole has misrepresented herself. She is not the mild-mannered librarian you believe her to be. Instead, she is an insurrectionist and was arrested and jailed as such."

An audible ripple of shock and dismay surged through the crowd.

"That's right!" Mayor Hensen cried. He pointed at Ms. Cole. "She is a criminal and not fit to serve public office."

Lindsey's jaw dropped as the room erupted into chaos.

CHAPTER

17

BRIAR CREEK
PUBLIC LIBRARY

Beth strode forward to the podium, intent on protecting Ms. Cole. Questions were being shouted from
the crowd while Milton, who'd been sitting up front,
rose and began to stride toward the mayor, looking like
he was intent on injuring him, which was shocking for
the peace-loving yogi. Bob Spielman, who was also in
the crowd, joined him. Emma let out a colorful cuss-
word and jumped up from her seat to head them off.

Ms. Cole didn't bat an eye at the mayor's accusation.
Instead, she calmly raised both of her hands to indicate
that everyone should calm down. The room was slow
to take the direction, but as Ms. Cole stood there so
calmly, the energy in the room began to change until it
became quiet.

Lindsey held her breath, wondering how Ms. Cole
was going to navigate this accusation.

"What the mayor says is true," she said.

The rumble in the room started up again, and the mayor looked quite pleased with himself. Meanwhile, Milton spun around to stare at her, and Bob tipped his head to the side as if he'd known what she was about to say and wondered how far she'd go with it.

"When I was an impressionable young teen, I read Rachel Carson's *Silent Spring*. It stayed with me, as all good books do. And when I became a college student, way back when dinosaurs roamed the earth"—she paused for the few chuckles that met that statement—"I believed in one person's ability to change the world. An advocate for protecting the environment, I attended rallies, I campaigned for politicians that I believed in, and I marched. Peacefully. I was very antipollution, and I still am. I think we can all agree that pollution is bad."

She glanced around the room, and slowly the merchants in attendance nodded.

"As merchants of a seaside town, you know how important it is for our bay and shoreline to be safe to fish, swim and boat in. Our livelihoods, and our very lives, depend upon it." She paused and more people nodded as the enthusiasm grew. "In my wild youth"—she made a face that was clearly making fun of herself—"I went all in saving Long Island Sound."

The laughter was genuine now. "The arrest that Mayor Hensen is referring to occurred on a particularly hot day when I and several of my environmentally engaged friends decided to stage a protest outside of a factory known for dumping raw sewage into the Connecticut River that was then churned out into the Sound. Did you know that Atlantic salmon used to run up the river to spawn, and that in the sixties there was a movement to bring the salmon back? Sadly, the ecosystem was so irreparably damaged by the Industrial Revolution, and the world wars that followed, that the dream was never achieved.

"On the day that the mayor refers to, I had decided that the best way to make myself heard was to dress up as a salmon." She gazed out at the crowd, her expression a mix of rueful and humorous as she continued, "I did not take into account that the factory owner would be so unhappy with us for standing on the curb in front of his factory, which turned out to be private property. Nor did I factor in my inability to run while wearing a tapered fishtail. When the other protesters fled from the security guards that he unleashed upon us, I was left to hop. Unsurprisingly, I did not get very far."

Lindsey snorted. She couldn't help it. The visual of Ms. Cole—Ms. Cole!—dressed as a giant salmon trying to outrun security by hopping. It was too much. She saw Beth laughing and noted that just about every merchant in the room was as well. It took several minutes for everyone to calm down, and Lindsey was relieved that even Milton and Bob had stopped their charge toward the mayor and were chuckling. Emma, who had positioned herself in front of the mayor, was smiling, but trying not to.

"The security officers detained me, and when the police came, I was cited for trespassing," Ms. Cole said. "Yes, that is the extent of my criminal past. I do hope you won't hold it against me. I believe in taking care of the planet that takes care of us, and I ask you for your vote so that we can revamp the infrastructure of Briar Creek and make it a cleaner, safer and happier home for us all, even if I have to dress up as a giant fish again to do it."

Applause drowned out anything else she might have said. Ms. Cole beamed. She tried to thank the merchants, but the applause grew, and soon people were on their feet and someone—Lindsey suspected Beth—started chanting, "Vote Cole!"

Lindsey stood and joined the cheers. When she glanced back at the mayor, she noted that he was gone and the door was just swinging shut. She suspected this was not going to go well for her.

The library wasn't even open yet when Lindsey put her handbag in the bottom drawer of her desk and her office phone rang.

"Hi, this is Lindsey Norris. May I help you?" she asked. She wondered what it would be like to answer the phone as Lindsey Sullivan. She was still undecided about changing her name. On the one hand, Sullivan was a great name and she liked it, but on the other, she'd been a Norris her whole life and wasn't sure why she'd change it. Maybe a hyphen. Hmm.

"Lindsey, this is Mayor Hensen." Even to Lindsey's caffeine-deprived ears he sounded mad.

"I'd like to see you in my office immediately."

Then he hung up. So, this was a glorious start to her Monday.

With a sigh, she left her office and headed out the door to the main library. Ms. Cole was at the circulation desk, talking to Paula and Ann Marie.

"I have to run to the town hall," Lindsey said. "I'll be back shortly."

Ms. Cole glanced at her over the tops of her reading glasses.

"He's going to chew you out for Friday evening's merchants' meeting, isn't he?"

Lindsey raised her hands in the air in a *whatever* gesture. "Maybe he's going to approve my budget request for surveillance cameras."

"Check the label on your blouse," Ann Marie said.

Lindsey glanced down at her pale blue cotton dress shirt. She was relieved she'd chosen today to wear it with her navy skirt and pumps since she was unexpectedly getting called onto the carpet and looking professional could only help.

"Why?" she asked.

"You want to be sure it's flame retardant," Paula joked. She and Ann Marie exchanged a high five and laughed. Ms. Cole gave them a quelling look but she was smiling, too.

"Ha ha, very funny," Lindsey said, but she was grinning when she said it. "All joking aside, if I'm not back in thirty minutes, can you call me with an 'emergency'?"

"Roger that," Paula said.

Feeling that at least she had an out if things got too sticky, Lindsey left the library and headed to the town hall. Thankfully, it was a glorious April day instead of a rainy one. The previous winter had been bitterly cold and long, and she was delighted to feel the warm sun on her face as she walked toward the brick building in the distance.

She strode up the steps and through the main doors. It was quiet today. She thought about stopping by the assessor's office to say hi to Janice and see if she'd learned anything about the call from her office, but she figured it wouldn't do to keep the mayor waiting.

She climbed the staircase and strode down the hallway to his office. The door behind the administrative assistant's desk was open, and Lindsey didn't even get a chance to pause and say hello to Pearl before he called her inside.

"Lindsey, you're here. Great. Come on in."

Pearl smiled at her and waved. Lindsey waved back as she passed her desk to go into the mayor's inner sanctum.

"Have a seat," the mayor said. He gestured for Lindsey to sit down while he stuck his head out the door, and said, "Two coffees, please."

Then he shut the door and strode back across the room to his desk. He took a seat and leaned forward, clasping his hands together. Lindsey waited. He had called her here. She wasn't going to be the one to fill the silence with chatter. The nice thing about being a shy introvert was that she preferred quiet and never felt the need to fill it with a meaningless word salad.

"Well," he said.

Lindsey stared at him.

"I suppose you're wondering why I asked you to drop by," he said.

She nodded.

He glanced down at his hands and then back up. "I've been considering your request for a larger library budget, including the security cameras you requested."

Lindsey almost fell out of her chair. "I'm sorry. Could you repeat that?"

Pearl came in with a tray with two coffees, a pitcher of milk and a sugar bowl. She set it on the edge of his desk and the mayor thanked her warmly.

When the door closed behind her, he said, "I've surprised you."

Lindsey took the coffee he held out to her. The cup felt hot in her hands, and she welcomed it because it gave her focus.

"I had thought you were very clear that the video cameras I'd requested for the library were out of the question. You didn't think there was a need for them."

"Given recent events, I've had a change of heart," he said. He grinned, and Lindsey was temporarily blinded by his overly white teeth. It was a politician's smile. She noted that his right-hand man, Herb Gunderson, wasn't here for this meeting. She found that odd. Herb was always in every meeting.

She began to feel uneasy about what was coming next.

"I'm relieved to hear it," she said. "But you didn't need to invite me here to tell me this. You could have detailed it in an email."

"And I will," he said. "I just need you to do one thing first."

Thump! Lindsey assumed that was the sound of the other shoe dropping.

"And what would that be?" she asked. She took a sip of coffee, hoping she looked calmer than she felt.

"Quite simply, if I approve of the new budget, I would expect that you would encourage your current staff to maintain their situations. A turnover would be so disruptive to the well-being of the library, don't you think?"

Lindsey put her coffee back on the tray. She narrowed her eyes at him and asked, "Are you trying to bribe me?"

"Not at all," he answered as smooth as butter. "I'm tying no strings to the security system and am merely encouraging you to do all you can to keep your current staff so as to keep the disruption in service to a minimum."

Lindsey clenched her jaw in frustration. He was just so smarmy. He thought she'd actually keep Ms. Cole from running for mayor for a handful of security cameras?

"Thank you for the coffee," she said. She rose to her feet. "Was there anything else?"

He studied her. Her lack of reaction clearly puzzled him. Good. Because what she really wanted to do was tell him off, but she wasn't going to give him anything. Let him wonder and worry.

"No," he said. His voice was clipped, his annoyance obvious. She was halfway across the room before he spoke again. "But if I may offer a word of advice?"

Lindsey did a slow pivot and regarded him with a steady gaze.

"Don't take too long with my offer. It won't last forever."

"I don't need forever," Lindsey said. "The answer is no."

She turned around again and slid through the door without looking back.

Anger fueled her steps to the library, and she decided to take the long way around to burn off some of her fury. When her staff asked what the mayor had wanted, she needed to be able to say *nothing* and look like she meant it. She absolutely did not want Ms. Cole to know about the mayor's offer. She was loyal enough to the library that she might actually withdraw from the race for some video cameras, and Lindsey wasn't about to let that happen.

She crossed Main Street and took the sidewalk that ran alongside the town's beachside park. It was a chilly morning, but the parents were out in the play area with their kids, and the sounds of shouting and laughter filled the air. It soothed her.

She passed the real estate office and Schmitt's building office. She thought about walking the length of the pier to talk to Sully but she remembered that he had a full day of water taxi riders and wasn't likely to be in.

Instead, she turned and went by the small grocery with the attached bakery. The tables outside were full as residents enjoyed their morning coffee and muffins. It hit Lindsey then how fiercely she loved this town and how much she wanted to protect it. Ms. Cole would make an excellent mayor. She absolutely was not going to let anyone interfere with her campaign.

Newly resolved, she walked on past the historical society building and the cluster of offices near it. One office had a VOTE COLE poster hanging in the window, and Lindsey took it as a sign, literally. She chuckled at the bad pun but felt better for it.

Ivy Kavanagh was just stepping outside of the office and Lindsey called out, "I like your sign."

Ivy grinned. "Vote Cole!" With a wave she headed in the other direction, leaving Lindsey to return to the library with renewed optimism for her town.

* * *

H e did not!" Robbie cried.

"Yes, he did," Lindsey said.

They were having afternoon tea in her office. Robbie had brought Nana's Cookies, this time the salted caramel chocolate chunk, and Lindsey was trying not to make a pig of herself over them.

"What did Ms. Cole say when you told her?"

"I didn't."

"Why ever not?" he asked. He had a cookie halfway to his mouth as he stopped to stare at her in exasperation.

"Because Ms. Cole is loyal enough to the library that I think she might actually withdraw from the mayoral race just to make sure we got our cameras. And I'll bet Mayor Hensen knows that about her, too."

"You're right," he said. "She might very well do that. Frightfully loyal of her."

Lindsey sipped her tea, trying to find some calm. She'd been agitated ever since her meeting with the mayor. She hadn't told Ms. Cole what the mayor had said, but she had told Beth and Emma. Beth was predictably furious but agreed they shouldn't tell Ms. Cole. Emma had said it was an interesting bit of insight into just how desperate Mayor Hensen was to be reelected.

"Speaking of Emma, here she is," Lindsey said. She pointed out the window of her office to the main library.

Chief Plewicki had entered the building with Officer Kirkland. They were standing at the circulation desk talking to Ms. Cole. Emma handed her a piece of paper, and Ms. Cole took it with a frown. After she read it, she gestured to the workroom.

"Uh-oh," Robbie muttered. "This can't be good."

"What do you mean?"

"That expression of Emma's," he said. "That's her serving-a-warrant face."

"She has a face for that?" Lindsey asked.

"Yes," he said. "See the frown line between her eyes? That's her serious face, but if you add in the tightened mouth, that's the serving-a-warrant face."

"You're very observant," Lindsey said.

"Actor." He shrugged.

"But why would she give a warrant to Ms. Cole?" Lindsey asked. "I mean, if she's searching a section of the library, she should come to me."

Lindsey put down her mug and rose from her seat. She and Robbie left her office and met Ms. Cole and Emma as they entered the workroom.

"This shouldn't take long," Emma said. "You're welcome to stay and observe."

"Thank you," Ms. Cole said.

"You're searching Ms. Cole's office?" Lindsey asked. She tried to sound calm, but her voice came out higher than she would have liked. "Why?"

"It's in the warrant," Emma said. She gestured to the papers in Ms. Cole's hands. "We got an anonymous tip and the judge okayed a search. Why don't you start with the desk, Kirkland?"

Lindsey looked at her in astonishment. She couldn't be serious.

"I can't treat Ms. Cole any differently than I would another suspect," Emma said. She glanced at her boyfriend, Robbie. "You know I'm right about this."

"Of course I do, love," Robbie said. He glanced at Lindsey. "She is."

"I know," Lindsey said. "I just think that given the

conversation you and I had a few days ago, that you know and I know that some people are desperate to get other people to pull out of the mayor's race and would do anything to make that happen."

"I know," Emma said. She looked annoyed. "That's why I'm here, ruling it out."

"Oh, so you didn't believe the tip?" Ms. Cole asked. She looked relieved.

"Of course not," Emma said. "But we have to follow the protocol."

"Um, Chief," Officer Kirkland said. He was on his knees, looking at the underside of Ms. Cole's desk.

"As librarians, I'm sure you both appreciate that there is a proper way to do things and you can't take shortcuts or do favors, you have to follow the proper procedure—" Emma said until Kirkland interrupted her again.

"Chief, I think we have a situation," Kirkland said. He was a big, rawboned redhead, and he'd hunkered down to look under Ms. Cole's desk, barely fitting his broad shoulders into the opening.

"What do you mean?" Emma asked.

"There's something taped on the underside of the desk," he said. "Just like the caller described."

"What?" Emma crouched down beside him.

They all leaned in close as Kirkland maneuvered his way back out. He had on blue latex gloves and in one hand had a computer cord.

"What was that doing under my desk?" Ms. Cole asked.

"I think the bigger question is, what is it?" Robbie asked.

"It's a cable that we use for the computers," Lindsey

said. She looked at Ms. Cole. "Didn't one of those go missing the other day?"

Ms. Cole paled. "Yes, the same day I found Henry in my car." She turned and looked at Officer Kirkland, who was putting the cable into an evidence bag. "Oh dear, I think you've found your murder weapon."

M s. Cole, we'll need you to come to the station,"
Emma said.

"Why are you taking her in?" Lindsey asked.

"I have to," Emma said. "If she's right and that cable
is the murder weapon, then I have to figure out what it
was doing under her desk."

"You know what it was doing," Lindsey cried. "It
was planted there to make Ms. Cole look guilty."

"Well, mission accomplished," Emma said. She
glanced at Ms. Cole. "Sorry. Obviously, I consider the
anonymous tip sketchy and am taking you to the station
merely as procedure."

"No, it's all right," Ms. Cole said. "I'd do the same."

"Should I cuff her?" Kirkland asked. They all stared
at him. "That's a no, then."

"I'll just grab my purse," Ms. Cole said. She opened
the lowest drawer on her desk and took out her handbag.

It was in a remarkable shade of red much like the rest of her outfit.

"I'll come with you," Lindsey said.

"No, you need to be here," Ms. Cole said. "There's no one else authorized to be in charge at the moment. If you wouldn't mind calling Milton and letting him know, I'd appreciate it."

"Of course," Lindsey said. "I'll be there as soon as I can."

As they left the workroom, Lindsey gestured for Emma to take the hallway that led to the back entrance. There was no need to make this a public show. Emma gave her a quick nod.

"I'll just go make a spectacle of myself, shall I?" Robbie asked.

Ms. Cole smiled. "That would be much appreciated."

"Anything for you, Ms. Cole," he said. He disappeared out the workroom door to the front of the library and they could hear him, greeting people out front.

Lindsey walked them to the door that led to the back hallway and held her breath while they slipped out the staff entrance.

Lindsey was now quite certain that Ms. Cole was being framed. But by whom and why? The mayor was her obvious choice because of the anonymous call that appeared to have been made by the mayor's wife or her friend, his bribe to Lindsey and now the anonymous tip about where the murder weapon could be found. The mayor had access to the library. He certainly could have planted it or had someone plant it for him. The thought that Mayor Hensen could be responsible was chilling, because if he had planted the murder weapon, that meant he was in possession of it in the first place, which meant he was the murderer. She hadn't really believed it until right now.

The rest of the afternoon crawled by. Lindsey wanted desperately to close the library and dash over to the police station and free Ms. Cole. She wanted to convince Emma that the mayor must be responsible, but she was stuck on the reference desk, helping patrons and pretending everything was normal. It was brutal.

Just before closing, the phone in her office rang. It was Andrea Spalding, the head of the town council.

"Lindsey, I'm so glad I caught you," Andrea said.

She was a pleasant woman, a frequent library user who enjoyed the crafts section. She and Paula were forever sharing their most recent discoveries on YouTube for new and unique crafts.

Their latest endeavor had been several projects involving washi tape.

"Hi, Andrea," Lindsey said. She was impatient to get out of the building and find out what was happening with Ms. Cole. "What can I do for you?"

"There's been an emergency town council meeting called for this evening," Andrea said. "Mayor Hensen wanted it to be closed to the public, but I feel we'd be better served to be transparent with our constituents, and I'd like for you to be there as it directly affects the library."

Lindsey felt her heart beat hard in her chest. "Can I ask what it's in regards to?"

Andrea was silent for a moment. "Yes, the mayor is requesting the termination of one of your employees."

An expletive slipped out before Lindsey could catch it. Horrified, she said, "Sorry."

"No need," she said. "That's exactly what I said

when I heard." Her tone was dry. "Tonight at the town hall at seven thirty."

"I'll be there," Lindsey said.

The town hall was full to bursting. Lindsey and Sully arrived ten minutes early to get seats, but since most of the town was in attendance, it was slim pickings. Lindsey saw Beth was already in attendance with Aidan. They were seated up at the front with the rest of the crafternooners. As they approached, Violet waved to them, pointing to the two seats she had saved by throwing her jacket over them.

Sully and Lindsey hurried up the aisle and claimed the two seats. They were in the row behind their friends, seated beside Milton and Ivy Kavanagh and several members of the Friends of the Library, including the president, Carrie Rushton.

There was no sign of Ms. Cole. When Lindsey had called Emma to ask what was happening, Emma said that Ms. Cole was still at the police station. Lindsey had protested that Ms. Cole needed to be released. Emma had cut her off and said that she wasn't comfortable letting her go off on her own. She didn't say it but Lindsey sensed she was afraid that harm might come to Ms. Cole outside the purview of the police department. It was a chilling thought.

Whispers filled the small auditorium, and Lindsey felt an anticipatory buzz fill the crowd as if they were here for dinner and a show.

Sully leaned close and whispered, "I wonder if this is what public hangings felt like back in the day."

"I was just thinking something similar," she said.

He squeezed her hand in reassurance. "It's going to be okay."

The town council began their meeting promptly. Lindsey noted that the mayor sat in the center of the table with three council people flanking him on each side. He looked over the crowd in annoyance. Lindsey wondered if he was regretting his decision to get Ms. Cole fired now that there was an audience who would require accountability.

The council ran the meeting using *Robert's Rules of Order*. Once the opening business was tabled, Andrea turned to the mayor and said, "Mayor Hensen, as we are here because you've requested an emergency meeting, please tell the council your concerns."

The mayor moved the shared microphone in front of himself and addressed the room. "It was my hope to have this meeting in private, but perhaps having the townspeople bear witness will give us the transparency that is generally lacking in government."

"He gets that he's government, right?" Sully whispered.

Lindsey shot him an amused look.

"It has come to the attention of the mayor's office that we have employed a person of questionable character," he said.

Beth and several others made an audible grunt of protest, which the mayor ignored, raising his voice to be heard over their protests.

"Today, Ms. Eugenia Cole was taken into custody for the murder of her lover, Mr. Henry Lewis, founder of Nana's Cookies and one of Briar Creek's most prominent former residents."

Lover? Lindsey frowned. The man had been her fiancé almost forty years ago. Why did the mayor pick a descriptor that made her relationship with Henry Lewis sound tawdry and illicit and recent? Because he was trying to make her look as unfit as possible. She felt her annoyance spike.

She glanced at Milton and noted that his bald head was slowly turning red and that the expression on his face was sliding from unhappy to very angry.

"She hasn't been charged," Andrea said, correcting him. "It was my understanding that she was merely taken in to answer questions, making this 'emergency' meeting hasty in the extreme."

Lindsey wanted to go and hug her. She resisted.

Mayor Hensen raised one of his eyebrows as if he couldn't believe her impertinence. Andrea didn't bat an eyelash. In fact, she kept speaking.

"I would like to make a motion to dismiss the council," she said. "Pending further information from the chief of police."

"No!" Mayor Hensen cried.

The crowd shifted restlessly. This was the drama they had come for. Lindsey saw the crafternoon ladies sit up straighter in front of them as if bracing for a fight.

"Excuse me," the mayor said. He flashed his white teeth. "I didn't mean to sound so forceful, but the safety and well-being of the townspeople is something *I* take very seriously."

"Which is why he won't give us security cameras," Paula muttered.

Beth nodded at her but the mayor didn't hear them and continued.

"Imagine a murderess being in our library," he said. "She has access to all of your personal information. What materials you check out, whether you owe fines, and she sees your children when they come into the building." He paused. His concerned gaze swept the room as he caught the eyes of the crowd, and then he said, "She even knows where you live."

A ripple of unease swept through the room. Lindsey could hear people shifting in their seats. He was vilifying Ms. Cole, and there wasn't a damn thing she could do about it. It was maddening.

The door at the back of the room opened and everyone turned to see who the latecomer was. It was Ms. Cole. She was dressed all in black, thank goodness, and she strode to the front of the room with purpose in her step.

"What are you doing here?" the mayor asked. He looked incredulous, as if he had no idea how to pivot now that the person he was trying to slander was standing right in front of him.

"Apparently, I'm defending myself," Ms. Cole said. She stuck out her chin and said, "Surprise!"

Beth looked like she wanted to leap from her seat and start applauding. Instead, she leaned over the back of her chair, closer to Lindsey, and said, "I wish we had some of those yard signs now. We could make a wall of them. Too bad the police took them all as evidence."

Lindsey nodded. It would make an impressive visual of support. She frowned.

She leaned close to Beth and said, "What was that?"

"We should have the yard signs," she repeated.

"No, after that."

"The police took them all."

"*All* of them?"

"Every single one. Really dinged my campaign budget."

Lindsey slumped back in her chair. It couldn't be. What would have been the motive? She took her phone out of her handbag and opened up her internet browser. She typed in her search and waited. There were several hits, one of which made her catch her breath.

"Are you all right?" Sully asked.

Lindsey nodded. She thought about standing up and sharing what she'd learned, but the mayor didn't give her the chance.

"It's good that you're here, Ms. Cole," the mayor said. "I like to be up front about things. Even if feelings get hurt, I find it's best to be direct and honest."

Ms. Cole stopped in front of the long table. Several of the council members didn't make eye contact with her but Andrea did. In fact, she smiled.

"Your timing is commendable, Ms. Cole," Andrea said. "I'm sure you know what this emergency meeting is about."

"I was informed," she said.

"The mayor has requested that we relieve you of your position at the library," Andrea said. She glared at the mayor when she said it.

"May I ask what argument he made?"

"I can tell you myself," the mayor said. He was clearly unhappy with the way the vibe in the room had changed. "You are a danger to the public and need to be removed forthwith."

Ms. Cole blinked. "That was direct."

"I believe in taking a forceful stance when the good of the community is at stake," he said.

Ms. Cole nodded. "So you've said. Is that why you won't approve a traffic light at the corner of Main Street and Jersey Court? The same location where we've had three fatalities in the past five years?"

The mayor gaped at her.

"Or how about replacing the equipment in the town playground? Your constituents have been asking about it for seven years, and the requests keep getting denied even though there are clear safety violations in the children's play area."

Several moms, the ones who'd been lobbying the mayor, burst into scattershot applause.

"This is not the time or the place—" the mayor began, but Ms. Cole interrupted him.

"I'm still speaking," she said.

Lindsey wanted to do a fist pump, but she held it in, not wanting to take away any of Ms. Cole's glory.

"This meeting is a sham," Ms. Cole said. "You're trying to force me out of my job in the crazy hope that if you accuse me of murder enough times, you will ruin me and I won't run against you. Well, that's not going to happen."

"Bravo, Ms. Cole," Ivy Kavanagh cheered.

Lindsey looked at Ivy in surprise.

"It is going to happen," the mayor insisted. "You are a murderer and you will go to jail. You had the means, the motive and the opportunity." The crowd shifted restlessly in their seats as if they thought the mayor might be privy to information they didn't have and they were eager to hear it.

"Care to explain why the murder weapon was found in your possession, Ms. Cole?"

She tightened her lips. There was no way she could answer because she didn't know.

"You see?" the mayor called out to the room. "She is a cold-blooded killer, and anyone who says otherwise is either crazy or a liar."

That did it. It was now or never. Lindsey rose from her seat. "I'm not crazy or a liar, but I know who killed Henry Lewis, and it wasn't Ms. Cole."

CHAPTER
19

BRIAR CREEK
PUBLIC LIBRARY

The audience made a collective gasp as all eyes turned to her. For a second, Lindsey's dislike of public speaking almost made her sit back down, but she saw Emma across the room. She had obviously come in a different door than Ms. Cole to make it appear that Ms. Cole was not in custody. She gestured for Lindsey to continue, so with a quick squeeze of Sully's hand, Lindsey made her way to the aisle to stand with Ms. Cole.

She glanced back at Emma, who subtly signaled to Kirkland to block the only other exit. Good. It was a show of faith from the chief of police that Lindsey much appreciated.

"Mrs. Sullivan," the mayor began.

"Mrs. Norris-Sullivan," Lindsey corrected him. It didn't sound half bad. She glanced back at Sully and found him grinning at her.

When she turned back, the mayor sent her a look of irritation that she ignored.

"Ms. Cole is an employee of yours," the mayor said. "Given your partiality, I don't think anything you say can seriously be considered by the council."

"Even if I tell you who the murderer is?" she asked.

Again, the ripple of anticipation swirled through the room. Lindsey ignored the feeling of eyes upon her. *Breathe*, she told herself, *just breathe*. Ms. Cole must have sensed her distress, because she reached over and patted her arm.

"Go ahead, you can do this," she said.

Lindsey swallowed her nerves and said, "Well?"

The mayor looked as if he was about to refuse, but Andrea got there first.

"Do tell us, Lindsey. Who is responsible for the death of Henry Lewis?" she said.

"There were several suspects in the beginning." Lindsey turned around and scanned the room. "The first person I suspected was Bob Spielman."

Bob's eyes went wide with surprise and the woman next to him, presumably his wife, looked outraged.

"Sorry," Lindsey said. "But you were his business partner. You wanted to sell and he didn't, and three hundred and something million is a pretty big incentive to . . . remove obstacles."

Bob looked hurt. "Henry was like a brother to me. I would never."

"I know," Lindsey said. "It became apparent very quickly that it wasn't you. My next suspect was the other person who obviously had something to gain by the removal of Henry Lewis. Curtis Schmitt."

"Hey!" Curtis, who was sitting at the back of the

room, protested. His wife also sent Lindsey a nasty look.

"Curtis had a motive," Lindsey said. "Henry was fighting his latest development as his new exclusive townhomes would flatten Henry Lewis's family home—the same house that is on the iconic label of Nana's Cookies. Curtis stood to lose a fortune if he didn't get the Lewis family home."

"I didn't—" Curtis protested.

"No, you didn't," Lindsey agreed. "It wasn't Curtis. He was helping his wife show a house out on the islands. That's a tough alibi to break."

There was a lot of grumbling in the crowd and they were getting restless, but Lindsey knew she had to stay the course so that everyone understood the who, how, why and when.

"Next, I thought it might be Lenny Lewis, Henry's only remaining relative," Lindsey said.

"Me?" Lenny Lewis was sitting up toward the front of the room. His straw-colored hair was in its usual disarray, but his eyes were large and, Lindsey thought, a little hurt.

"Sorry, Lenny, but you are Henry's last remaining relative, and you did admit that you wanted to sell the house but he forbade it, which was unfair since it was your house to do whatever you wanted with," she said. "And you wanted to buy a boat and sail the seas, didn't you?"

"Yes."

"And now you have a boat."

"I do, but I—" As if sensing everyone was staring at him, he stopped speaking and gazed down at his lap.

"Would never harm anyone," Lindsey finished for

him. "I know. Which is why you didn't kill Henry either."

"I didn't?" Lenny asked. Then he nodded vigorously. "That's right. I didn't."

"I notice Ms. Cole isn't one of your suspects," Mayor Hensen snapped from the dais.

"No, of course not," Lindsey said. She turned and addressed the room. "I was with Ms. Cole on that horrible day. We went to the parking lot to get the campaign signs out of the trunk of her car. If she had killed Mr. Lewis, why would she bring all of her friends and colleagues out to her car where she'd left his body?"

"As a cover, of course," the mayor said. "So she could feign surprise and act shocked that the man she'd just killed was stuffed into her trunk."

Lindsey shook her head. The crowd wasn't buying it either. She scanned the room. Everyone was sitting forward on the edge of their seats. Now she needed to bring it on home.

She glanced at Ms. Cole, who was watching her patiently and quietly, actively listening and engaged. She was going to make an amazing mayor.

"Ms. Cole didn't murder Henry Lewis," Lindsey said. She met the mayor's gaze and held it while she said this. "Although, it would be awfully convenient for our current mayor if she did, seeing as how she's much more likely to win the upcoming election than you are."

"How dare you—" he began but Lindsey cut him off.

"Shall I tell them how I dare?" she asked. "About anonymous phone calls to my office, accusing my staff of murder, or should I mention the bribe?"

"Meeting adjourned!" the mayor cried. He half rose

out of his seat, but Andrea stopped him with a hand on his arm.

"Sit down. I'm the only one who can adjourn this meeting. And I, for one, want to hear what Lindsey has to say."

"I really thought Mayor Hensen was the murderer," Lindsey said. The mayor gasped and she shrugged. "Sorry, but you were so determined to kick Ms. Cole out of the mayor's race that I thought you must have known about her prior relationship with Henry and decided to use it against her. Murdering Henry Lewis and having your rival take the fall for it would save you not only from losing your mayor's position but also the fortune you invested in Curtis Schmitt's new development."

The mayor turned a brilliant shade of red, and Lindsey knew she had him on the defensive.

"Just because I invested in Curtis's project doesn't mean I murdered Henry Lewis. Likewise, just because my opponent had a relationship with Lewis does not mean I was going to try and pin a murder on her. I mean, what sort of man do you take me for?"

"A man who has been mayor for eight years and whose identity has become wrapped up in being the mayor. That has to be a hard thing to give up."

"Who says I'm giving up?" he asked.

Lindsey managed to contain her eye roll. When everything came out about the mayor—that his wife or her friend had called Lindsey demanding Ms. Cole be fired, that the mayor had tried to bribe Lindsey to get Ms. Cole to abandon her run, topped off by this emergency town council meeting meant to preemptively fire

Ms. Cole—the man wasn't going to stand a chance at reelection.

"In any event, despite your many issues, it turns out the killer is not you either," Lindsey said.

The mayor looked surprised and then nodded. "That's right, it's not me." He looked relieved, which rolled right into belligerence. "Of course it's not me."

Lindsey paced. She moved to the end of the row where the killer was sitting, right in the middle in a cherry red sweater, her white Peter Pan collar just visible above it. Her spiked white hair was perfectly styled, and she looked every bit the professional. Her face was serene as if she had absolutely no idea that her cover was blown.

"Perhaps it's best if the killer explains why she did what she did so we can all understand," Lindsey said. The room responded in a flurry of whispers. Heads were turning as people were looking for whoever the killer might be. Lindsey didn't look in the killer's direction, but in her peripheral vision she noticed her obvious attempt to look casual. When the curiosity reached a fever pitch, Lindsey spun around and pinned Ivy Kavanagh with her stare.

"Tell us, Ivy, why'd you do it?" she asked. "Why did you murder Henry Lewis?"

The crowd reacted with shock and dismay. Ivy Kavanagh was one of the pillars of their community. Her charity, Dig Deeper, was known for single-handedly reforesting great swaths of wildfire-damaged acreage. That Lindsey would stand there and accuse her of murder was clearly an outrage.

"I have no idea what you're talking about," Ivy said. Her demeanor was serene and her gaze full of pity, as if she was sad that Lindsey had clearly gone cuckoo, and so publicly, too.

"Really?" Lindsey asked. "I think you do."

"I'm going to leave now," Ivy said. She rose from her seat and began to walk toward the exit. Officer Kirkland was there. She turned and headed for the other exit but Emma blocked it. Ivy looked agitated. "You can't stop me. You have no reason to detain me."

Emma tipped up her chin. "If you're innocent, hearing what Lindsey has to say shouldn't be a problem then, should it?"

Ivy's gaze swept the room as if she was looking for other exits. There were none.

"I have to say," Lindsey said. "You were never on my radar. You've lived in Briar Creek all your life, you were a childhood friend of Henry's, and the two of you formed an amazing charity together. After he was murdered, you were distraught about his death. After all, you had plans to reforest the entire planet together, and Henry was one of your biggest sources of funding, wasn't he?"

Ivy didn't say a word, with her mouth set in a grim line and her eyes darting from side to side, avoiding Lindsey's steady gaze.

"Henry told Bob that he was coming to Briar Creek to see to some old unfinished business," Lindsey said. "Bob assumed that he was referring to Ms. Cole, but he wasn't, was he?"

"I'm sure I wouldn't know." Ivy tipped her chin up in defiance.

"No?" Lindsey asked. "Well, do you know that according to a source that rates charities, yours is ranked as one of the lowest in the nation? That of the twenty-four million you've taken over the past ten years, only three percent has actually been spent on planting trees? Three percent of twenty-four million is seven hundred and twenty thousand. Where did the rest of the twenty-three million two hundred and eighty thousand go, Ivy?"

"There is a lot of overhead. You wouldn't understand," Ivy snapped. Lindsey shook her head slowly from side to side. "I do not have to justify my charity to you. Henry understood. Henry got it. He was committed to reforestation until the day he died."

"You mean until the day you killed him," Lindsey said. "He was taking your charity out of his will, wasn't he?"

"No!" Ivy retorted. "He would never."

"Yes, he would," Lindsey said. "In fact, he was planning to sell his business and retire here to live out his days in Nana's house."

"That's insane," Ivy said. "He didn't want to sell out."

Lindsey looked at Lenny. "Do you remember your conversation with Henry? When you told him you wanted to be free, what was it that he said?"

Lenny sat up straight and said, "Uncle Henry said I had no idea how lucky I was that I hadn't been betrayed by someone I trusted."

"That's right," Lindsey said. "When you told me, I thought it was Henry's way of telling you not to betray him by leaving, but I think he was talking about someone else."

"You can't prove anything," Ivy said.

"I think I can," Lindsey said. "Because you made one mistake."

Ivy gave her side-eye, as if trying to determine where the strike was going to come from.

"You knew about Henry's past with Ms. Cole. You knew they'd had a terrible breakup and hadn't spoken for years. I imagine if Henry believed he was going to settle back in town, then he wanted to reconnect with Ms. Cole. Before he had the chance, you decided to use their former relationship to your advantage. After you killed him, you figured she would be the perfect person to blame for his death. How long did you follow her to make sure you intercepted Henry before he talked to her?"

Ivy's lips twitched, which was just enough of a tell to let Lindsey know she was right.

"Henry was going to the library that day to see Ms. Cole, wasn't he?" Lindsey asked. "You wanted to head him off, because you knew he would probably tell her all about you and your fraudulent charity. They were old friends. He would confide in her and you would be ruined. Never mind the fact that you had to kill him before he changed his will. The clock was ticking. The day he arrived at the library, you panicked. You stole a cable from one of the library's computers and you headed him off in the parking lot."

"This is ridiculous," Ivy said. "I mean, look at me. How could I, so petite and tiny, take on a full-grown man?"

"She attends CrossFit in the same place where Milton conducts a yoga class," Ms. Cole said. "I've seen her flip tires the size of small cars. She could absolutely lift up Henry Lewis."

"Thank you, Ms. Cole," Lindsey said.

"This is all speculation," Ivy said. "You can't prove any of it."

"Except for one thing," Lindsey said. "You have a VOTE COLE sign in your office window."

"So?" Ivy said. "I'd think you'd be pleased that I'm backing her, which I can assure you I won't be after this."

"I would be pleased, but there's a small problem," Lindsey said. "All of the signs that Ms. Cole had made were taken by the police as evidence—every single one. You are actually the only person in the entire town with a VOTE COLE sign, and the only way you could have gotten one is if you'd taken it from the murder scene."

Ivy's face drained of all color. In a flash, she was charging the door that the chief was blocking. Despite all of her CrossFit, Ivy went down hard.

"Lies, it's all lies," she said.

"Then why did you feel the need to run?" Emma asked as she wrestled a pair of cuffs onto Ivy's wrists.

"You can't arrest me," Ivy cried. "I am committed to the environment and reforestation and saving the earth."

"More like manicures, pedicures, wax treatments and facials," Shana, the local hairdresser, said. "You convinced me to give you beauty treatments for free so that you would look your best to schmooze the donors for your charity. Do you have any idea how much I've personally invested in your appearance?"

"And how about me?" The local car dealer, Sam Fordyce, jumped up. "I've let you run around in a Mercedes for free so you could 'hold your own' with the country club set. And here you've been pocketing *millions*?"

The room broke into a frenzy of shouting, and Ivy shrank back behind Officer Kirkland, who'd joined Emma in the arrest.

"It's not my fault!" Ivy cried. "If Henry had just kept making donations like he was supposed to—but no, he had to hire a retirement adviser who went through all of his books and decided that I wasn't representing my charity authentically. Jerk! And then Henry wanted his money back! I panicked. I was in the library and he texted me that he was going to see Ms. Cole. I couldn't risk that he'd tell her. I did what I had to do. For the trees!"

The entire room went silent. Would she admit it? Was this the moment that Ivy confessed?

"Of course, you had to think of the trees first. So, what did you have to do?" Emma asked. Her tone was gentle as if she were leading a wild animal to shelter.

"I was waiting for Henry at the library, and I saw Ms. Cole park her car. I noticed that her trunk was up and I peeked inside to see why. Henry had said he'd be there that morning, so I waited. I realized I needed to convince him to listen to me. I had the idea that I could tie him up so he'd hear me out, but I didn't have any rope, so I borrowed a cable from one of the computers.

"When I saw him park his car, I met him in the parking lot. I walked him to Ms. Cole's car to show him the campaign signs in her trunk. I wanted him to understand that she had moved on to bigger things, like running for mayor, and she wouldn't want to see him, but he didn't listen. He kept telling me that he was done with me and my scam of a charity. He was so angry." Ivy took a deep breath. She began to cry. "I had no choice. He was going to ruin everything we'd built together, so when he leaned into the trunk to look at the campaign signs, I shoved him hard in the back, knocking him down, then I wrapped the cord around his neck.

"I only meant to frighten him, to show him that he couldn't just toss me aside, but when he stopped fighting, I didn't let go. I thought he was faking me out. When he went limp, I thought he'd blacked out. I panicked and lifted his legs into the trunk, then I tied it shut. No one had been in the parking lot while we were there, so I figured he'd wake up in there and reconsider his decision to abandon me."

"Why did you take one of the signs?" Emma asked.

"Because if I had one in my window, then no one would suspect me of trying to frame Ms. Cole for his mur—" Ivy broke off.

"Murder," Emma said. "You've just admitted that you knew he was dead."

"No, I didn't. This is all your fault," Ivy snapped at Ms. Cole. "He only came back here for you."

The look Ivy cast Ms. Cole was dark, and Lindsey felt Ms. Cole stiffen ever so slightly. Like flipping a switch, Ivy blinked and turned her wide eyes to Emma. "I didn't mean to kill him, I swear. It's not my fault."

"What about the threatening picture that was mailed to Ms. Cole?" Lindsey asked. "Was that you, too, Ivy? Where did you get it?"

"Henry had it in his pocket." Her voice dropped and her expression turned mean. "He shouldn't have betrayed me."

"So, you cleaned out his pockets after you tossed him in the trunk, making it difficult for us to identify him," Emma said. "You knew exactly what you were doing."

Lindsey felt her stomach twist. There was something purely terrifying about a person who believed they had the right to take the life of another when they didn't get their way.

"Ivy Kavanagh, you're under arrest for the murder of Henry Lewis," Emma said. Her voice was grim. She took Ivy by one elbow while Kirkland took the other and they led her out the door, Emma citing her Miranda rights as they went.

"You can't arrest me!" Ivy yelled. She sounded frantic and started to buck and kick. "Think of the trees. The trees!"

When the door closed behind them, Lindsey felt a pent-up breath whoosh out of her.

"Well, I'll have to commend Beth on her suggestion of yard signs," Ms. Cole said. "I had no idea they could be so useful."

Lindsey glanced at her, and as she took in the indomitable Ms. Cole, she started to laugh. The crafternooners had gathered around, and they looked at Lindsey and then at Ms. Cole in confusion.

"I have no idea why she's laughing," Ms. Cole said. "I merely stated that I had no idea how useful yard signs could be."

This time it was Beth who started to chuckle, and after the tense few moments with Ivy terrorizing the community, the chuckles became contagious. Ms. Cole stood in the middle of it, looking benevolently upon them. When the laughter started to wind down, she approached the table where the town council still sat, and said, "If it's quite all right with you, I'll be going now."

"Perfectly all right," Andrea said. She pushed back her chair and rose to stand. "And if you'd allow me, I'd like to buy you a drink at the Blue Anchor. Goodness knows, I could certainly use one."

"That would be lovely," Ms. Cole said.

"Meeting adjourned," Andrea announced.

Lindsey watched the two women leave, thinking that was the beginning of a beautiful new friendship.

CHAPTER

20

BRIAR CREEK
PUBLIC LIBRARY

"But if Mayor Hensen resigns, who is going to take his place?" Beth asked. She and Lindsey were setting up the crafternoon room. It was Beth's turn to provide the food. When she unpacked a heaping basket of fried dill pickles and ranch dip, mini cream puffs, and chicken wings battered in Parmesan and garlic, Lindsey didn't say a word. She figured the menu was at the mercy of Beth's cravings.

Two weeks had passed since the arrest of Ivy Kavanagh and word had gotten out around town that the mayor's wife had used the tax assessor's office phone to call Lindsey to demand that she fire Ms. Cole. Lindsey had also approached the town council about the mayor's blatant bribe for security cameras if she would convince Ms. Cole not to run against him.

"Herb Gunderson will step in as interim mayor," Lindsey said. "He's appalled by the revelations about his boss and has already made it very clear that he won't run for mayor himself. It appears Ms. Cole might be running unopposed."

"Mayor Cole," Beth said. She clasped her hands together under her chin. "I'm so excited."

"We are, too," Nancy and Violet said as they joined them in the crafternoon room. They were sporting matching T-shirts that read *Vote Cole*.

"I love it," Beth cried. "Where did you get those made?"

"Paula made them for all of us," Nancy said. She opened a bag and Violet reached in and handed a shirt to Lindsey and one to Beth. Then she reached in again and pulled out a baby onesie that read *Vote Cole*. Beth's eyes watered as she hugged it to her chest.

"Aw, thank you, the baby will wear it with pride," she said.

Ms. Cole entered the room carrying a jug of sweet tea. She took in the scene at a glance and said, "Oh, my."

"Pretty great, right?" Paula asked as she followed her into the room.

"I . . . I'm overwhelmed," Ms. Cole said. "But it's six months until the election. Things could change a lot before then."

Lindsey met Ms. Cole's gaze and said, "'She knew things that nobody had ever told her. For instance, the words of the trees and the wind. She often spoke to falling seeds and said, "Ah hope you fall on soft ground," because she had heard seeds saying that to each other as they passed.' Don't worry, Ms. Cole, you've already fallen on soft ground."

"Oh, that was perfect," Nancy said. She held up her copy of Zora Neale Hurston's *Their Eyes Were Watching God*, their book selection of the week.

"It's my favorite passage in the book," Lindsey said.

"I'm going to say that to people when I wish them well," Violet said. "I hope you fall on soft ground—such a lovely sentiment."

"And appropriate," Beth said. "Despite the tragedy of Henry Lewis's death, you managed to land on soft ground, Ms. Cole. I think most of the townspeople know who you are and what you stand for now and I think they will happily vote for you."

Ms. Cole smiled. "We'll see. Life doesn't always turn out as we expect."

Lindsey wondered if she was thinking about how her younger self had been engaged to Henry Lewis and what her life might have been like if she'd chosen him.

"Did you know that Zora Neale Hurston was married three times?" Lindsey asked the group.

"None of them took," Violet said. "Which reminds me of Janie's character in her book. She's married three times, too, and only finds true love in the third marriage. I wonder if being a writer made Hurston more of a career woman than the men back in the day could handle?"

"Probably," Beth said. "She was also one of the darlings of the Harlem Renaissance in the nineteen twenties. Why settle down when there was so much art and music happening as Black artists began to discover their autonomy?"

"She wasn't just a writer. She was also an anthropologist. I read that she won the Guggenheim Fellowship in nineteen thirty-six and traveled to Jamaica and Haiti to study voodoo rituals," Nancy said. "Can you imagine what that must have been like in the thirties? It's also where she wrote *Their Eyes Were Watching God.*"

"And thank goodness she did," Violet said. "Sadly, she never made much money from her work and died in poverty in an unmarked grave. Alice Walker was the one who made certain that her grave was marked and named her the 'Genius of the South.' She is primarily responsible for the recognition of the legacy of Zora Neale Hurston's work."

"Women looking out for other women," Paula said. She raised a glass of the tea Ms. Cole had poured, and the others joined in her toast.

"Speaking of legacies, has anyone heard what's happening with Nana's Cookies or the Lewis house since Ivy was charged with Henry's murder?" Beth asked.

"Yes," Lindsey said. "Lenny is committed to the sale of the house and plans to set sail on his boat for points unknown. However, he has agreed to donate all of Nana's cookbooks and several artifacts to the Briar Creek historical society. As you can imagine, Milton is thrilled. Curtis is moving ahead with the development. And Bob is selling Nana's Cookies to the giant food corporation that made the three-hundred-and-something-million-dollar offer."

"Wow, that's a lot of pocket change," Beth said.

"I heard from Emma that Bob Spielman is donating the half of the sale that would have been Henry's to the remaining charities in his will. Apparently he's found a legitimate reforestation charity to take the place of Ivy's and he's donating her cut to them," Lindsey said. "Also, because he knew Nana's house meant so much to Henry, Bob is having it moved to a new location where the town historical society will offer tours and offer samples of Nana's cookies. Bob said it was just a marketing ploy, but I really think he did it for his life-long friend."

"That's only fitting," Ms. Cole said. Her voice was tight. "As it's what Henry would have wanted."

"Is there anything we can do to help you honor him?" Lindsey asked. She sensed that Ms. Cole was having a hard time letting go of the past, the road not taken, and that she rued the missed opportunity to have made peace with her old friend.

"What do you mean?" Ms. Cole asked.

"You didn't get to say good-bye," Beth said. Her voice was tight and a tear dropped down her cheek. "No matter how things ended for you, knowing that he was coming back to talk to you and that you never got the chance has to hurt."

Ms. Cole put her hand over her chest. "Yes, it does," she said. "You wouldn't think so after forty years apart and with harsh words being the last between us, but it does."

"We thought it might," Lindsey said. She took Ms. Cole's hand in hers and pointed to a tree, newly planted, on the library lawn. "That tree, that red maple, is for you, Ms. Cole, from all of us. We planted it in memory of Henry Lewis, and we're going to have a bench put beneath it with his name on it."

Ms. Cole put her hand over her mouth. Her eyes were watery and her voice tight when she said, "It's beautiful and perfect and he would have loved it so. I will sit there often and I will think of him."

Lindsey gave her a quick side hug. "That's what we hoped you'd say."

The rest of the crafternooners joined them by the

window, each of them hugging Ms. Cole in turn. Beth was the last one. She hugged the lemon close and said, "And with the bench right there by the library, you'll have an excuse to pop in and say hello to us when you're the mayor. Remember, your friends are always right here."

Ms. Cole turned and looked at her. Her face was full of affection when she said, "We're not just friends, Beth. The crafternooners are family and we're the best sort of family because we've chosen each other."

"So true," Nancy said. She opened her arms and they entered into a group hug.

There were tears and laughter, and when they broke apart, Lindsey glanced at her friends and the gorgeous day outside and said, "Come on, let's go introduce Ms. Cole to her tree."

And so they did.

Crafternoon Guide

Want to host your own crafternoon? All you need are some booklover friends, a really good book, delicious snacks and a craft you can all enjoy! Here are some suggestions to get you started.

Readers Guide for
Their Eyes Were Watching God

by Zora Neale Hurston

1. The protagonist, Janie Crawford Killicks Starks Woods, evolves from a compliant teenager into a woman in charge of her own destiny. How does this change come about?

2. The disparity between men and women is evident throughout the book. What are some examples of this? How does this inequality shape Janie?

3. Janie is married three times. What does she gain and lose from each marriage? Which is the love of her life? Why?

4. What significance does the horizon hold for Janie? What does it mean in the context of the novel?

5. Throughout the story, Janie challenges convention. In what way does she make her own decisions and control her own destiny? Have you ever defied anyone's expectations of you?

Craft
Ribbon Bookmarks

⅝-inch ribbon clamps (2 per bookmark)
⅝-inch velvet ribbon cut into 9-inch lengths
Flat-nose pliers
Needle-nose pliers
Jump rings
Charms (you can repurpose old pendants or earrings)

Place a ribbon clamp on the end of the ribbon. Use the flat-nose pliers to clamp it tight onto the ribbon. Repeat on the other end of the ribbon. Using the needle-nose pliers, open the jump ring and attach a charm to the jump ring. Then attach the jump ring to the ribbon clamp. Repeat on the other end. That's it!

Recipes

CHEDDAR-BROCCOLI TARTLETS

Crust

1 cup butter, softened
6 oz. cream cheese, softened
2 cups all-purpose flour

Filling

16 oz. frozen chopped broccoli
1 large egg, slightly beaten
1 can (10¾ oz.) condensed cream of celery soup
¼ cup milk

¼ cup mayonnaise
½ cup shredded sharp cheddar

In a medium bowl, cream butter and cream cheese until smooth. Slowly mix in flour until a dough forms. Divide in half and shape each into a ball. Cover and refrigerate for an hour until firm. Preheat oven to 350. Shape dough into one-inch balls and place in greased mini-muffin tins. Press the dough into the bottoms and up along the sides.

Cook the broccoli according to the directions. Drain the broccoli. In a large bowl, combine the egg, soup, milk and mayonnaise. Stir in the cheese and broccoli. Spoon the mixture into the mini-muffin cups.

Bake until the edges are golden brown, 17–21 minutes. Cool in pans for five minutes. Remove and serve warm.

MAKES 48.

LEMON CHEESECAKE SQUARES

2¾ cups finely crushed shortbread cookies
1 tablespoon granulated sugar
6 tablespoons butter, melted
12 ounces cream cheese, softened
1 cup powdered sugar
2 tablespoons fresh lemon juice
½ teaspoon lemon zest
2 teaspoons vanilla extract
2 large eggs

Preheat oven to 350 degrees. Grease an 8 x 8 inch baking
dish and set aside. Combine crushed cookies and sugar, then
mix in melted butter until mixture is thoroughly moistened.
Evenly press into the bottom of the baking dish. Beat cream
cheese with powdered sugar until smooth. Mix in lemon
juice and zest. Put aside ¾ cup of the mixture and refrigerate.
Add vanilla to remaining mixture and beat in the eggs. Pour
filling over the shortbread crust. Bake for 23–26 minutes.
Cool completely, then pour the remaining mixture on the top.
Refrigerate until firm (about 2 hours). Cut into squares.

SERVES 16.

Acknowledgments

Thank you to reader Michelle (Micky) Cox for coming up with the fabulous title for this book—you're brilliant and I am ever grateful.

Eternal gratitude to my editor, Kate Seaver, and my agent, Christina Hogrebe. Your wisdom and support are so appreciated during every stage of the writing process. Truly, I couldn't do it without you. To my amazing team at Berkley: Jessica Mangicaro, Natalie Sellars, Brittanie Black and Dache' Rogers, thank you so much for all of your amazing work on behalf of the books. You really are the loveliest people, and I'm thrilled that I get to work with you.

Hats off to the art department and artist Julia Green for another brilliant cover. These covers are pure genius.

Special shout-out to my crafty, uber-talented personal assistant, Christie Conlee, whose beautiful handmade ribbon bookmarks inspired the craft in this book! Thank you for being your amazing self!

Three cheers to my plot group buddies Kate Carlisle and Paige Shelton. You always drop whatever you're doing and lend me a hand when I'm stuck and I so appreciate it. Also, big thanks to Hannah Dennison, who gives the best pep talks of anyone I know. And many, many thank-yous to my blog sisters, the Jungle Red Writers—Hank Phillippi Ryan, Hallie Ephron, Lucy Burdette, Deborah Crombie, Rhys Bowen and Julia Spencer-Fleming. I feel so very fortunate to have you all in my daily life with your boundless wit, wisdom and friendship.

High fives to the McKinlay's Mavens and the Fans of Jenn McKinlay—two of the nicest places I've ever visited in the wide world of social media—I'm so happy to call all of you my friends.

To my families, the McKinlays and the Orfs, thanks so much for your unwavering support. I'm so lucky to have you all in my life. With extra thank-yous to Chris Hansen Orf, Beckett Orf and Wyatt Orf for being patient and kind and truly hilarious whenever I need it most. You three are my whole world and I love you to pieces.

Turn the page for an exclusive look at Jenn
McKinlay's next Library Lover's Mystery . . .

THE PLOT AND THE PENDULUM

Lindsey Norris, director of the Briar Creek Public Library, was seated at the reference desk gazing out the window that overlooked the bay and the archipelago, called the Thumb Islands, within it. The large maple tree on the front lawn of the library was in its final stages of autumn vibrancy and the leaves were dropping like colorful confetti every time the ocean breeze stirred the tree's limbs.

October was here. For Lindsey this indicated that shorter days were coming, which meant winter would follow soon after with fires in the fireplace and days spent reading while the snow piled up outside. Bring it on.

She glanced around the library, watching the comings and goings of the patrons and staff. She liked to pause every now and then and try to see the library from a visitor's perspective. Was it engaging? Colorful displays of books greeted patrons when they first arrived and seasonal displays decorated the windows. Lindsey tried to change them out regularly to keep them interesting. Was the building clean? Yes, the town had an amazing cleaning crew and the staff made it a practice to sweep through and gather materials left on tables several times per day.

Was it friendly? Lindsey glanced at the first point of contact for patrons. The circulation desk.

Ms. Cole, the head of circulation, was stationed on the desk. She was wearing a white blouse with navy slacks in a shocking departure from her usual style of monochromatic dress in which she wore all shades of blue, whether they were complementary or not. Formerly, Ms. Cole had been nicknamed "the lemon" for her puckered personality, but she'd mellowed over the past few years and was presently running unopposed in next month's mayoral election.

Lindsey was resigned to losing Ms. Cole and despite the many ups and downs their relationship had endured since Lindsey's arrival, she found that she was going to miss Ms. Cole and her pragmatic ways. There was a steadfastness about Ms. Cole that was rare in employees these days.

Before she could get too maudlin, a scarecrow wandered past her desk, leaving a trail of leaves in its wake while a pack of children followed, collecting the leaves with the excitement only a group of toddlers could bring to such an activity. Lindsey met the scarecrow's gaze and he winked at her over the heads of the children.

Aidan Barker, the library's temporary story time

person, was dressed in patched overalls that sported wide flannel pockets sewn onto his knees and bib, a flannel shirt and a straw hat that was perched on his head. The kids gathered the leaves and raced back to him, stuffing his pockets until they were bursting.

A young boy who looked to be about three shoved a handful of leaves into one of the pockets on Aidan's knee, patted the flannel and said, "Here's your insides, Mr. Scarecrow."

"Thank you, young man," the scarecrow said. Then he did a little jig as if adjusting his leaves. The boy laughed and scampered off to find more.

The child's mother smiled and said, "This is brilliant. Maybe I can get him to do some leaf pickup in our yard when we get home."

The scarecrow tipped his hat to her as she chased after her son.

Lindsey smiled and said, "Wild guess here. You're reading about scarecrows in story time?"

Aidan said, "Correct. We're reading *The Scarecrow's Hat*, *Scaredycrow* and *Barn Dance!*"

"The kids will love it," she said.

"I hope so," he said. "My wife is a tough act to follow."

Aidan was the husband of Beth Barker, the library's regular children's librarian, who was out on an extended maternity leave with their newborn daughter Beverly, named for Beverly Cleary, the beloved children's book author. During Beth's final stages of delivery there had been some labor-induced talk of naming the baby Ramona or Beezus, but Aidan had prevailed and Beverly won out.

"How are Beth and the baby?" Lindsey asked. In addition to being her children's librarian, Beth was also Lindsey's best friend, and while they talked often, Lindsey had been giving the new mother some space, mostly to rest around the rigorous nursing and diaper-changing schedule she'd been maintaining for the past few months.

"Amazing," he said. "They're just amazing." His voice held a note of awe. "But Beth is ready to get back to the library. Thank you for arranging a job share so she can come back part-time. I don't think she'd be willing to leave baby Bee otherwise."

"I'm glad it worked out. And thank you for filling in for her story times. I don't think she'd trust anyone else," Lindsey said.

"Thankfully, my library director is a new parent, too," Aidan said. "She gets it."

Aidan was a children's librarian in a neighboring town, and he and Beth had met while doing dueling story times.

"Is there any chance we'll see Beth today for craft-ernoon?" Lindsey asked.

"She read this week's book, P. G. Wodehouse's *The Code of the Woosters*," he said. "So, she's planning to attend but it's really up to the baby."

Lindsey nodded.

"Mr. Scarecrow, can we have stories now?" a little girl asked. She had pigtails and was trailing a very grubby and clearly well-loved blanket behind her.

"Of course," he said. He shrugged at Lindsey. "Duty calls."

He clapped his hands in a short pattern and the

children stopped what they were doing and clapped back. And just like that, they gathered the last of the leaves and left the main area of the library and headed toward the story time room in the back.

The quiet that followed their departure was short lived.

"Hot dish. Hot dish. Coming through," a voice announced.

Lindsey turned to see Paula Turner walking through the main room of the library. She had two oven mitts on her hands and was cradling a casserole dish that was giving off steam. She was headed toward the meeting room where they held their weekly crafternoon sessions.

"Go ahead," Ann Marie Martin said as she joined Lindsey behind the desk. She was Lindsey's adult services librarian. Mother to two rambunctious tween boys, she considered this job her oasis from the chaos. "I've got the desk."

"Thanks. I don't have any questions to turn over to you. Other than a visit from a scarecrow, it's been very quiet."

"I'll take that as a good omen for getting my adult programming calendar done, then." Ann Marie smiled. Quiet moments in the library, which was the center of their small community, were rare.

Lindsey hopped up from her seat and hurried ahead of Paula to make certain the meeting room door was open for her.

"What is that?" Lindsey asked as she caught up to Paula. "It smells amazing."

"Sweet potato casserole with a crunchy pecan streusel," Paula said.

Lindsey opened the door and Paula entered the room. The table where the crafternoon members gathered to discuss a book, work on a craft and eat was fully loaded.

"You've been busy," Lindsey said.

"Don't tell the others, but you are my test subjects," Paula said. She put the casserole dish down on a trivet on the table and tossed her vibrant orange braid over her shoulder. Paula tended to dye her hair with the seasons or her mood, whichever motivated her the most when she was getting it done.

"Test subjects?" Lindsey asked. She wasn't sure she liked the sound of that.

"My parents are coming for Thanksgiving and my dad is a meat-and-potatoes guy," Paula explained. "I'm hoping I can serve a vegetarian meal and he won't be disappointed. So we have the casserole, figs in a blanket, salt-and-pepper radish chips, and cornbread, because cornbread goes with everything."

"Agreed." Lindsey nodded. "You're a braver woman than me. I would never subject anyone to my cooking by hosting a holiday meal."

Paula laughed. "Good thing your sister-in-law owns the Blue Anchor restaurant so you don't have to."

"I married up," Lindsey agreed.

She glanced out the window at the town pier, hoping to catch a glimpse of her husband, Mike Sullivan, known as Sully to his family and friends. He piloted the local water taxi that serviced the residents of the Thumb Islands and ran a seasonal tour boat as well. The pier was empty so she assumed he was out. This was another reason she enjoyed winter. More time with her husband as his tour schedule diminished.

"Are we late?" Violet La Rue asked as she and Nancy Peyton arrived.

Like the retired Broadway actress she was, Violet entered the room dramatically in her usual flowing caftan with her silver hair held back in a bun at the nape of her neck. With her deep-brown skin, large dark eyes, and prominent cheekbones, she was a strikingly handsome woman and people always turned to watch her when she crossed a room.

"We can't be. We're never late," Nancy Peyton said. Short with wavy hair that was slowly turning pure white and sparkling blue eyes, Nancy was a "Creeker," meaning she'd been born and raised in Briar Creek and had never left. Widowed young, she owned an old captain's house on the water, which she'd converted into three apartments, one of which Lindsey had lived in when she first arrived in town.

While technically senior citizens, both Nancy and Violet were incredibly active in the community. They were also two of Lindsey's favorite residents and had been with the crafternoon club since the beginning.

Lindsey noticed that they both carried their crochet bags. She sighed. The only part of crafternoon that she didn't care for was the craft part. She was equally awful at all crafts and no matter what she tried she just couldn't craft to save her life. Recently, they'd been working on crocheting bucket hats. It was excruciating.

"Where's your project?" Paula asked, looking pointedly at Lindsey's empty hands.

"Did you know Sir Pelham Grenville Wodehouse was called 'Plum' by his friends and family?" Lindsey asked.

"She's changing the subject," Nancy said to the others. "That means she's made a muddle of her crochet."

"Who made a muddle of their crochet?" a voice asked. They all turned to the door to see Beth arrive, pushing a stroller.

"Baby Bee is here," Nancy cried, keeping her voice soft in case the baby was sleeping.

Any talk of crochet was forgotten as they all gathered around to admire the baby, for which Lindsey was grateful. She really didn't want to trot out the tangle of yarn that was supposed to be a hat in front of her friends. She joined the group as they gazed in wonder at Beth's little girl.

At five months old, Bee was a pudgy butterball of unparalleled cuteness. She had her mother's dark hair and pert nose and her father's dimpled chin and pretty eyes. She blinked up at them, not at all alarmed to have so many faces peering down at her.

Beth unfastened the strap that held her in and hefted her out of the stroller. Nancy was there with her arms outstretched and Beth handed her over, clearly happy to share. Bee gurgled at Nancy, who looked enchanted.

Beth stretched and sat on one of the sofas in the room, looking relieved to have a rest for a minute. Nancy walked the baby about the room with Violet by her side.

"I knew it was a genius idea to read this week's book," Beth said. "Now I can sit here and eat lunch without interruption for the first time in months."

"I hope you like sweet potatoes," Paula said.

"Love them," Beth assured her.

"Lindsey, there's a man waiting out in the lobby for you," Ms. Cole said as she entered the room, clutching her crochet bag and a copy of this week's book.

"Oh?" Lindsey asked. Ms. Cole appeared agitated, which was unusual for the normally unflappable librarian.

"I would have sent him away but I believe he's *William Dorchester*," Ms. Cole explained in a hushed tone.

Nancy gasped. Her eyes were wide and stared at Ms. Cole as if she couldn't believe what she'd just heard.

The rest of the crafternooners glanced between the two women. Violet took the opportunity to lift the baby from Nancy's arms and it showed how distracted Nancy was that she let her.

"Are you sure?" Nancy asked Ms. Cole.

"Not one hundred percent," Ms. Cole admitted. "I tried to get his name but he said he preferred not to give it."

"That's weird," Paula said.

Lindsey silently agreed.

"Oh, dear," Nancy said. "If it is William, why do you suppose he wants to see Lindsey?"

"No idea," Ms. Cole said. "He was very circumspect."

The group was silent taking this in, and Lindsey wondered if she was about to deal with an overly aggressive salesman or an aggrieved patron. Neither one of which would be good for her digestion.

"Not to make it all about me, but I have a casserole here that's getting cold," Paula said.

At the mention of food, the ladies adjusted their

priorities accordingly and moved to take their seats at the table.

"Before I go out there, can I ask why the arrival of William Dorchester, if that's who this man is, is so shocking?" Lindsey asked.

Nancy looked at Ms. Cole, who nodded while spooning some of Paula's casserole onto her plate.

"Because he's the son of Marion Dorchester," Nancy said. "You know, the old lady who lives in the broken-down old mansion on the edge of town. As far as I know, he hasn't been back here since . . ."

"The runaway bride went missing," Ms. Cole said.

"I was going to say nineteen eighty-nine," Nancy said. She looked annoyed to have her thunder stolen.

"Runaway bride?" Beth asked. She was munching on a fig in a blanket. "Tell us more."

Lindsey glanced at the clock, aware that she was keeping the man waiting. "Abridged version, please."

"William Dorchester was in love with Grace Little, but his mother, Marion, refused to let him marry Grace as she deemed her unsuitable, or more accurately too poor," Nancy said. "Grace married Timothy Hartwell instead—"

"The Little League coach?" Paula asked.

"Yes," Nancy said. "But then Grace went missing six weeks after she married Tim. He and William had a terrible fight as William accused Tim of killing Grace. Tim naturally denied it."

"How have I never heard of this?" Beth asked. "I've known Tim for years."

"There was never any proof," Ms. Cole said.

"William left town, swearing to his mother that he would never marry—to spite her—and he left."

"He hasn't returned once in all these years," Nancy said. She frowned. "I wonder what brings him here now?"

Lindsey blew out a breath. "Well, I suppose I'll go find out."

Ready to find
your next great read?

Let us help.

Visit prh.com/nextread

Penguin
Random
House